Happy Ch

This is a different
viewpoint about
your favorite
islands
Luna
July
19

Queen

of the

Island

Poor writing
interesting Topic

Queen of the Island

❖

Jo Ann Mazoué

Wilderness Adventure Books

© **1993 by Jo Ann Mazoué**

Library of Congress Number: 93-060468

ISBN: 0-923568-30-1

Cover Art by David M. Bredau

Historic Map used with the permission of the
Beaver Island Historical Society

Wilderness Adventure Books
Post Office Box 17
Davisburg, Michigan 48350

Manufactured in the United States of America

To my sons

Author's Note

This is a historical novel, so some liberties have been taken with historical fact. The events that took place on Beaver Island during the summer of 1850 have been preserved, but the dialogue is based on my own interpretation of history.

Special Appreciation to:

> Shirley Ann Grau
> Caroline Gordon
> Walker Percy
> Alan R. Frederiksen

About the Author

Jo Ann Mazoué spent her childhood on the shores of Lake Michigan. Her lifetime fascination with the islands of the Great Lakes led to the study of James Strang and Beaver Island. Jo Ann is an avid writer, and her short stories and articles have been published in *The Literary Review*, the *New Orleans Times-Picayune, The Detroit Free Press, The Backstretch, Horsemen's Journal*, and *Good Housekeeping*. When she's not busy writing, she enjoys tennis, swimming, fishing, and photography.

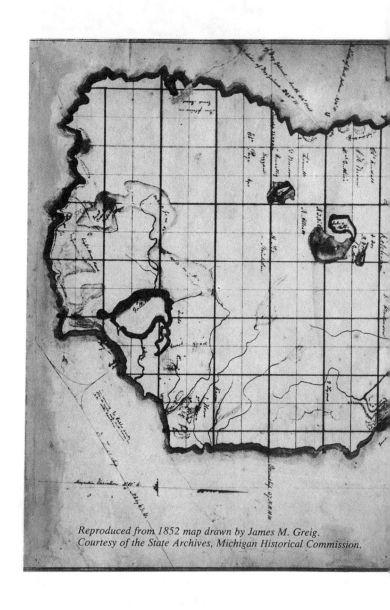

Reproduced from an 1852 map

Drawn by James M. Greig

Prologue

 $\mathcal{A}$ ll roads led to Nauvoo, Illinois in 1844. Tourists and pilgrims traveled by stagecoach, carriage and horseback to the new metropolis created by Joseph Smith, the founder of Mormonism. Nauvoo had been a marshland until brick homes, shops, and a grand temple were constructed to rival Chicago. One curious lawyer who arrived from Burlington, Wisconsin was James Jesse Strang.

Strang was born in Scipio in Cayuga County, New York on March 21, 1813. When Strang married Mary Abigail Perce, her brother, Benjamin Perce, moved to Racine County, Wisconsin, and proselytized the Mormon religion with great enthusiam. He claimed land near Voree that became Strang's Garden of Peace. Soon all the family connections arrived and it became a large Mormon community.

When Strang visited Nauvoo, he impressed Joseph Smith because he was a well-educated lawyer and had great knowledge about geography.

After receiving Mormon instruction at Nauvoo, Strang was baptized by Joseph Smith on February 25, 1844, into the Mormon faith. A few months later he was ordained an elder. Back home in Wisconsin Strang mailed a detailed report to Smith regarding the new Mormon center that Mary's brother had settled.

To understand Strang, one must realize that he imitated Joseph Smith in many ways. Joseph Smith was born in Sharon, Vermont, and when he was ten years old his family moved to Palmyra, New York. In 1820, at age fifteen, he claimed the first two persons of the Blessed Trinity appeared to him. Three years later he announced the Prophet Maroni talked to him. In 1827, Smith said Maroni directed him to a hill, Cumorah near Palmyra, where he found gold plates buried there from the Fifth Century A.D. On the plates was engraved the history of the ancient civilization of the Western World.

Smith reported the cryptography on the plates was a Reformed Egyptian religion. Buried with the plates he found the Urim and Thummim, two gems that changed color. When the high priest in the Old Testament entered the Holy of Holies, he used the Urim and Thummim that indicated God's judgment on the matter under consideration. Smith translated the records he unearthed by using the Urim and Thummim. Those translated writings became the *Book of Mormon*. On April 6, 1830, Smith founded Mormonism with a church in Fayette, New York. Following a revelation in 1831, he moved to Kirtland, Ohio, and established another settlement in Missouri. Four years later he selected Twelve Apostles and a council of seventy men. Eventually the governor of Missouri demanded the Mormons leave the state. They traveled to Nauvoo, Illinois in 1838 when Martin Van Buren served as President.

Three years before Strang became a Mormon, Joseph Smith sent Brigham Young on a mission to England. Before he left,

Young suffered from malaria-like symptoms of chills and fever called ague. Smith preformed a faith healing in 1839, praying over Brigham, "in the name of Jesus Christ arise and be made whole."

Young had joined the Mormon Church in 1832 in Kirtland, Ohio. When Smith sent him to England, Young prostylized for almost two years. While there, Young baptized eight thousand people and distributed five thousand copies of Smith's *Book of Mormon*. Later four thousand English Mormons booked passage to the United States, and settled in Nauvoo. Upon Brigham's return in 1835, he was ordained in the Council of Twelve.

Smith sanctioned polygamy in 1843. At first it repulsed Brigham, but he remained faithful to Smith. He stayed in the Church and accepted Smith's revelation of plural wives.

Smith campaigned to become President of the United States and wanted to end slavery. Dissension increased among Mormons. Apostate Mormons operated a press, the *Nauvoo Expositor*, and waged attacks against Joseph Smith and his followers. Trouble also continued for two years with non Mormons. When Smith was accused of treason, he and his brother, Hyrum, surrendered and were incarcerated in a Carthage jail.

On May 24, 1844, Samuel Morse invented the telegraph and sent his famous message between Baltimore and Washington, D.C. "What hath God wrought!" A month later, on June 25, 1844, Smith and his brother were murdered by a mob in that Carthage jail. The telegraph did not send the news of the Mormon leader's assassination. Instead newspapers reported his death. By August, Brigham ruled the Mormons. He was appointed President of the Church because he convinced the Twelve of his position second to Joseph Smith. Opposition to Brigham came from Smith's son, Joseph, who began the Reorganized Church of Jesus Christ of Latter Day Saints.

Others demanded to take over the leadership, including Strang, who had only been a Mormon for five months. Brigham belonged to the Church for twelve years, and had returned from England after a successful mission. His accomplishments did not hinder Strang who sent Moses Smith and Norton Jacob to Nauvoo with a copy of his alleged "letter of appointment" signed by Joseph Smith.

Strang claimed that Smith wrote the letter before his murder. The letter designated Strang to inherit all Smith's spiritual and temporal powers. Fearing for his life, Strang did not take the letter to Nauvoo and Brigham Young, but sent the two men.

Brigham denounced the letter as "a wicked forgery." He excommunicated Strang and delivered him over "to the buffetings of Satan." Brigham also excommunicated Joseph Smith's brother, William, who published a booklet labeling Brigham, "the most licentious man in the world."

Strang accepted the challenge from Brigham, won over the Kirtland Mormons and dispatched men to England to enlist Brigham's followers to join Strang. Strang continued to make progress in Philadelphia, New York and Boston. Brigham and the Nauvoo leaders became greatly concerned about their future strength when Strang captured the allegiance of Mormons from Illinois to the Atlantic seaboard.

Strang's apostles encountered rejection in England. On November 15, 1846, a Liverpool newspaper, *Millennial Star*, labeled the Strangites: "Polecats, swine and sons of Satan." Much of this resulted from the unsavory antics of a Strang disciple, Martin Harris, who destroyed Strang's English Mission. Instead, monetary contributions and people arrived from England to support Brigham and Mormons preparing to settle in the West. Because of this, Strang could no longer be a rival of Brigham Young. His only recourse was to leave Voree, and settle at a new paradise, Beaver Island.

On September 1, 1845, fifteen months after Smith's murder, Strang testified that an Angel appeared to him in Voree and gave him the Urim and Thummim. The angel anointed his head with holy oil and escorted Strang to a hill near White River and revealed to him plates buried under an oak tree.

When Strang returned to the tree after twelve days, he brought four witnesses to prove the ground wasn't previously excavated. After the four men dug near the tree, they found a case containing three small brass plates.

Using the Urim and Thummim, Strang deciphered the plates and claimed they were the writings of Rajah Manchou of Vorito. According to the Manchou script, it was revealed by God: "The forerunner men shall kill, but a mighty prophet there shall dwell. I will be his strength and he shall bring forth thy record. Record my words and bury them in the hill of promise."

On September 21, 1845, Strang introduced the four witnesses to a large crowd inside a barn to testify to the unearthing of the plates. C. Latham Sholes, a newspaper editor and developer of the first typewriter was present, but Sholes remained neutral about Strang's discovery.

During mid-October Strang turned into Brigham's most bitter rival. He reported in his newspaper, the *Voree Herald* the news about the plates and the letter of appointment from Joseph Smith naming Strang as his successor to lead the Mormon Church. He included a testimonial by the four witnesses of the plates and Strang's translation of the plates using the Urim and Thummim. A thousand copies of the newspaper raised suspicions if the Twelve and Brigham should be in charge of the Church. Strang gained support from a prominent Mormon, Reuben Miller and three hundred Nauvoo Mormons. After that Brigham and the Twelve felt threatened that Strang would seize their leadership. Brigham and the Twelve denounced Strang for giving false revelations and labeled him a wicked liar. Strang first visited Beaver Island in 1847. He decided to settle there saying, "This is where I will come to build up my kingdom."

1

July 4, 1850

From Chicago to Mackinac, schooners on Lake Michigan sailed past Beaver Island. The general store was closed for the holiday, but a strange ship headed straight for the island.

Virginia saw the ship with a side paddle wheel early that morning when she took cherry pies to the buckboard. She was sixty-five years old, of medium height, slender, with brown eyes and grey hair braided neatly around her head. In one hand she carried a starched sunbonnet that matched a calico dress that almost covered her high button, black leather shoes.

Right away she decided not to tell Bill about the ship. He'd wait for it at the wharf. Her picnic plans would be ruined. Other days when he hung around the dock she had complained, "You're wasting time."

"I gotta know who's aboard," he had said. "Chase the scallywags off Beaver."

Virginia walked alongside the cabin. She heard Bill yell,

"Let's go, Ginny. We're late." He stood behind the wagon and tied an American flag to the tailgate while puffing on a corn cob pipe. The day was hot. The seventy year old fisherman wore a naval cap to shade his eyes. He was a foot taller than Virginia, thin and spry. Dressed in brown pants and a light blue shirt, his sleeves were rolled up on arms tanned from pulling oars, setting nets and hoisting sails.

They were the last to leave the village with eight log cabins built on each side of a wide sandy path. Whitewashed fences divided land and log cabins. Today, Virginia saw bright summer flowers reflecting on cabin windows like stained glass in church. The stillness turned this moment into something special. *How wonderful*, she thought. *Bill and I are all alone. No barking dogs. No screaming kids. Just peace and quiet.* Her tranquility ended when Bill took the pipe from his mouth and sang:

> "If the clouds seem scratched by a hen,
>   take your topsail in.
> When the wind shifts against the sun,
>   watch her boys for back she'll come."

She enjoyed his baritone. Seeing her stand at the open cabin door, Bill called out, "Ready?"

She stood as tall as the lavender hollyhocks blooming on each side of the doorway. "No. Got to feed my hens." She lifted up the long skirt and stepped down.

When she reached the bottom of the steps, she walked on a path made from flat limestones hauled in the wagon from the beach. Bill met her, "Hold it, Ginny. I'll feed them." He headed for the corn, stored in a burlap bag outside the hen house, when a dog barked. Other mongrels down the street joined in.

Virginia asked, "Who's coming?"

Bill looked toward the road, and walked over to the picket fence. Virginia followed. When they stood at the front gate, she saw a tall man in a black suit hiking along the center of the sandy street. He carried a long stick. At times he stopped and turned around to swing the stick at two barking dogs who trailed a few paces away. She asked, "Who's that?"

Bill took off his cap. Fingers callused from hauling in nets twisted the tarnished braid on a visor. He looked at Virginia and said, "He's all in black. He's a Mormon."

Bill put the cap back on his bald head. The couple watched the stranger approach, a silhouette against the bright July sky. Bill opened the gate, stepped out and yelled at the dogs, "Git! Git home! Git!" The animals retreated.

The stranger's black silk top hat matched a frock coat that reached his knees. As he trudged wearily toward them, he kicked up sand from his dark boots. When the thin man stopped at the fence, he tugged an index finger inside his white shirt collar.

Virginia watched how Bill's eyes met the fellow's stare. The stranger's dark eyes blazed feverishly, as raven-black as his short curly beard. On his left lapel a miniature silver cross caught the sun's bright rays and glittered. He jerked off the hat, wiped a dingy handkerchief over a perspiring forehead and the back of his neck. In a deep voice he said, "Thanks for chasing them kyoodles, mister. I'm Deacon Ebenezer Wright."

"Howdy. I'm Captain Ryan." Bill jerked a thumb toward Virginia, "Mrs. Ryan." Ebenezer stopped rubbing his neck and bowed his head at Virginia. She figured Ebenezer had hiked the length of the island by the look of his dusty hat and suit.

After the stranger wiped over his hat brim, he shoved the cloth inside a coat pocket and set the hat level over shoulder-length black hair, slicked down with goose grease. He smiled tiredly at the couple, "Lake's rough. Ain't it?"

"How come you're here?" Bill demanded, ignoring the

man's question. "I seen you plowing fields. No time to chew the fat. Why today? What's up?"

"I come to town to—"

Bill didn't let him finish. "Buy shelf goods? That's greed, mister. God don't like greedy folks. I don't nohow. Trappers hiked to town Tuesday. No lard. No flour at Shanahan's. Mormons bought out the store. Know what they said?"

"What?"

"Trappers told Shanahan they'd toss him and all youse Mormons in the drink next time. They wasn't hiking ten miles again for nothing."

Ebenezer studied the lake, "Sure is rough. Ain't it?"

Bill said, "That ain't rough. Ain't no blow. Just whitecaps kicking up a bit. Dancing a jig. Wait 'til September. Waves twenty feet high. That's rough."

Ebenezer stared down the street where the village stores faced the harbor and asked with amazement, "Say, where is everybody?"

Bill opened the gate and stepped into the street. Virginia followed. He walked a few steps to where his chestnut team was hitched to the wagon, then bent over and hit the pipe bowl several whacks against a wagon wheel. Next he pointed to the tailgate where the American flag rippled gently in the soft morning breeze. "Don't you know? It's the Fourth of July."

Ebenezer frowned and pressed his thin lips tighter as if afraid to say the wrong thing. He pulled out the handkerchief again, propped a foot on the wagon spokes and swatted hard at first one dusty boot, then the other. Once finished, he straightened up. "Sure, I know."

Bill leveled his gaze. "What are you in town for? Store's closed. It's a holiday."

"Looking for a ship."

"Harbor's closed. From Manitou to Mackinac skippers don't anchor here. They know we picnic on the Fourth."

Ebenezer looked toward the lake at the end of the road, and stroked his curly beard several times. He smiled and replied in a friendly tone, "My preacher's coming."

Virginia leaned against the wagon and twisted a sunbonnet ribbon. "Who?"

Ebenezer kept his tired eyes on the harbor as he announced proudly, "Reverend James Jesse Strang."

Bill nudged Virginia in the ribs with an elbow. He hoped she'd take the hint and shut up. He'd heard all about Mormons. If she hadn't baked so many durn pies, they'd be at the picnic. They should've left this Ebenezer to the dogs.

Virginia smiled and asked again, "Who is he?"

Ebenezer looked from the quay to Virginia and said, "Greatest preacher alive. Faith healer too."

"Really!"

"Who shot the breeze to you?" Bill asked.

"Got news last mail call."

"Damn sneaky. How come you ain't told nobody?"

"Reverend Strang wrote not to talk 'til the Fourth. You folks are the first to know. I waved at the others. They kept moving."

Bill said, "I don't blame them guys." He looked at Virginia and saw a gleam of excitement in her eyes. Now she had news to tell the women. Bill rubbed over his damp forehead, turned to Ebenezer and said, "This picnic's a big shindig. We've got to get moving."

Ebenezer walked over to the team and patted a horse soundly on the rump. The animal stopped whisking its tail, turned and stared sleepily. Bill reached up and untangled the reins. Ebenezer eyed the front yard. "Got a well? I'm plumb thirsty."

Virginia said, "I got cold milk. Want a glass?"

Ebenezer grinned, "Sounds good."

Bill pushed open the gate. The trio walked through the yard

past the iris, red geraniums, and the tall hollyhocks at the front
door. Bill shoved the door open. They entered one at a time.
At each side of the door, twelve small panes of glass formed
a large picture window. Sunlight filtered through white muslin
curtains, heavily starched and ironed neatly. The odor of
cherry pie baked that morning perfumed the air. Sunlight filled
the cabin to reveal a pine floor scrubbed clean. Bill said, "Sit
down, mister."

Ebenezer picked up his coat tails and sat on a chair like a
hen settling gently over a nest of eggs.

Virginia asked, "Who's coming with your preacher? How
many folks? We need women for quilting bees."

Bill sat, took off his white cap, and placed it on the table.
He slapped his callused right palm against his cheek and rested
his elbow on the table to prop his face. He impatiently tapped
the fingers of his left hand on the table and grumbled, "Hurry
up, Ginny. Give him the milk. I gotta get to the picnic. Throw
horseshoes. Knife target too."

Ebenezer ignored Bill. "Whole company. Folks far away as
New York."

Virginia gasped, "Really! New York!"

Bill stared sullenly at Ebenezer. "How many old Mormons
sailing here to croak—fill up our graveyard?"

Virginia frowned, "Bill, that's a terrible thing to say."

"No harm. Your husband takes the Gentile attitude. He
fears our strength in numbers dead or alive."

The men remained silent while Virginia walked to the
kitchen. She returned with a glass of milk and set it down in
front of Ebenezer, "Much obliged."

She asked Bill, "Milk?"

"No."

Virginia sat across from Bill as he stuffed tobacco into his
pipe. With a wave of her hand Virginia apologized, "I'd offer
you cherry pie, but it's packed."

Ebenezer swallowed a long gulp of milk, then put the glass down. "This is fine. Hits the spot."

Bill studied the skin on Ebenezer's cheeks that stretched as he drank. Although Ebenezer wiped his tongue across his lips, the fuzz above his upper lip remained white until he rubbed over it with the back of a hairy hand. Virginia leaned forward, with arms crossed and rested on the table. "How many folks in a company?"

Ebenezer stared at their bedroom where a bright coverlet had been neatly smoothed over the four-poster and a Crazy Quilt folded at the end. Next, he gazed at the two armchairs with white embroidered doilies on the arms and the back that faced the fireplace. "No telling. A hundred Mormon souls or more. Reverend Strang goes first class."

Virginia uncrossed her arms and placed her elbows on the table. With her chin cupped in her palms she asked, "What's first class?"

He set the glass down and replied, "Our ship, *Zion*, is real fancy. Three staterooms and carpets in the dining room. Captain and crew all good Mormons."

Bill wished Virginia didn't get so friendly. Did she forget how those other Mormon women treated her last year? Four Mormon families had landed and settled while he and Virginia had rowed to Garden Island early that spring. He didn't know that Mormons would arrive in Paradise Bay when he wasn't home. Virginia needed maple sugar from nearby Garden Island. The couple rowed the short distance, not just for sugar, but also because she always enjoyed visiting with the squaws.

Bill scoffed, "Good Mormons. That's a laugh. Last year Mormons landed. I heard they rented horses and wagons at the livery. Hauled stuff ashore and settled. Remember Ginny? You and Mrs. Smith took them fresh bread and strawberry jam. Never had nothing to do with you." He looked at Ebenezer and asked, "How long is this bunch staying?"

Ebenezer rubbed his beard and looked out a window. "Ask Reverend Strang. I'm just a deacon." He grinned, shook his head and bragged, "He's the best preacher in the whole wide world. Wait 'til you hear his voice—sweeter than honey. I swear. Folks walked over ten miles, in deep snow, just to hear him preach. His voice rings clearer than a silver bell."

Bill passed a rough hand over his short beard while his elbow stayed propped on the table. "Sure, I remember him. Tall. Red hair and beard. Red like the devil."

"Reverend Strang is a lawyer, newspaper editor, and debater. Mormons will kill for him."

"Makes us even. I'd kill for Beaver. My old man settled Beaver. Ought to call it 'Ryan Island.' Fishermen and trappers respect me. Call me Captain Ryan. You better too."

Ebenezer drank, then in a slow, determined voice said, "Beaver's big enough for Mormon and Gentile."

Bill glared. "Don't call me Gentile."

"We call others Gentile."

"That Strang was a snooper. I wish I'd kicked him out."

"It's a free country. Beaver's not private land."

"Last May he snooped all over the island. Wrote down our catch of trout. Net size. How we cut ice. He measured streams. Drew maps. Asked about animals. If I was you, I'd get off Beaver fast. Tell that shipload of Mormons too. I heard yesterday that a rough bunch of cutthroats is sailing here to chase Mormons off. What trouble was you in back in Wisconsin? Whittling, greasing and swallowing? Burn barns? Tar and feather? Ride a man on a rail?"

"We moved too much. We run no more. Beaver's our last place on the Lord's green earth. We will stay here if we have to be crushed as a people and swallowed up in one common ruin rather than sacrifice each other. Beaver Island is our paradise."

Bill shook a finger, "You listen. I'm telling you and them

guys too. That gang is coming here from Crooked Tree. Ship docked here yesterday. Sailors told me all about those roughnecks sailing here. Landing any time." Bill looked intensely into Ebenezer's eyes and said, "Real mean critters."

Ebenezer laughed and put on his top hat. "We ain't been scared of renegades at Whiskey Point. Some more rascals don't matter."

"This bunch is worse. Got hate in their gullets for Mormons. Ain't right for island folks to get hurt. Those rats can shoot me and the missus. Think we're Mormons. I can see it all. A big fight. Beaver blasted to bits. Folks murdered in their sleep. Cabins set on fire."

A nerve twitched on Ebenezer's cheek. "Ryan, you're talking looney."

Bill stood up, raised both hands and implored, "Why don't you listen to me?"

"You're a typical Gentile. You're trying to scare my brethren off the island."

"Mormons can't land here. Sail to the Manitous. Good soil over there."

Ebenezer stood up. "Ah-ha! That's it! You want us to get out. Pull up stakes. Leave big gardens. Corn fields. Hit the road. Sail away. Pan gold at Sutter's Mill?"

Bill raised his voice, "Mormons ain't wanted here. You buy out the store. No flour. No lard 'til a shipment came from Pine River." He hitched up his brown pants with both hands and cried out, "Why don't you listen?"

Ebenezer's face flushed. He said in a loud, heavy voice, "Mormons will meet those roughnecks head on. That scum will be pushed into sand and ground out with the heel of our boots."

Virginia stood. Ebenezer handed over the empty glass and in a quieter tone said, "Thanks, madam. Appreciate the milk." Both men shoved their chairs back, then walked to the door.

Bill put on his cap, looked sullenly at Virginia and demanded, "Let's shove off."

After the trio stepped down the log cabin stairs, Ebenezer
tipped his top hat and said, "Good day."

They watched him hike toward the wharf. When he was out
of hearing, Bill faced Virginia. "You were nicey-nice." In a
falsetto voice he imitated, "Have some milk. Sorry, pies all
packed." In his normal voice he insisted, "He's a Mormon. He
eyed the whole blame house."

She placed a hand on his bare arm. He looked down and
saw the hairs rise up like the fur on a scared animal. As he
pulled away she said, "I felt sorry for him. It's hot. He came
a long way on foot."

Without a word, Bill walked back to the cabin. He jammed
a sturdy bolt across the rear door. "I'm locking up. Mormons
can clean us out." He stomped about the cottage, pulled the
muslin curtains together at the bedroom window and dragged
a braided rug over the kitchen trap door that opened to a fruit
cellar underground.

Virginia stared icily and snapped, "Get that rug away. You
know I hate it there. I'll break my neck on it." She pushed a
wisp of grey hair from her forehead. "Who's going to steal my
shelf goods? Who are you afraid of?"

Bill walked to the front door with a set of large keys. He
selected the biggest one, turned around and shook it. "That
Strang and his gang. Mormons will land like rats off a sinking
ship. Better safe, not sorry."

"Get the roses. I want to leave," Virginia said. She walked
down the steps. He locked the front door and jiggled the knob
several times. After he climbed down the steps, he walked to
the shady side of the cabin. He returned carrying a wood
bucket of red and yellow roses in one hand and zinnias in the
other.

When he reached the wagon, he placed the buckets inside

and said, "Flowers are a durn Jonah!"

"Don't say that. The flowers are for your father. Dead sailors too."

Bill shoved his cap further back, then cupped his hands alongside his mouth. "Hear that, Beaver Island? Ginny Ryan's chewing out her old man."

She looked down, picked up her long calico dress, and placed a foot on the first wagon step. "Folks aren't home. You can't shame me." She climbed up to the front seat.

He got in, sat next to her, and picked up the reins. He slapped the rawhide across the horses' rumps and they lurched forward. Virginia squealed, "Take it easy. My pies! They won't be fit to eat or win a prize."

He wrapped the leather straps around his knuckles. "Blame the horses, Ginny. Not me."

At first the wagon wheels moved steadily through the sand, but when the roadway became stony, the wagon bounced. Virginia looked back at the pies and lunch. "Well?" Bill asked.

"Nothing spilled. Oh! My hens! You didn't feed them."

"Don't worry. They'll live." He hit the horses with the whip. They trotted faster.

Virginia glanced a second time at the rear of the wagon. Suddenly she yelled, "Slow down! The roses. Go easy. They almost tipped over."

He slowed the team and looked at her brown eyes under the sunbonnet. "We'll die on the way. Got flowers for our graves."

She stared back. "Don't talk looney."

He let out the reins and touched the whip lightly on the horses. "After Mormons land, we ain't gonna be safe."

Virginia let out the bonnet ribbon and retied it into a neater bow. "Don't be so gloomy. I'm not worried. More the merrier, I say."

"If my old man had sense, he'd have land-claimed Beaver

before he died. I'd own it now."

Virginia's sharp eyes darted at him, "Bill, don't say that. God rest the poor man's soul."

Bill raised the whip and flicked it lightly against horse-hide, and coughed. Then he leaned over and spat at the side of the road where dandelions grew alongside bluebells. He looked skyward and pleaded, "Pa, why didn't you fix things legal? Make Beaver mine. Not U.S. government?"

Virginia ignored him. She was tired after baking pies, and had been apprehensive that Bill would wait for the ship to land. She closed her eyes and held onto the side of the wagon. Soon she'd be with lady friends, enjoying a wonderful picnic.

Deep ruts in the road made the seat vibrate. Bill stared at the trail ahead. "Sneaky Mormons. Told nobody 'til now. That Ebenezer sure let the cat out the bag."

Virginia opened her eyes, and squinted in the bright sun. "When's that gang coming?"

"No gang. Tried to set a fire under him. When Strang lands, my men will kick him out. Strang won't set foot on Beaver."

2

*J*ames Strang stood alone at the ship's bow. A stocky man, five feet, seven inches tall, he studied the distant outline of Beaver Island. Strang had a large head, a high prominent forehead, and henna-colored hair and beard. He wore a black suit, dark green vest and white shirt beneath a black cape that covered his broad shoulders. Around his neck on a chain hung a Sixth Century Byzantine gold cross with small sunburst wheels.

It was midmorning and sunlight made his hair and beard glow bright red. He anticipated the moment when the ship steamed into Beaver's landlocked harbor later that afternoon. He'd greet the Mormons he'd brought to the island last year. They'd be dockside waving white handkerchiefs to welcome him. At first sight, the handkerchiefs would be small white dots, as snowy as the tips of the waves hitting each other playfully all over Lake Michigan, and as pure as the white sails of the fishermen's mosquito fleet.

Ahead waited Beaver, the Emerald Isle, and behind his last home, Voree, the Garden of Peace. Beaver would be a far better place than that Wisconsin settlement.

It had been a twenty-seven-mile wagon trip from Voree to Racine. When the *Zion* sailed from Racine, the passengers remained topside for almost an hour. Each wanted to be the first to spot the sea monster reported by Strang's elders on other trips. They had insisted, "We are sure that if unmolested, the monster is not dangerous."

Before this voyage talk circulated again about the sea monster, and it almost frightened the Voree brethren not to sail. "O fudge!" Strang had exclaimed. "If I see it, I'll believe. It's pure humbug!"

For the moment Strang treasured his solitude; he inhaled the frigid air and studied the lake. That helped erase all thoughts of the troubles he'd endured. At age thirty-one, he became a convert in the Mormon Church. At Nauvoo, Illinois in 1844, he was baptized by Joseph Smith, the founder of Mormonism. By creating a permanent settlement at Beaver, he'd escape memories of Joseph Smith and Brigham Young. Brigham had destroyed all his plans to take Smith's place. He often pondered what his life would be like if Brigham Young had not taken over as president of the Mormon Church after Joseph Smith was murdered.

When the breeze blew nor'west aboard ship, the wind wafted barnyard sounds. Strang heard cackling hens, mooing cows and the whinny of a horse. The collection of animals was tied up inside temporary stalls at the ship's stern. While Strang remained topside enjoying the solitude, he knew he'd made the right choice to live isolated on Beaver. Waves splashed on his hands as they clutched the railing. He grinned—it reminded him of the thirsty Mormons led by Brigham Young four years ago on that desert wagon trail headed West. He thought they probably longed for cool drinking water while Strang's followers never became thirsty. Later he'd persuade thousands of brethren to join him on Beaver. He'd build up a strong Mormon empire. He'd make Brigham sorry he excommunicated James Strang.

3

$\mathscr{A}$ white railing with a narrow red trim on the first deck encircled the wood burning ship. Two black metal smokestacks were in front of the center mast, one third the distance from the bowsprit. This July morning most passengers remained in the dining room when the seas turned rough midway. On the ship's shady port side, two men sat on a bench tied down by ropes. A few gallant souls stood topside and leaned against the railing looking at the distant island while the strong breeze tousled their hair.

The ship pitched hard up and down with a steady tempo and hit the blue waves crested by foaming tips. Men staggered to walk the deck. Two middle-age women in black dresses and sunbonnets sat on a wood bench chained to the ship. They squinted in the bright sunlight. One asked the other, "Is she still down there?"

"Who?"

"Sister Mary. She's been in that fancy stateroom the whole trip. Too good for us."

"No. You're wrong. I remember she worked hard at the store. Kept the credit books. Waited on customers."

Directly below the women, Mary Strang sat in a maple rocker in her cabin. Tired of sewing on a quilt, she folded it and placed it over the chair's side.

Mary got up and walked to the wall mirror hung above a small shelf. Royal blue eyes stared back at the young woman wearing a grey cotton dress with dainty white lace at the collar. She raised her arms and patted her slim fingers over her dark hair that was braided and twisted into a loop on each side. As the twenty-eight year old woman stood there, she tucked stray hairs into place, and scratched her oily scalp. She recalled how she had said to her husband, "How awful! No water to wash my hair on the wagon trail. Now I see all this lake water and still can't wash my hair."

Mary remembered the luxury of a comfortable home where she'd taken washing her hair for granted. She'd given up a wonderful house in Voree for that island, called a new paradise, but now just an ink blot below the horizon. She had been exposed to gossip about polygamy on the wagon trip. The word, "polygamy" merged with the wagon wheels and became a monotonous singsong in her head. Mary had explained to the women, "Brother Strang will not allow plural wives on the island. He doesn't care what Brigham Young does in Utah. My husband will not allow spiritual wifery on Beaver." She had met those gossips face to face, and didn't care that they disliked her for admonishing them.

At twilight on the trail when Strang checked out the water supply and feed for the animals, Mary had tucked her children into bed. The ugly thoughts of polygamy haunted her.

She had told James, "At breakfast the women cook oatmeal and gossip. The old women look at the girls strangely. They

try to find a hint of sin in their eyes. As if those girls slept
with their husbands."

He had laughed and said, "We're too busy for such
tomfoolery. They don't dare sin around me."

Mary walked back to the rocker, picked up the quilt and
began to sew. When the ship's bell sounded, she glanced at the
clock on the bulkhead. Eleven o'clock. After the bell stopped,
she heard footsteps and men talking in the passageway. She
hoped their voices didn't wake up Myraette and William
sleeping in the bunk. Mary got up, opened the door a crack
and peeked outside. Immediately a cool lake breeze from the
open stairwell chilled her cheeks and light pink lips.

She saw a group of men standing outside Strang's stateroom. Before she closed the door, she saw Strang standing at
the top of the open stairwell. Bright sunshine illuminated his
red hair. She watched him climb down fast, always impatient
to reach his destination. Once below, he pulled off the black
velvet cape, and handed it to an elder who folded it carefully.
They all walked inside Strang's cabin.

Mary closed the door and sat in the rocker again. She
glanced at her plain gold wedding ring. So often she complained, "I'm always forgotten. Talks with your men are more
important than being with me. Why do I have to sacrifice?"
The clock ticked away. She watched the brass pendulum
swing, and thought, *This is how my life with him has been. On
the move. Never together.* Before the trip he had told her, "I
need my own stateroom. I conduct meetings and write."

Mary picked up the needle and worked the white thread in
and out of the small quilt with her slim fingers. This was the
same quilt she sewed when a note tied to a rock had been
thrown on her porch in Voree. The rock landed with a heavy
thud and frightened her. The crudely printed message disguised
the handwriting. The words were engraved in her heart and
mind forever. If only she could forget and drop them like

pebbles into a deep river. But she would always remember the note: "Mr. Strang's secretary ain't his nephew. Charlie is a girl."

She rocked and the chair kept time with the thumping paddle wheel. As she moved back and forth, her face flushed to recall that day. At first she felt rage. After the shock wore off, her hands stayed icy for a long time. Strang had returned from an Eastern speaking tour with Charlie and had told her, "Charlie is my seventeen-year-old nephew from New York." Strang paid Charlie's board at a rooming house.

Mary calculated what she disliked about Charlie: the slim figure, soft like a woman, and the aloof personality. Charlie copied speeches for Strang, answered letters and wrote articles for the newspaper. It annoyed Mary that Charlie also acted as Strang's valet; he brushed suits, polished boots, and carried James' best silk top hat in a round box for special occasions. Charlie avoided talking to Mary, but Mary detected a trace of femininity in the voice. Although Charlie wore a gentleman's black suit and had short dark hair, he had a smooth complexion with no hint of a mustache on the upper lip. The male disguise didn't fool Mary. It aggravated her when Charlie and Strang sat together at the table in Voree writing newspaper articles.

One evening as she was washing dishes, Mary had snapped at Strang, "How can you afford a secretary?" When she glanced up from the dishpan, she saw her husband smile, wink at Charlie and say, "Charlie is worth far more to me than anyone will ever know."

Charlie gazed at Strang with hazel eyes. Mary knew that Charlie was a girl. Anger and hurt welled up inside her with that certainty. They were sneaking around to be lovers.

Mary's soft black boots pushed against the oval hooked rug as she rocked. At Voree she had kept busy by purchasing a year's supply of flour and other staples for this trip. She bought small items like safety pins, thread, and spices. Boxes

had to be marked and she had to decide what to pack for the
long buggy ride from home. *Home! Where is my real home?*
She asked herself. She had said to Strang, "Every time I
furnish a house, we move on. I have to make that stateroom
comfortable. I can't stand a bare room. Not even for the lake
voyage."

This cabin became a real pleasure for Mary after traveling
like a gypsy in a spring buggy over rough trails. When they
stopped, Mary helped the women cook over campfires. The
men had snapped whips at horses and cows. At last when they
reached the *Zion*, women had screamed nervously at children
to get aboard.

"Where's the island, ma?" a little boy had asked. His
mother ordered, "Get up there and shut up."

Mary said, "James, I hope you have a decent log cabin
picked out." She knew she would forget that note if she kept
busy after they landed. She never discussed it with James. He
had kept busy as a lawyer; he closed land sales and advised his
followers what to bring to Beaver and what the ship could not
transport. Mary wanted to help with the newspaper. Strang had
said, "No. Stay home with the children." Another time he
said, "I'm too tired to talk. Read the *Gospel Herald* about
moving to Beaver. There's a good poem printed this week."

Mary read the poem:

"Let me go to Big Beaver in Michigan Lake;
Let me have dear friends and relatives take.
My wife and my children and brethren also,
To keep God's commandments, O there let me go."

While sitting inside the stateroom, she heard the loud waves
spilling over the revolving paddle wheel, just like memories
rushing to mind. Strang had gone to Charlie's boarding house
in Voree. "Myraette and William bother me. I must concen-

trate on paper work." How many times had he said that? Mary lost count.

The ship's clock reminded her of another clock, one she watched as she waited for Strang to return home. Toward evening she became so weak after reading that note, she had barely enough strength to walk to the fireplace and burn it. While she watched the hot coals turn the paper into black tissue, she felt as if she had aged fifty years. Later she begged Strang to let her stay in Voree until the new house was built on Beaver. Charlie remained back at Voree. He insisted that Mary go with him.

Mary rocked and thought of all the nights and the heartache when she sat alone and read. She had finished reading Hawthorne's *The Scarlet Letter* and two chapters of Dickens' *David Copperfield*. She hoped to finish it on the boat to Beaver. Whenever she waited up for Strang, she covered herself with a blanket and sat in front of the fireplace. She wanted to welcome Strang with a glowing fireplace, roast beef, freshly baked apple turnovers and warm apple cider. That might make him forget Charlie. When he didn't come home, the food turned cold. She went to bed.

The next afternoon he returned and Mary asked, "Where were you all night?"

He had replied in a nasty tone, "I don't have to explain my absence. Where I go and what I do is my business."

Mary sighed with relief knowing that Charlie stayed back in Voree. She rocked faster and asked herself, *How will James treat me when Charlie comes to Beaver?*

4

*B*efore the Puritans reached Plymouth Rock, the French of Champlain's colony at Quebec landed at Beaver Island, part of an archipelago in Lake Michigan northwest of Pine River.

In 1647, the French explorers with Father Joliet and Father Allouez called it "Isle du Castor." By 1755, it was renamed Beaver, resembling a beaver skin stretched out to dry. Thirteen miles long and six and a half miles wide, and located four miles off the Chicago steamboat route, Beaver attracted ships with a two-mile broad harbor. Its channel, three-fourths of a mile wide between the entrance reefs, with a strait ninety rods wide between headlands, separated the inner and outer harbors. Paradise Bay, almost a mile long, was landlocked and nineteen fathoms deep. If the harbor became crowded with ships, passengers walked down a gangplank next to the land.

On the west coast tall trees covered fairly high hills. On the east grew a thick forest of pine, cedar, ash and hemlock. Six lakes varied in size from forty to sixty acres with deep pure water, clean sandy beaches and plenty of fish. Rich in timber, the interior remained dense until sunlight cascaded between the branches of sugar maple, birch and fir. Fisheries spread over the lake fifty miles north and forty miles south.

Steamboats named *Michigan*, *Lady*, *Scotia*, *Ohio* and *Troy* tied up to buy ice, fish and firewood, then sailed north to Mackinac Island, named Michilimackinac or "great turtle" by the Indians.

When shrill steamboat whistles blew at Paradise Bay, black bears lunged from the lake shore into the island's refuge of fifty-eight square miles. A sandy road circled the island where the waves washed playfully over the top deck of an old shipwreck. Back from the road, wind-formed ripples covered a sandy knoll on the dunes and below it grew juniper bushes. After the dunes, there were grassy hills, another forest, a swamp and more inland lakes. Throughout the interior of the island, trappers lived in log cabins. Fishermen settled in the village near Paradise Bay and tied up boats not far from fishing shacks. On Beaver the villagers bought shelf goods at Shanahan's general store.

The ship was filled to capacity with cargo and passengers. All the Mormons aboard had sold their homes in Voree, Wisconsin, each built on a quarter lot 4x10 rods and purchased for $12.50. Now they'd resettle on free land at Beaver Island, which they called, "our paradise."

Zion reached the middle of Lake Michigan when Strang greeted four men inside his stateroom. As the ship's bell sounded, Strang reached inside his waistcoat, took out a pocket watch, and glanced at the time. He faced Praiseworthy Van Dusen, an elderly man with white hair and a long beard. His hands had bright blue veins under flesh as thin as dry onion skin.

After Strang spread out a large map on the table, he looked over at the elder. Praiseworthy spoke in a raspy voice, "I was a big man at Nauvoo. The brethren came to me for help. Joseph Smith was always busy. I was ready to run for mayor. Joseph said he'd back me." He took a deep breath, and coughed so hard his white beard shook.

Immediately Strang pounded his ruby ring against the table and called out, "Order elders. Order. Let's open with a prayer." The men shoved chairs back from the table, stood up, and bowed their heads. Strang raised his hands, then clasped them together at his waist and lowered his head. After a few moments of silence, he prayed in a sonorous tone, "O Lord, enlighten your humble prophet, James Jesse Strang, to do Your holy will. Grant wisdom to Your servants gathered here that they may have the courage, health and industry to make Beaver Island their new paradise. This we ask in the name of Your servant, James, and all his beloved elders. Amen."

"Amen," the men echoed devoutly. They sat down and Strang glanced around, wondering if he'd made the right choice for Church elders. Praiseworthy was too old to work, but rich. Frank Bowers sat at the left of Praiseworthy. Frank, a one-time actor and preacher, had toured Europe and met royalty. Dr. Hezekiah McCulloch sat next to Frank and worried Strang. At Baltimore he had been pro-Mormon, then anti-Mormon. Strang wouldn't want him to make trouble, but he needed a physician.

Nathan Bates sat to the right of Praiseworthy. Tall like the doctor and Bowers, he had been Strang's printer at Voree. Strang needed Bates to print the *Northern Islander* once the printing press arrived on the next ship.

Praiseworthy rubbed saliva from his lips with the back of his hand and asked, "Brother Strang, how many log cabins?"

"Enough," Strang replied.

The old fellow shook his head and the little pouches high up on his cheeks moved like soft jelly. He said, "I better get a good one. Can't stand drafts. Got sore bones."

Strang said, "You'll get a good fireplace. Don't worry. Nothing has changed since I came last year. My brethren wrote me faithfully all winter and spring."

"What if the cabins are taken? Then what?"

Strang pressed his lips tight and stared at the man. He said, "No new settlers. Nothing to worry about."

Praiseworthy leaned his elbows on the table and supported his knuckles under his white beard. "Who owns the empty cabins?"

Strang sighed, provoked that the old man kept pestering him. "No one. They're free."

Praiseworthy clasped his hands in front of his chest. "What if settlers object?"

When the old man folded his hands over his thin chest, Strang thought, *That's what he'll look like laid out in a coffin. I suppose he sleeps like that. Practices for his death. He'll die on Beaver and I'll give the funeral oration listing his good work as a Mormon at Voree and Nauvoo. Ought to start writing his obituary. He won't survive winter.*

Brigham Young had tried to sign up Praiseworthy for the trip West. It had been Strang's great triumph to win the old fellow away from Brigham by convincing him the lake breeze would benefit his wife's poor lungs. Strang put up with the old man's complaints only because of his money. Strang replied, "They won't. You forget about my petition to Congress. I want the government to give Beaver to Mormons."

Dr. McCulloch asked, "What if Congress votes no?"

Strang didn't like the doctor's interference. He wished he'd kept this meeting strictly for the elders. He clenched his teeth, then grinned slightly at the doctor and replied, "If not, then we take land. Consecrate it for the Lord."

McCulloch raised his black, bushy eyebrows slightly, stroked his dark beard thoughtfully, and asked, "Steal? God's wrath will be upon us."

Strang glared. "No. I repeat, consecrate. Use what is needed to build up our kingdom. It's all revealed in the Plates of Laban. Besides, I'm a lawyer. I know what I'm doing. There are many ways to skin a polecat."

McCulloch tapped the long fingers of his right hand on the table and asked, "What if the Gentiles want my medicine?"

Strang said, "Forget the Gentiles. They've lived for years without a doctor. I doubt they'll come to you for tonics and pills. I hope, doctor, you brought enough general merchandise to stock your store. The brethren will build shelves for your goods and medicine."

"I did. Where's my store?"

"Here." Strang pointed to a place on a map. "Between the cooper and my print shop."

McCulloch shook his head and frowned, "That's too far from the dock."

Praiseworthy burst out laughing, "Far! You call that far? A few rods, doctor."

McCulloch scowled, "I wanted my store closer."

Strang said, "You're right. The closer the better for ships and Gentiles."

Praiseworthy asked, "If this is our island, why sell to Gentiles?"

Strang held up his right hand. "Brother Van Dusen, we can't take over the island the first day."

The old man's head shook slightly from palsy, and strands of hair fell over his forehead. "You promised it was ours. I didn't give you all my money for trouble."

In a firm voice Strang said, "No trouble. Our brethren will keep coming and the Gentiles will be outnumbered. Soon

Beaver will be ours."

Praiseworthy blinked his fine white eyelashes slowly as his Adam's apple jiggled in his throat each time he swallowed. He asked, "Where's my cabin?"

Strang pointed at the map with the tip of his pocket knife, "All the big X's are empty cabins. You and the wife can live here next to my future temple."

"I thought you told me the village."

"Later. Fishermen live there now. First we settle in empty cabins in the woods, plant our gardens, and live off wild animals and fish. After more brethren sail in, we operate our sawmill, fish, and ice business for the lake boats. Before long, not one settler will stay." He looked at the men who listened intently and continued, "When we tie up at Beaver, I want order. I don't want folks running off to explore whatever catches their fancy. Unload the ship fast. The captain sails back for my printing press, livestock, and a company of fifty."

Praiseworthy's dull grey eyes stared at Strang. "When's he sailing?"

"Tomorrow. Early. Thousands of our brethren in Voree are itching to relocate here."

Frank Bowers twisted his thin lips into a sneer as his lanky body slouched in a chair. "I get the feeling Brother Praise-worthy is losing faith, Brother Strang."

The elder shook a fist at Frank. "You young upstart. I worked hand in hand with Joseph Smith. Faith! I got more in my little finger than you got in your whole lazy body."

Frank smoothed a silk brocade tie and grinned at the angry Praiseworthy. The old man raved, "You're just a penny ante actor."

Strang cried out, "Stop! This meeting is to make plans. Not to bicker and slander."

"I speak the truth, Brother Strang. Frank thinks because he acted in Europe, he's a big shot." He smacked his lips, then shouted, "I curse the day he got baptized a Mormon!"

Frank jerked up straight in the chair and turned his head. He stared at Praiseworthy with narrow set dark eyes, then turned to Strang and asked, "Brother Strang, do I have to be blasphemed by this old reprobate?"

Strang stood up, his face flushed the shade of a wild rose. He called out loudly, "Stop! Save your wrath for Gentiles. We are Mormon brothers united in a serious obligation. Be at peace with one another. The journey has been long and difficult. Look out the portholes.

"When my eyes first rested on Beaver Island, I knew it was the most beautiful place on earth. See Beaver. Right there in blue waters—at peace with the world, away from the strife at Nauvoo. The Mexican War that our country is foolishly engaged in will never bother us. We will live fully forever, loving the Lord, God with all our hearts, and our brethren as ourselves. Gentlemen, put aside any anger you feel toward a brother. Do not let Satan follow us to Beaver and live in our hearts. There will be no unfruitful works of darkness born of hell and begotten by Satan.

"Reach out. Touch your brother. Take his hand. Forgive any wrongs he has done in word or deed. I promised you a miracle. There it is. Beaver Island. Soon we will land. Let us grasp each other's hand in a bond of renewed love, faith and loyalty to the Church and each other.

"Gentleman, I propose a toast to Beaver Island." Holding a silver pitcher in one hand, Strang poured liquid first into his gold chalice, then each man's goblet.

Dr. McCulloch asked, "Wine?"

Lines formed on Strang's oversized forehead. Bright henna hair neatly brushed fell slightly below the tips of his ears. He replied, "It's apple juice. Liquor is the abomination of the devil."

After he finished pouring, Strang set down the pitcher on a

small table. The men stood up. Strang raised his chalice and said, "For our success at Beaver. Nauvoo was destroyed by Brigham Young, the Council of Twelve, and the Nauvoo Legion. Beaver will be our paradise with men of righteousness. Our peace lies a few hours away. My paradise. Your paradise. Today, we are making history. Soon all the world will respect our settlement on Beaver. No one will ever remember that cursed Brigham Young. The name of James Jesse Strang will be known by all generations. Elders of the first Mormon Church on Beaver Island, Michigan, I give you a toast to our promised land, a Nauvoo born again by God's holy will."

He raised the gold chalice high in the air in front of the men. Streaks of light came through a porthole, reflected on his goblet and glittered on the white bulkhead. Strang called out, "To Beaver Island."

The four silver tumblers clicked against the gold chalice as the men joyfully shouted, "To Beaver Island!"

After they finished drinking, a loud knock sounded on the stateroom door. Strang opened the door to admit Zenas Caldwell, a short man about thirty years old with black hair tousled by the wind. He wore a dirty buckskin jacket and dark pants and reeked of body odor. His skin was deeply tanned and his short dark beard was speckled with grey. Below a hawk-like nose, his lips were thick and bleary eyes stared wildly at Strang as he pleaded, "Brother Strang, my wife is sick. Come quick. Pray over her."

Dr. McCulloch eyed the man, then turned to Strang. "I gave her sarsaparilla. No need to go."

Holding a hat in one hand, Zenas stepped closer to Strang. He held out his right hand like a beggar and implored again, "Please come. Put some holy oil on her. She'll get well. I know you can cure her."

Strang recalled how Zenas had loaded a section of the ship wrong. Because of his mistake, the cargo had to be restacked.

Valuable time lost. He didn't like Zenas telling him what to do. Strang replied, "Go back to her. I'll be there shortly."

Zenas quickly slapped the dirty hat on his head, walked to the door and jerked it open. He said, "Come quick. She's in the dining room."

The door closed, and Frank Bowers picked up his black hat from the table and fanned the air. "Whew! He stunk. No wonder his wife's sick."

The men laughed. Except Strang. He stared out a porthole and said, "Takes all kinds to pioneer. He's a good worker, when he does the job right."

Frank said, "I hope he won't live near me. I've smelled sweeter polecats."

Strang frowned, annoyed at Frank's remark, and said, "This meeting is over."

Praiseworthy remained seated after the others stood up. Frank picked up the silver tumblers and placed them on a small side table. Praiseworthy said, "Brother Strang, I'll watch your faith healing."

Dr. McCulloch said, "I'll go too. If the Lord doesn't hear you, Brother Strang, the woman should take more sarsaparilla. I'm satisfied she's not a contagious patient."

Strang resented the doctor's advice. He didn't want the brethren to believe in Dr. McCulloch's testimonial about "Dr. Townsend's Sarsaparilla," called "The Most Extraordinary Medicine in the World." Dr. Townsend claimed it cured fever and ague, spitting blood, consumption, fits and canker in the mouth. The label on the bottle stated sarsaparilla dosages were more pleasant to swallow than quinine and codeine. Strang did not want his healing power to compete with medicine. Of all times, now was the moment to show the doctor up, but the physician would be handy on Beaver Island to set broken bones and deliver babies.

Before the sailors had lifted the anchor, Strang heard

complaints of toothaches, sore throats and bronchitis. He had
no time to do faith healing then; he sent them to Dr. McCulloch. Later on the island he'd cure them faster than the doctor's
pills and tonics.

Strang took out a set of keys from his pants' pocket. He
knelt down, unlocked an oak footlocker, lifted the top, and
removed a small silver jar. When he stood he said, "Come on.
Let's go to the sick Hortense."

When they reached the ship's dining room, Zenas stood
near his wife stretched out on thick blankets on the floor.
James noticed that Zenas had taken off his buckskin jacket and
dirty hat. He wore black pants and a blue denim shirt with
long sleeves and buttons missing at the cuffs. His wrinkled
clothes looked like he'd slept in them for months.

The moment Zenas saw Strang approach, he stepped
forward and whispered, "She's worse. Fever's got her bad."

Dr. McCulloch rushed ahead, followed by Strang and
Praiseworthy. An elderly woman caring for Hortense got up
from where she sat on the floor next to the sick woman. A wet
cloth had been placed on Hortense's forehead and neck. Her
swollen lips mumbled incoherently as her arms rested limply
at her sides. Her shoes and black cotton stockings were
removed. Strang watched as she rubbed her bare feet together,
first one then the other at the ankles.

Dr. McCulloch knelt down and removed the cloth from her
forehead. He felt her face, turned to Zenas and demanded,
"Get ice from the galley."

Strang ordered, "No. You asked me to come. I'm here to
pray over her. Every gift of God is good."

Zenas looked from Strang to the doctor. His dark eyes
widened and a look of bewilderment flooded his face.

The doctor took a deep breath, then commanded once again,
"Get ice."

Strang raised his right hand. "No. I will call upon the Lord

to heal her." He knelt down next to the woman, clasped his
hands, and bowed his fiery red head to pray. "Lord, I ask you
to heal Sister Hortense. Blessed are they that keep Thy
commandments, that they may have the right to the tree of life,
and may enter through the narrow gate into the city. Help
Sister Hortense recover, Lord." While he knelt, he opened the
silver container, dipped his right thumb inside and wiped oil on
her forehead. Then he stood up, turned to Zenas and asked
softly, "Has she been baptized?"

Zenas nodded. "Twice." All the while his eyes stared at
Hortense, searching for any indication of improvement.
Praiseworthy stood nearby as the doctor leaned against the
bulkhead.

Strang heard the waves slap hard at the side of the ship, and
the thump of the big paddle wheel. Hortense stopped rubbing
her feet. Next, Strang placed the ointment on her cheeks. For
a second time he spread it over her forehead. He closed the
jar, turned to the others and announced with great confidence,
"She's better."

The doctor agreed in a matter of fact tone, "Of course.
Crisis is over."

Strang eyed the physician and sternly replied, "I repeat.
Every gift of God is good. Do you deny my power of faith
healing?"

Dr. McCulloch grinned slightly, and folded his arms over
his chest. "No. There's enough sickness in the world for faith
healing and medicine. It's a matter of choice. God gives me
power to heal in many ways." He turned to leave, then halted.
"She's young. That's in her favor."

Zenas knelt next to Hortense. She opened her eyes and tried
to sit up. He placed a hand on her shoulder and said, "Rest.
You will be all right." When he stood he smiled broadly with
relief. He grabbed Strang's free hand and shook it soundly.
"We got six kids. What would happen to them if she died? I'll

do anything you want. Any job."

Praiseworthy stepped next to Strang. "Can't we find a bunk for this poor soul?"

Strang addressed the sick woman, "Sister Hortense, I will find a more comfortable place for you to rest." The woman remained too weak to reply, but Strang knew she understood by the way she gazed at him.

Praiseworthy faced Zenas and said, "You're lucky the Lord heard. I was on a ship near Erie. Had a sick elder. Five prayed with me. We were in and out of that sickroom eight times before the Lord heard our prayers. It was Brother Edward Comstock, sick with *Cholera morbus*. Think of it! Eight times! Finally I said, 'We're not handling this right.' I got all the congregation together and we prayed. Even the church sisters joined. Before we docked, he got well. That night we celebrated. Had a feast on sugar. A new face was on all of us."

He laughed, "We were so happy. Sang hymns all the next day. I'll never forget. Folks living along the Erie Canal raised windows to hear our singing. There was Elder Loomis with his violin and Elder Rogers, a baritone. What a sight! All those heads poked out of house windows, just to hear our singing."

Strang tugged at the old man's sleeve, "Let's go. Sister Hortense needs rest. I must set up a stateroom for her."

Praiseworthy held up a blue veined hand, "One more thing." He turned to Zenas, "Keep faith in Brother Strang, young fellow. His laying on the hands and anointing with oil is far better than pills. I remember when Mother Van Dusen had a high fever."

Strang interrupted, "We must let the good woman rest." As they walked out of the dining room, Strang noticed Zenas' stride. He paced the deck like a tiger Strang had once seen in a zoo, moving nervously back and forth in a cage. Zenas stopped. He waited for Strang to catch up, then he walked closely beside him. Strang walked faster towards the stairwell to get topside and breathe fresh air—not this man's body odor. Zenas said, "Brother Strang, I'll work for you day and night."

"I'll need you," Strang said. "Feisty Irish settlers on Beaver. I'll meet the scoundrels head on. If I have to, I'll grind them in the sand with the heel of my boot."

5

$\mathcal{A}$fter he left the sick woman, Dr. McCulloch climbed topside. A tall, lean gentleman, forty-five years old, he wore a dark brown suit with the jacket unbuttoned over a white shirt. A few streaks of grey highlighted the black hair that hung down to his collar, and a dark beard almost covered his maroon tie.

The physician stopped in front of two buckboards turned upside down. He watched how the wheels spun in the breeze. Next he passed a buggy with a shiny black leather top, and feed sacks blocking its wheels to hold it steady. He saw boxes inside marked FRAGILE in bright red letters.

He edged past a collection of household furniture—small sofas, chairs, tables, and mattresses stacked on top of barrels and crates. The ship's bell rang again as he walked along the narrow path left open next to the wood railing, until he came near two young seamen who sat on top of wood crates.

When the last echo of the ship's bell drifted away in the wind, the sailors jumped down and hurried toward the stairs that led to the dining quarters below.

Dr. McCulloch looked at the ship's side wheel that churned the water into a continuous wake. The froth next to the half-covered wheel pushed above the waves like a bubbly fountain. He walked to the bow and eyed the figurehead, an austere image of an Old Testament prophet carved out of cypress and painted like gold. While the bow cut into the lake, water splashed high up at the sculpture's carved hands, which held a cross with a snake chiseled upon it.

How appropriate, he thought. *This figurehead of Moses is like Strang leading his people onward—not over deserts and mountains like prophets of old, but bounding over waves, as if all this water will keep trouble away—separate Mormon from Gentile and gain peace. No more persecution.*

He saw Strang at the other side of the bow and called over, "Going to lunch?"

Strang walked over to him and said, "Never eat much at sea. Get mal-de-mer."

Dr. McCulloch grinned. "I wish the passengers ate less. I brought plenty of peppermint tonic. Cures seasick."

Strang said, "Lake's getting rougher."

The doctor sensed by his tone that what had passed between them earlier with Sister Hortense was forgotten. He agreed, "Yes, it's gusty."

The ship vibrated suddenly, and the doctor watched as Strang reached out to grab the railing. The sun beamed directly overhead and illuminated Strang's ruby ring. Strang looked down at his hand and smiled at the strange glare. He turned his wrist and shone the red glow upon his other hand. Here he wore a gold ring with a small raised figure of a coiled snake. When the doctor glanced up at the sky, the ship became gloomy as a cloud passed over the sun.

After a few seconds the sun returned. Strang turned away from the rail, leaned his back against it, and reached into his side pocket for a watch. His arm brushed against a gold chain that hung across his waistcoat.

Dr. McCulloch saw a dozen charms. "What's that?"

Before he could reply, a high wave splashed up at the side of Strang's face. The doctor watched as Strang frowned, quickly reached into his pocket and took out a large, white linen handkerchief with his initials embroidered in one corner. He turned from the lake and wiped his face and red beard. Next he held up a row of charms, silver figures fastened to a chain around his waist. Strang proudly said, "It's my momento chain." He fixed his gaze on the doctor and said, "Each charm is a gift from someone I've cured." He grinned and eyed the doctor, "There isn't one family aboard I haven't cured at one time or another. That's why my brethren follow me to Beaver Island."

Dr. McCulloch stood with hands clasped behind his back, and bent his knees to balance as the boat lurched up and down. He said, "I wish you'd cure them of sea sickness. I ignored the lunch bell. Can't watch them eat. They'll come topside. Lean over the rail, vomit, and want more tonic." It pleased the doctor that no Church Elders were present. He was tired of hearing their pet expression, "winning souls." He pointed at a red and white flag at the stern and asked, "Whose flag?"

Strang replied, "Mine. My wife sewed it."

"I've hardly seen Mrs. Strang this voyage. I trust she's feeling well."

"She's fine. The children worry her. She's afraid they'll fall overboard. She keeps them in her stateroom."

The doctor couldn't understand the change that had come over Mary Strang. He recalled her as a lively young woman back at Voree—good conversationalist, but now withdrawn. When they came aboard, he spoke to her, but she replied briefly about the weather and trip as if she wasn't the least bit interested. Perhaps she was afraid of this voyage or maybe she didn't want to leave the mainland. Instead of being excited to sail to Beaver like the other women, she looked greatly depressed.

The doctor rubbed his hands together. They were getting colder from the raw lake air. "This is a splendid sea boat. Your first trip?"

"No. Sailed to Beaver a year ago with a small group. Rented a schooner. We changed ships at Cheboygan. Second ship was late. Got off at dark. The wharfinger charged me eight dollars. I had a company of three families. Women and children spread blankets to rest on that cold dock."

"How long?"

"All night. Terrible. Miserable time. Next ship was long overdue. The temperature dropped to thirty-two."

Dr. McCulloch tucked his hands under his armpits and exclaimed, "That's freezing."

"It was rough. Water splashed up between planks. Women were cold and sick. Babies cried. Made up my mind. Never again. I prayed to the Lord. He heard me. Elder Praiseworthy's generous donation and my brethren's tithes at Voree paid for this sturdy water craft."

Dr. McCulloch shivered as the wind blew strong. "That wharfinger was a scum."

Strang nodded. "He wanted more money. I told him I'm an editor. I reminded him of the power of the press. After I said that, he lowered his price."

The doctor shook his head, "Amazing what men will do for a dollar. Money means nothing to me or I'd be in Chicago right now working with John Bennett."

"Why didn't you?"

The doctor shook his head with disgust. "I'd make a small fortune, but be at the mercy of whining, rich old women."

Strang cleared his throat, leaned over the railing and spat into the lake. When he straightened he said, "I suppose all Bennett's patients are females."

"Ninety percent. Rest are kids. Men don't go to doctors." He studied Strang's hazel eyes, a deep green like patches in the water.

Strang asked, "Do you know why Bennett left Nauvoo?"

"Heard rumors. All humbug."

"Not humbug. Did you know Bennett tried suicide? Drank poison."

"No!"

"Gospel truth."

"What antidote saved him?"

"Milk at first. After that a doctor gave him a warm water enema."

"What else?"

"Ferric hydroxide from carbonate of soda and tincture of iron. Morphine stopped pain and spasms."

"I always use that treatment."

"The rascal took a small dose of poison."

"Why? He helped Joseph at Nauvoo."

"I know. I was there. In eight months Bennett was Major General of the Nauvoo Legion, second only to the U.S. Army. Nauvoo Saints were ready to take over the Nation. Joseph could be the president of the whole country."

"I don't understand. Never did. What did Bennett do wrong to fall from grace with Joseph?"

"Bennett was rotten to the core. Seduced innocent women. He had a reputation as a great physician. He was president of the medical faculty and professor of the Principles and Practice of Mid-Wifery and the Diseases of Women and Children at Willoughby University of Lake Erie."

Strang laughed. "His specialty was abortion. The rascal promised abortions to women if he made them pregnant.

Claimed to be a bachelor. When Joseph found out he had a wife and children in Ohio, Bennett took poison. At the Programma Militaire, Bennett was in charge of a sham battle as Major General. The Twelve weren't in the reviewing stand. Bennett should have known something was up. Joseph rode a black stallion protected by guards on horseback. Before he arrived, Joseph claimed a still small voice delivered a warning that Bennett would kill him. Bennett was forced to leave Nauvoo."

"Why did you ask Bennett to Voree?"

"I needed an intelligent man. I thought he'd change."

"A leopard can't change its spots."

"I know. In October 1847, we excommunicated Bennett for apostasy, falsehoods, and immoralities like performing abortions. He's in Plymouth, Massachusetts now raising chickens. No secrets at Voree. News travels fast. I'll know who gets an abortion on the island."

Dr. McCulloch held up long, tapering fingers, slim as candles with the palms free of calluses. "I won't do any. I'm glad you need me as a doctor." He let his hands fall to his sides, reached into his pants pocket, took out a white handkerchief, wiped his eyes, then put the cloth back in his pocket. "In the past I was forced to do abortions. My duty." The handkerchief dangled from one hand and his eyes widened as he exclaimed in a nervous, quivering voice, "Infection. They'd die by inexperienced butchers. I had no choice."

There was no response from Strang. The doctor stared at the lake and asked, "What if a woman comes to me on Beaver for an abortion? Shall I tell her to find some Indian midwife to butcher her up?"

"I won't allow the evil of abortion on Beaver."

The doctor nodded in agreement. After a few moments of silence he said emphatically, "Nauvoo. What would have happened if Joseph Smith wasn't murdered?"

Strang leaned forward against the railing and turned the large cross on his chest to the right side. He said slowly, "I don't know. Forget Nauvoo. You are headed for a better Nauvoo."

When the sun slanted, it reflected brightly on the water like sprinkled bits of glass floating all the way to Beaver's harbor. Strang squinted. The doctor shaded his eyes with one hand and asked, "What do you mean?"

"As leader, I will order a church built and the brethren will pay tithes. My temple will be grander than Joseph's at Nauvoo. You will thank the Almighty you settled at Beaver."

Dr. McCulloch grasped the balustrade, then he reached in his pants pocket again, and took out the white handkerchief. He wiped his hands slowly and asked, "What if Gentiles make trouble?"

Strang turned from the brilliant sun with a sly grin. "We are isolated. There are a few islands nearby with Indians. If anyone wants to bother us, they have to set sail from Pine River on the mainland or as far away as Sleeping Bear."

"What about settlers?"

"A few fishermen. My brethren have lived there the past year in peace. I printed their letters in the *Gospel Herald* at Voree."

"That's what convinced me to come. I read all the reports about pure air, good crops, and herbs."

Strang asked, "Herbs?"

Dr. McCulloch grinned slightly and explained, "I collect herbs for medicinal purposes. The best tonics are learned from Indians. They know the good of every herb and weed."

Strang shook his head, "Don't bother. I have a list of every flower, weed, and tree on Beaver Island."

"As a doctor, I've found cures for poison ivy, stomach disorders, and rheumatism with herbs. There's a great future in herb medicine."

Strang laughed so hard his beard shook. "Are you going to traipse through the woods picking weeds?" He laughed harder and his broad shoulders shook. "Doctor, you better not let folks see you with a bouquet of weeds. What will they think?"

Dr. McCulloch hadn't expected this sarcasm. "I don't care who calls me a looney. I live as I please. Not to suit others."

Strang stopped laughing and grinned, "You will be too busy with patients. *Zion* will bring more brethren all summer. If you want to know about weeds and herbs, come to me. I can tell you. I'm writing a book for the Smithsonian Institute about Beaver. I let you come to be my assistant. If the Lord doesn't answer my prayers to heal the sick, you hand out medicine, deliver babies, and bandage gunshot wounds. I can't be everywhere at once."

Dr. McCulloch said, "The ladies like to reach for tonics and pills."

Strang looked deeply into the doctor's grey eyes and recited sternly, "The Lord gives me the power to heal body and soul."

The two men stood a while in silence as the big paddle wheel thrashed at the water and lugged the ship toward its destination.

Dr. McCulloch watched as Strang pulled at his black velvet cloak and reviewed their conversation. He didn't want to establish a spirit of camaraderie; he might not like Beaver Island. He felt something unsaid existed by Strang's quiet manner as they looked out at the lake.

The doctor spoke, but a gust of strong wind carried the sound away like a feather in the wind. Strang asked, "What?"

Dr. McCulloch spoke louder over the wind and the sound of waves thrashing the sides of the ship. "Beaver. What about polygamy?"

Strang rubbed his fingers over his serpent ring and held up his left hand. "See this?"

"Yes."

"This sir, is to remind me of the devil. Polygamy is the abomination of the devil."

"Church leaders practiced it at Nauvoo."

"There will not be plural wives at Beaver Island. I repeat, polygamy is born of hell and begotten of the devil."

The doctor asked in a surprised tone, "Never at Beaver?"

Strang wet his thin upper lip with his tongue, and stared at his companion for a brief moment, then looked at the lake. He raised his voice above the thumping ship's side wheel, "I will fight against polygamy with every fiber of my body." He angrily hit the palm of his hand against the ship's rail. "I will not allow that abomination practiced like at Nauvoo."

He turned back and looked intensely at Dr. McCulloch. "Sir, I printed an editorial in my newspaper, 'Polygamy Not Possible in a Free Government.' One of the Church officials signed a statement. He had questioned me for days and verified my opposition to polygamy. I call it the devil's work. During August 1847, my statement was printed. In the last years of my ministry I have traveled to large Mormon congregations in the biggest cities. No man or woman lives who ever heard me say one word or do one act in favor of polygamy. My opinion of it is unchanged and unchangeable." In a low menacing voice he demanded, "What about you?"

The doctor stood, head down as Strang talked, and listened carefully. Now he raised his head and glanced at the end of the ship where the large red and white flag flapped in the strong breeze. "I'm against polygamy."

"There are decent people aboard," Strang cautioned. "I have hundreds—thousands—sailing to settle on Beaver. Don't speak that hellish word, polygamy. I don't want tongues to wag. We must settle. I don't want internal discord. Polyga-mists can join Brigham Young out West."

Dr. McCulloch laid a hand on Strang's shoulder. "I wouldn't be here if you favored spiritual wifery. You are a

holy man. You are the true successor of Prophet Smith. Not
that rascal, Brigham." He took his hand away and gripped the
railing, for his head felt light from hunger. He had surprised
himself by falling under Strang's spell. He had heard about the
man's charisma and sincerity, and the power in his strong
voice and determination in his hazel eyes.

Beaver Island, the ideal location for Mormons, lay ahead,
growing larger by the minute and now a definite green. He had
heard Strang preach on the Sabbath in Voree. Now standing
next to him, he felt a stir of giddiness in his heart. Excitement.
To think of being on the ground floor of this fantastic movement. An island just for Mormons. He breathed the cool
breeze deeply and hoped to cool his cheeks, flushed from this
first intimate conversation with Strang.

After a few moments McCulloch asked, "Didn't you work
with Brigham Young?"

"Never. He was jealous of Joseph and me." Strang edged
closer to McCulloch. He squinted and recited in a confidential
tone, "They were all jealous of me at Nauvoo. I knew Joseph's
modus-operandi, who he could trust, and who were his
enemies."

McCulloch asked, "Why do you think Nauvoo failed?"

"Many reasons. The big mistake was Joseph's revelation of
polygamy. No one wanted it. Next, the Gentiles burned down
over one hundred homes. Called them wolf hunts. Joseph
allowed dancing and plays. He set his mind and energy to
campaign for U.S. President. He was anti-slavery. That didn't
help him."

Strang stepped aside and looked at the lake, then glanced
back at McCulloch. "It wasn't Joseph's assassination in that
Carthage jail by a mob that split Nauvoo apart. No. It all
began earlier. Internal discord. Jealousy. The greed for
power." In a more contemptuous voice he snarled, "The hate."

When he took a deep breath, he felt the cool air in his

throat. Clasping his hands tightly over his waist, he said, "I'm convinced hate and greed destroyed Nauvoo. I should have been on top of the heap. Over all the elders, the vice presidents and that rascal, Brigham. He turned the brethren against me. I didn't go back to Nauvoo after Joseph was murdered. Too many Brighamites. I sent Moses Smith and three elders from Voree. They kicked them out of the Church. Brigham ruled with an iron fist. No one could speak my name. One man did. He disappeared."

"How did Brigham take over Nauvoo when Joseph died?"

"First he got Joseph's mother on his side. Promised her a new carriage and land. Said he'd support her the rest of her life."

"What about Emma? She was Joseph's real widow."

"Emma and her sons gave Brigham big trouble. She argued with Brigham over Joseph's estate, and hated plural wives. Brigham doesn't. He practices Joseph's revelation of polygamy, but my heart and soul rankles against it. He won't engage in revelation, but I do."

Dr. McCulloch said, "You were in the Church only six months when Joseph died. Brigham worked twelve years with Joseph. He was a missionary in England. Why would the Council elect you Church President over Brigham?"

Strang's first reaction was anger. He wanted desperately to give the doctor a tongue lashing, and call him a hair-brained liar. Others had said the same words. Pure humbug. Instead he explained, "I am a lawyer. I'm highly intelligent and better educated than Brigham. Brigham can't spell his own name correctly. Joseph told me that. I have Joseph's letter appointing me to be President of the Mormon Church."

"I believe you, Brother Strang." The doctor paused. "Joseph left a militia of four thousand men. Why did Nauvoo fall apart? I'd like to know what happened after he died. Is it true Abraham Lincoln helped the Mormons?"

"Yes. Joseph composed the Nauvoo Charter for self government with the Nauvoo Legion, an army of 4000 men. He got help from Abraham Lincoln to get it approved by the Illinois legislature. After Joseph was murdered the Gentiles started more wolf hunts. Set fire to homes and barns. Things got worse when the Illinois governor forced our brethren to give up their shooting irons. The Nauvoo Charter was repealed in 1845. Brigham formed a whittling and whistling society with three hundred deacons. They chased strangers from Nauvoo."

"That's what ruined Nauvoo?" McCulloch asked.

"No. Plural wives ruined Brigham. They say he took fifteen wives in nine months. He had twenty, but it got so he couldn't keep it a secret. Then, Joseph's killers were tried. Found not guilty. More violence at Nauvoo. Brigham knew he had to move West."

"Did he sell Nauvoo?"

"Yes. Took a big loss on everything. Homes and property sold for next to nothing. I got back at Brigham with the power of the press. I exposed how the brethren died on his Westward wagon trail."

McCulloch looked Strang in the eyes and in a candid voice said, "I'm on your side. I will do all in my power to help you and our brethren."

Strang pointed to wagon wheels on two overturned buckboards. "Look at those wheels spinning in the breeze."

The doctor turned, surprised at how fast they moved. Strang said, "I'm like a wheel moving towards my goal of royalty and power. Soon Beaver Island will be mine. Those wheels will haul logs and fish, carry our brethren to cabins and to hear me preach. Wheels of all sizes will roll on every road leading to my future tabernacle. I'll preach loud as thunder, praising our God of Israel. Wagon wheels move like me. Just as the wind pushes them, so too the Lord inspires me. Got much to accomplish. Great plans for Beaver." Strang took out his pocket watch and looked at the time. "Excuse me. I have a special appointment."

As he walked away from Dr. McCulloch, he sighed with relief, glad to end talk about Brigham Young. He'd never forget Brigham's sarcasm, "Let Strangism alone. It is not worth the skin of a flea." Worse yet was Brigham's letter dated January 24, 1846. Brigham signed it after the Twelve wrote, "James Jesse Strang is an excommunicated member of the Church and a wicked liar."

While he waited for the visitor inside his stateroom, Strang sat at the table and wrote:

Aboard *Zion*   July 4, 1850

Dear Charlie,
We left Pine River this morning at 8 o'clock. Having a splendid run with fine weather. We didn't sail early yesterday for at daybreak the wind sprang up from the north. It got stronger 'til noon with heavy seas and the lake white. After the wind subsided today, we set sail. Passengers are cheerful. A few brethren seasick and Dr. McCulloch dispenses elixir for mal-de-mer. I will look forward to the next issue of the **Gospel Herald** *entrusted to your brilliant editing in my absence. Your arrival at Beaver is highly anticipated. Respectfully yours,*
                    James Strang

As he sealed the envelope, a gentle tapping sounded on the cabin door. Strang called out, "Come in, my dear."

6

*W*hile her children slept, Mary planned to read *David Copperfield*, but Strang had forgotten to give her the book. She walked to his cabin, opened the door and immediately smelled pungent lilac perfume. Sunshine flooded the room. Mary saw Strang stretched out naked on the bunk next to a dark haired woman. He sat up quickly and shouted, "Get out!" Mary did not recognize the female, who quickly pulled a blanket over her bare body.

Mary screamed. Her cry sounded like an animal trapped in a deep well. The ship rocked. Grey waves splashed against the portholes, and the cabin became dusky like a lantern turned low. When the steamship leveled, daylight returned. Mary stared horrified at her naked husband with his tousled red hair that matched the red fuzz on his bare chest.

"Out!" he yelled. His hazel eyes glared with anger.

He swung his legs over the side of the bunk, stood up and

grabbed Mary by the shoulders and shook her like a rag doll. She smelled the lilac perfume on his skin, and felt his fingernails dig into her flesh as her knees weakened. He turned her around, opened the door and shoved her out. The latch clicked, and she stood in the passageway, stunned.

Her black slippers seemed filled with lead as she walked slowly toward the ship's stairwell where sunlight glowed. She grabbed hold of the wood railing and slowly pulled herself up one step at a time to reach the top deck. It was empty of passengers; they were in the dining room.

She cried harder as she stumbled to a side bench. When she sat, warm tears streamed down her cheeks as she pressed her cold hands against her face. Her body trembled. Much later when the weeping ceased, she faced the stiff breeze with puffy eyes, and hoped the cool lake air would remove the swelling. She dreaded the next encounter with James. She thought, *I must avoid him until the hurt in my heart mends.* She wanted to think it had been a bad dream. She looked over the water where raggedy tips of whitecaps thrashed viciously against each other, and pounded steadily at the ship. All the while the huge side paddle wheel churned its foaming path from Racine to Beaver Island, hours away.

As the chilly wind whipped against her face, the past flashed to mind. She had ignored warning signs of his interest in women. His quick glance always picked out the prettiest woman in a crowd. It wouldn't have bothered her if he had kept his thoughts to himself, but no. He had turned to her so many times with the same remark, "That's a fine pippin of a woman."

At Voree a fat blond with too much lace on her dress monopolized James every Saturday as Mary waited in the buggy. There were school teachers and housewives, all good church women who wore a path to Mary's door for talks with James in his study with the door closed. At Thursday afternoon tea and banquets, she observed how many women gathered around him laughing and talking.

More women than men encircled James after every Sabbath service. Mary trusted his excuse about "consultation for a personal matter." She had to accept his association with women parishioners, but witnessing today's scene of adultery shocked her. While staring at the monotonous whitecaps, she recalled that scandalous episode over and over. How she had opened the door and saw the two as naked as Adam and Eve. Disgusting! The more she recalled it, the more she wished that this shaking lake boat was headed back to the mainland, and not to a strange place called Beaver Island.

Tears flowed again. She bent over and wiped them away with her grey dress hem. She wished she'd never gone to his cabin. Now she wanted him to pay dearly for the hurt she suffered. How could she ever look at him again? Live in the same house? Sleep with him? Nothing mattered anymore. Ten years of marriage had suddenly ended. Her love had died.

Like a strange malady, a hollowness invaded her body, and she didn't care if she lived or not as the seas rolled higher and the air turned frigid. Ahead lay a lonesome life on that wild island. Although that situation confronted her, she did not cringe. As she thought about her predicament, she gritted her teeth and accepted the challenge with great determination to survive. Here she was, Mary Perce Strang, age twenty-eight, pregnant again. Far removed from her mother, with an unfaithful husband and no trusted lady friends. On Beaver she'd be isolated from the mainland, except for mail.

She was too ashamed to write her mother. Even if she did, there was the possibility that James or someone else would open the letter. Mother would write back, "I told you so." Mother had disliked James from the start.

Mary's thoughts drifted back to the times spent helping her mother at the store. She knew her mother would miss her.

Mary kept records of accounts in the credit books and ordered merchandise. She worked from early morning, when the farmers walked in to buy seeds, to late evening, when she lit the lamps after waiting on customers all day.

Mary's soft voice always spoke words carefully and slowly. She developed an aloofness, priding herself that other women envied her position. Someday she'd own this store when her mother died. Mother depended more on Mary each day. At times when her mother suffered with ague, she sat in a wood rocker on the store's wide porch watching travelers ride into town in buggies and flatbed wagons.

On chilly days when no customers arrived, Mary sat near a potbelly iron stove with a small quilt wrapped around her thin body. When she smoothed back a loose strand of hair, silver bracelets jingled on her arm and sunlight from the front window shone on her ruby ring. Her mother said, "Mary, you look like a butterfly in a cocoon."

Her mother had always been good to her. When Mary was five years old, she had a custom built playhouse in the backyard and a palomino pony. At seventeen, she attended a private girls school in the city, and when she returned home at Christmas vacation, the townspeople noticed the education gave the storekeeper's daughter "airs." She still helped in the store, but the farmers and locals regarded her differently. She had lived in the city, and went to the opera and the ballet.

Mary visited the homes of wealthy girl friends on weekends. The homes had marble fireplaces imported from Italy, silver sets in a cabinet, china stored in a walnut sideboard, and gigantic glass chandeliers with hundreds of pieces that took a week for maids to clean. She knew they'd never have fine things like that at home; her mother was a woman of simple taste.

Customers were content to buy their dress material from flat bolts and wore plain ladies boots. Instead of imitating them,

Mary ordered fine silk and brocade to wear Sunday to the Baptist church service. Her boots were no longer plain black leather, but soft in a variety of colors with fancy stitching on the sides or decorated with rhinestones or imitation pearls. She owned ten pair of shoes that matched her dresses, the lightest shades of salmon pink and pale lavender. Her pocket books were made of hand-fashioned leather for daytime, but for evening dances she carried a string purse, either beaded or silver. She loved to be the envy of other women.

Mary wasn't like her mother. Mrs. Perce wouldn't hesitate to admonish a child buying food for the family. She would step forward, face the child regardless of customers, and yell, "You tell the folks to pay on their bill. They don't, no more food charged. Understand?"

When Mary's mother bought goods from salesmen, she appeared disinterested until he came down on the price and included a bonus gift of a pretty shawl or a pearl necklace. Mary heard a salesman remark upon leaving the store, "That Perce woman is tough."

On one occasion Mary watched her mother dash out the front door when a woman passed by the store holding a dark parasol, tilted to hide her face. Mrs. Perce ran after her and shouted, "Mrs. Smith, when will you pay your bill?"

The woman, highly embarrassed to be singled out in public, kept her face hidden in the parasol and promised, "I'll pay it."

"Better be soon. Two months overdue." Mary wished she could be aggressive like her mother.

The first time Mary talked to James Strang was on a busy Saturday night. At harvest the store became crowded with Mormons who had arrived from neighboring towns to help with harvest or to raise a barn. Mary became very tired and hungry. There had been no time to stop and eat dinner. "Next," she said, annoyed, then regretted it when the young man with red hair stood at the front counter. He was James

Strang. The way he looked at her and smiled made her think, "love at first sight." She never thought love would strike her so quickly. Immediately she became infatuated with his appearance, the short henna beard, sharp hazel eyes, and deep voice. She could tell he was well educated. As the days passed he stayed longer in the store. He told her that after he passed the bar exam, he'd work with an elderly lawyer in the next village.

Strang explained his Great Design, "My head is filled with projects." She listened to his aspirations to form a literary association, organize a military academy for young officers, print his own journal, operate a fur trade and enter the military himself. She also admired his religious interests. He claimed to have helped convert young people, but said, "Nearly half have already returned to their wallowing again."

One day he announced, "I've had some agreeable trouble. My seventy-five pupils found out they were on the wrong tiger track when they saw me with my brace of pistols. It was my turn to laugh at them for being frightened with an iron candlestick."

Sometimes he spoke of his past—almost losing his life on the floating logs at a mill one summer—and his success as a debater. As the months passed, she realized he was the man she wanted to marry. He was ambitious, a brilliant scholar, and dressed in fine clothes.

After he asked her to marry him, Mrs. Perce protested.

"Mary, he's a jack-of-all-trades. He'll never come to any good as a lawyer. He's got too many job ideas. A man should hold one job."

But in Mary's heart she knew James Strang would achieve success. There were times, however, when he became depressed. He said, "From infancy I've been taught that mankind was totally depraved. The heart of man is an impure fountain. If the depravity of man originated in his unnatural habits, a

return to those which are natural would effect a cure. What are
the natural habits? Evil is man's perpetual associate."

Sometimes she couldn't understand what he talked about,
and when he finished he always spoke about a paradise he
hoped to discover. "There I will live as God intended man
from the beginning. I have always had dreams of royalty and
power."

School closed early because the young boys were employed
in the sap works. Strang returned home when he became ill
after his final bar examination. Mary thought he'd die from
pain, purging and vomiting. His mother back in New York
thought he had Spasmodic Cholera that had broken out all over
Buffalo. After two weeks of rest and medication, Strang
recovered.

While home, his uncle left his wife for another woman.
When Strang saw Mary again, he had lost weight and was
pale. He said, "You wonder why I long for a place of peace
away from all the misery of this earth. Here was my father's
brother professing to be religious, but left Aunt Sally with
three sickly children and took half of their property. Now Aunt
Sally's days are spent in care and distress and her nights in
misery and mourning. My poor mother is too upset to come to
our wedding. You will meet her someday."

All those memories seemed so long ago. Questions came at
Mary from all directions like the whitecaps covering the lake,
What to do? Which way to turn? Like assorted snippets for a
quilt, no answer took shape, but slipped in and out helter-
skelter. She had no clear direction. At last she decided, *I can't
tell James I'm pregnant. He'll think I'm using the baby to
bring us together. I don't want a reconciliation. I must leave
before James suspects I'm carrying his child. I must escape.*

Oh God! Give me strength. Don't let me weaken or despair. My one hope is myself. I put myself into this mess. I married the wrong man. I'll get myself out. I won't live the rest of my life in misery.

She studied the island's long, jade outline that loomed on the horizon like a dragon, ready to leap and devour her child the moment it was born. *Time is against me. The baby will grow as I study the calendar day after day. I dread September. No ships sail after that. High waves. Later the lake freezes. No mail. Beaver will be cut off from the world. I must sail back to Mother as soon as possible. She's the only one who can help me.*

7

$\mathcal{A}$fter the woman dressed and left his cabin, Strang stayed inside. He dipped pen in ink and recorded his faith healing aboard ship. When a firm knock sounded he called out, "Come in."

Sundial Whipple, an elderly man with a thatch of white hair at the top of his bald head, entered. His forehead had two deep vertical lines slanting upward from the tip of thick white eyebrows. He was short and habitually raised his shoulders to stand taller. The fresh air turned his sagging cheeks rosy, and they hung like chipmunk pouches. His nose was long and his lips thin and pale. When he blinked, long lashes covered his brown eyes momentarily as if stuck together. He swallowed hard causing his Adam's apple to jiggle.

Strang hoped Sundial's high raspy voice wouldn't say, "My nephew, George," or "My cousin, Sam." That meant a long story followed. Strang had often been delayed by Sundial's eyes that nailed him, if he tried to pull away, Sundial would grab him by the arm. Besides being talkative, Sundial shook from palsy. Strang pointed to a chair and said, "Sit down. What do you want?"

"I got to know more about Beaver."

Strang slammed his notebook shut. "Can't you wait until we land?"

"It's not me. It's my wife. My poor wife. I told her it's our paradise. Not another Nauvoo."

Strang asked, "When were you at Nauvoo?"

Sundial sighed deeply. "Spent a long time there. Heard Brigham Young preach to The Twelve in the Temple. Wish you debated Brigham. You got a powerful voice. Good lungs. Hoped you'd get elected to the Presidency after that Missouri mob murdered Joseph."

Strang stared out the porthole and said, "Brigham! What a scamp. I heard he was on a Mississippi ferry boat when the Nauvoo temple was set on fire. Brigham said, 'Let it burn. The city is full of devils. I wish they were all burnt out.' No way to talk about our brethren. Good people at Nauvoo."

Sundial's head quivered as he gripped the chair with both hands. He said, "I sure liked Nauvoo. Great Mormon city." He grinned with thin lips, "I'll never forget the ships bustling with passengers; visitors jammed the streets and gawked at the Temple. The streets glittered gold after the wagons spilled grain. And the women!" He blushed. "I'm an old man, but I saw the prettiest females in the world at Nauvoo. Brother Strang, I wish the Twelve made you President."

Strang glanced out the porthole at Beaver, a flat dark oval. He said dejectedly, "I tried. I sent them a copy of my letter from Prophet Smith in his handwriting, giving me the power to rule upon his death." He turned and looked at Sundial. "No use."

Sundial gazed intently at Strang and asked, "Why didn't you

fight? You had followers."

"My church was in Wisconsin. I had responsibility. Joseph gave me that Voree stake. I had a common stock association of hundreds of brethren."

Sundial turned his shaky head, "How far now?"

Strang looked out a porthole. "I see Beaver. Look!"

"Got poor eyes. I take your word."

"You'll see it when we get closer. Looks like the mainland. When I see green, it's an hour away."

Sundial buttoned his jacket with fumbling hands. "Is it big?"

Strang picked up a ledger and replied, "I keep all my facts here." He opened the book, turned several pages and read, "Beaver is thirteen miles long and six and a half wide. Thirty-five thousand acres. I'm keeping records for the Smithsonian Institute. It's an island of contrasts. All around are sandy and cobbly beaches. West side slopes over one hundred feet. Rises above sea level.

"We will sell wood for ships until the end of time. Timber is plentiful. There's white and red pine. Even maple, aspen and birch. The swamps are filled with cedar, balsam and spruce."

"What are the nearest islands?"

Strang wished he'd leave. He tolerated Sundial for his money. Just like he put up with Praiseworthy. It bothered him the old man prattled like a school boy. Strang pushed back red hair from his forehead and said, "Garden is a mile north. High Island is eight miles west. Only Indians live there. Forget other islands. Beaver is by far the best place God has ever given us for temporal or spiritual blessings and prosperity. The best place for location and health."

Sundial wiggled into another position and asked, "Indians on Beaver?"

"No. Their burial mound is a short walk from the harbor."

"What tribe?"

Strang looked out the porthole where the green blob of the island became larger. Shortly he'd make out the large horseshoe harbor and stores. He wondered if Sundial wanted another laying on of hands and an anointing with oil to cure his palsy. The last time Strang's and the elders' prayers didn't work. He told Sundial, "Be patient. Have faith and pray."

"The tribe," Sundial repeated.

"First came the Mound Builders, then Chippewa and Ottawa. They say a Catholic missionary, Father Frederic Baraga—a Slovenian—was the first white man on Beaver."

"Are Indians still savages?"

"No. Some speak English. Live on Garden. They're not like the ones in 1762. Eighty-eight years ago Fort Michilimackinac had a massacre. Indians brought a white survivor to Beaver to boil and eat him." He knew that would scare the wits out of the old man.

Sundial cried out, "Good Lord! Cannibals! No wonder the whiteman hates them."

Strang stood up. "I have paper work. What is not done in season is apt to go undone. At best ill done."

Sundial stood up. "I'll leave." Then in a confidential tone, "I was surprised to see that doctor aboard."

Strang opened the cabin door. "Why? I need a doctor at Beaver."

Sundial's head quivered. "Sir, I have it on good authority he preformed abortions at Baltimore."

Strang declared angrily, "Slander is a vile sin. What proof of that? How can you rankle that in your heart?"

"I know. They told me."

"Who are they? The gossips in skirts? Sundial, don't believe all you hear."

"I know. It's true. Mrs. Whipple once had a housekeeper who worked for him. Said he always operated on the rich women. I want nothing to do with him. I'll die before that man touches me or Mrs. Whipple."

Strang said, "Put your potato on your fork and peel it quietly. Don't believe slander. I find the doctor a noble brother."

Strang watched Sundial leave. He closed the door, sat on the bunk and watched the rise and the fall of the waves outside the porthole. He pulled off his boots, and stretched his tired body on the gold bedspread. The moment he felt the richness of the material he recalled his preaching mission in the East. Elvira, alias Charlie, traveled with him. After breakfast at the hotel, they shopped, and she selected the bedspread. She had matched his stride as they walked from one expensive store to another looking for small scale furniture for this stateroom. By noon they found a sideboard and he had explained to the clerk with pride, "It's for my ship." While in New York, they decided to skip the opera, *Norma,* and instead marvelled over Barnum's Museum where they saw the African half-man, half-ape and an albino family. This was also the year of ventriloquism and dominoes. What attracted Strang's attention was spirit rapping, originated by Margaret and Katherine Fox. The sisters began a movement of spiritualism that evolved into a national cult.

One evening he took Elvira to hear Jenny Lind, the "Swedish Nightingale," sing at the Castle Garden. Jenny Lind toured the United States under the promotion of P.T. Barnum.

Strang continued to look at the lake where soon island trees would outline the sky like small black sticks. They'd unload cargo and hike some brethren to empty cabins before dark. He hoped the island Mormons had cleaned up the cabins for the tired passengers. *Sundial better not spread gossip*, he thought. *I need that doctor. My faith healing doesn't always work.*

8

*M*ary sat on a bench topside. She hoped the lake might help her forget the scene of adultery. Five men emerged from the stairwell and staggered along the deck to the bow where they grabbed the railing and faced the sprays hitting the prow. After a short time, Strang joined them.

She didn't want to look at her husband. The memory of Strang with that naked female tormented her. A sickness vibrated in her body as persistent as the ship's paddle wheel.

She had dreaded seeing Strang again. Now he stood majestic in black suit and cape. She thought, *That cape, pulled tightly about his body, encloses all his dark secrets. They don't know he's a sinner. How can he proclaim to be a holy man? How can he separate his personal life from what he preaches? Those stupid, ignorant people flock to him like moths to a lantern. He'll know the way I treat him what my true feelings are. He disgusts me. It's my great satisfaction he doesn't know*

I'm with child. Oh God! Give me strength. Don't let me weaken. Help me find a way to leave that island.

Strang did not see Mary. While his back was turned, she managed to slip unnoticed down the ladder and return to the stateroom where her children still slept. Mary sat down in the rocking chair and listened to the paddle wheel. It reminded her of the wagon wheels that brought her to this ship. On the wagon trail they traveled before dawn—before anyone saw them—and walked until dusk. It had been an ordeal to cook over campfires to feed the weary travelers.

Strang had ordered, "No one, not even a child talks to the townspeople. If they ask, 'Where you headed?' I'll do the talking."

Villagers had stared as the Mormons trudged past like a band of tired gypsies. Women complained, "My back hurts. Please stop. Rest a while." Children wandered away from camp and played in the woods at twilight. The men smelled of forbidden whiskey. When a wheel fell off a wagon, it caused a great delay. Strang rode his horse next to the buggies and wagons. When they approached the edge of Racine, he shouted, "Gee up! Keep moving!"

At last when the caravan had reached the ship, *Zion*, Strang had dismounted and ordered the men, "Load fast. I fear Gentiles more than rough seas."

Suddenly the stateroom door opened. Mary faced Strang sooner than she expected. He still wore a black suit and cape, but now a plug hat covered his red hair. He motioned for her to step outside. She followed him outside and shut the door gently. Daylight from the front stairwell flooded the passageway. She heard dishes in the galley and the smell of food drifted in wafts.

Strang took off the hat. He smoothed back red hair from a high rounded forehead with the palm of his hand. The jacket padding made his strong shoulders appear broader. Under the jacket he wore a blue shirt and green velvet waistcoat. He straightened the gold cross around his neck and did not look directly at Mary, but stared at the sun flooded stairwell. He said, "Leave your stateroom. There's a sick woman aboard."

"What about the children? I can't wake them up."

"You have to. Take them to the dining quarters," he insisted, pulling his cape tighter to his chest.

Mary folded her arms over her breast and in a clear voice demanded, "What about me?" He still did not look directly at her. "Am I to be evicted from the only place I've had peace and quiet the whole trip? I don't want to sit with those old harpies in the dining room."

Strang said, "Charity. We must help the sick."

Mary said, "Give her your stateroom. Or does it smell of perfume?"

He ignored Mary's words, took out a gold pocket watch, consulted it, and replied. "No. Can't use my cabin. I meet with the elders. *Zion* has three rooms. Yours, mine and Mother Van Dusen. Praiseworthy's wife is old and sickly." His hazel eyes dug into hers when he scolded, "Why can't you be agreeable?"

Mary leaned her head against the bulkhead and felt the ship's strong vibration. The breeze descended fresh and cool with a thumping from the ship's bow cutting the water. A woman's shrill burst of laughter echoed from the dining room. Mary's head hurt as if a band had been pulled tightly around the middle. She protested, "No. It's my room. I'm tired of moving."

"Do as I tell you," he demanded. "Leave your things in the cabin." He smoothed his red beard with one hand. She saw how the slanting rays of sunshine fell upon his fingers and a fiery glow appeared on his ruby ring.

She folded her arms across her breast and said, "You don't need me. You have all the women you want. They jump at the snap of your fingers. I'll never forget you with that woman. That hussy. Things will never be the same between us." Tears rolled down her cheeks.

He frowned and asked, "What's wrong with you?"

Mary could tell that he assumed that attitude to put blame on her. He acted innocent, as if the adultery in his cabin never took place.

"Are you ill from this lake voyage? Are you homesick for Voree? Grow up Mary. Don't be a child and hanker for home. Socialize with the ladies. Don't keep to yourself so much. Don't you care what the other women say about you?"

Mary felt the rage dry her mouth as anger forced a hard lump in her throat. "No, I don't. It's your congregation. Not mine."

"Be quiet," he ordered.

"Who for? Those old biddies. They stick their noses into everybody's business. Gossips. It will be the same on the island."

He looked anxiously towards the stairs with a strained expression and his cheeks turned pale. Mary wanted to say, "I hate you. I hate that woman in your stateroom bunk. Charlie too." She'd like to toss all these words at him the way she'd throw a bone to a hungry dog. Anger forced the lump in her throat to hurt more, as she promised herself that someday she'd get even with him. As the cool lake breeze drifted below, it chilled her whole body. The odor of boiled cabbage and the conversation with Strang made her stomach queasy. "When I needed a healing, your prayers never helped. Why not me? You cured others."

He looked solemnly at Mary and said, "You need baptism."

"I was baptized."

"As a Baptist. You need another immersion. Next time in the crystal clear Font Lake on Beaver. Your soul born anew as a Mormon."

She placed a hand on the cabin door knob and replied, "One baptism is enough."

"You see!" he exclaimed. "I want to help. You won't listen. If you won't be submissive, I'll get a wife who will. What kind of a Mormon wife are you?"

The smell of ham and boiled cabbage sickened Mary just like his words. He scowled and said in a low tone, "If my brethren talked to me like that, I'd punish them. You must respect me as the leader and your lawful spouse. My followers believe me. They come in a spirit of meekness like lambs behind the shepherd."

"How can you say that after what I saw in your stateroom?" Mary cried out.

"Enough!" he warned. "Move out. Hortense will rest in your cabin." As he walked away, his boots stomped hard on the wood deck.

Mary thought, *You hypocrite. I'll show you. Just wait and see.*

9

*M*ary woke up Myraette and William, and told them to find the girl who told stories. She pondered over all that Strang had said. She thought, *He won't make a fool out of me.*

Mary lifted up her skirt and climbed down the stairs to the ship's dining room. Most of the space inside the long chamber, illuminated by portholes, was taken up by a long oak table. Women sat on wood benches and on the table were bowls of cabbage and platters of beef.

An elderly woman called out, "Sit here, Sister Mary." She patted a wrinkled hand on the bench space next to her. Mary sat down and placed her white shawl between her and Sarah Bowers, who had a withered face and one front tusk in a toothless mouth. Sarah's complexion hadn't improved with the lake air, for it remained the same grey pallor and wrinkled like a dried crabapple. "Where are the babies?" Sarah asked.

"Not babies, Mother Bowers. Myraette is eight and

William, six."

Sarah looked around with hawk-like eyes and asked, "Where are they now?"

Mary pointed to a group of children sitting around a young girl with a book on her lap. "It's story time. They'd rather listen than eat."

When the women passed food, Mary took small portions. She saw their glances as she nibbled at bread, cheese, and a small helping of boiled cabbage flavored with bits of dried beef.

"Milk? Nice and cold," a woman said and placed a large silver pitcher before Mary. When Mary tried to lift the handle, it was too heavy.

"My, you're weak," a husky woman said. She lifted the pitcher and poured milk into a mug.

Another woman at the far end of the table remarked, "What a shame, Sister Mary. You had to leave your comfortable stateroom."

Mary smiled weakly and said, "It doesn't matter. I pray Sister Hortense recovers soon. She needs the cabin more than me."

"That's charitable, Sister Mary," Sarah praised. "You are kind and understanding."

As Mary drank her milk, she heard the storyteller's voice drone steadily as it mingled with a soft background noise of dishes washed by sailors in the galley. *Strange*, she thought. *Men doing kitchen work.* She recalled when they had first climbed aboard. Two women fascinated by the tiny, spotless galley asked to help, but Strang had said, "No. Deckhands cook and wash dishes."

"Bread pudding?" a young sailor asked Mary.

"No, thank you."

The women began to knit. Sarah opened her bag of yarn and needles, and the odor of moth balls seeped out. She asked,

"Where's yours, Mary?"

"I'm tired of sewing."

The old lady shook her head. She said, very emphatically for everyone to hear, "My dear mother always taught me idle hands are the devil's workshop."

Her words repulsed Mary who thought, *So are wagging tongues, you old meddler.* Mary got up and walked toward a porthole to watch the waves roll high. She wished there was some other place to sit, but all the benches were taken. She looked out the glass as if interested in the lake. She wished she had not come down here, but it was safe for the kids. Strang had demanded, "Be nice to the women, a model Mormon wife."

Sarah stopped clicking her long needles. She patted the bench again and said, "Come, Sister Mary. Rest." She looked at the other women and added, "As long as I've known the Strang family, they're always on the move. Busy, busy."

Mary sat down. Not to please Sarah, but because her legs felt weak at the knees. She smoothed out her grey dress and said, "I'm only a Strang by marriage."

Sarah knitted furiously. She attacked the yarn like an enemy, and her needles were instruments of death. She kept looking at the wool and said, "Yes, but you remind me of Brother Strang's aunt." She sighed, "Dear Rachel. My closest friend."

James' aunt! The very idea. Mary felt the ship tremble and roll slightly from side to side. She looked out a porthole on the shady side where the water turned the color of granite tombstones. The wind whistled softly through the stairwell. Cargo shifted across the upper deck with a screeching sound to remind Mary of a certain day long ago, exactly one month after her wedding day. A peculiar buckboard squealed just like that as the wagon carried a high load of household goods and pulled up to her cottage door.

She presumed the tired driver had lost his way. After the dust had settled, she saw her husband's buggy had stopped behind the buckboard, and seated next to him was an elderly woman.

Mary hadn't recognized the person, until Strang helped down the small lady with fine white hair brushed into a knot on the top of her head. He called out to Mary. "I fetched Aunt Rachel. Sister and kids are sick. We feared auntie would catch it."

Mary spent her days pleasing the aunt, whose routine became firmly established. Every morning she awoke late, hobbled to the fireplace, lifted up the back of her dress and said, "I'm warming my tailgate." The old lady's smell filled the room and sickened Mary. She made excuses to go outside whenever the aunt sat at the table, smacked oatmeal, and noisily sipped sassafras tea.

Mary watched the lake through the porthole as she remembered more—how the old lady slept until noon, complained the day too hot or too cold, the sun too bright or the wind too loud as it whistled through the window cracks. Aunt Rachel demanded acorn squash boiled and peeled and no seasoning on meat. She refused Mary's pastry, but ate thick apple butter on bread.

Days stretched into months when Strang's relatives never came for Aunt Rachel. The old lady lived there on Mary's first wedding anniversary. It was a beautiful day, with bright sun and fluffy clouds. First, Mary added dry maple to the kitchen stove. After a quick breakfast of a boiled egg and a corn muffin, she had quietly beaten cake batter with a wood spoon hoping not to wake up the aunt. After the two cake layers cooled, she made boiled frosting, tinted delicate pink with beet juice. She put one small candle in the center.

Next, she ironed clothes, being careful not to clang the flat irons on the stove. Before the aunt awoke, Mary had left the cottage, walked for a half a mile and picked a large bouquet of wild roses and bright buttercups. When she returned home, she arranged them in a cut glass vase next to the pink anniversary cake on the table covered with her best white linen.

When Aunt Rachel awoke and began chattering, Mary felt her perfect day being spoiled. She quietly explained, "I'd rather not talk, Aunt Rachel."

Immediately the old woman wailed, "Why are you mean to me?"

Mary felt her self-control slipping, "I'm not mean. I believe in being frank. This house is not big enough for two women."

Aunt Rachel insisted, "This is a big house. All my things are in your spare room."

Mary raised her voice as the anger tightened her throat muscles. She cried out, "If this was a fifty-room mansion, I couldn't live with you. I want my own cottage." She recalled how Aunt Rachel had cringed and became a shade paler at Mary's final words, "All mine. Not to share with another woman."

Everything came back to Mary. The old lady pulled a black shawl around her stooped shoulder blades, got up suddenly from the table and knocked over a cup of hot chocolate.

Mary gasped, "My best linen. I'll never wash that out."

Aunt Rachel glared hatefully and yelled back, "I wish my nephew never married a wretch like you! I'll buy you another tablecloth."

"You haven't a penny. Your daughter better take you home. I can't stand you another day. I married James, not his family." Mary recalled how Aunt Rachel tottered to her bedroom with lowered head, gasping to breathe.

Mary removed the cake and flowers from the table. She scrubbed the tablecloth in a tub of hot, soapy water, rinsed the linen and hung it on the washline. Then she walked to a field to pick more flowers and forget the scene. When she returned, she went to Aunt Rachel's bedroom to call her for lunch. The aunt's white head hung over the side of the bed and one arm touched the floor. Mary didn't stoop to pick up the black sunbonnet, a few inches from her hand.

Mary's first reaction was fright. How could she have been gone when the woman had the seizure and died? She wondered if Aunt Rachel had called out for her. Suddenly a sense of great deliverance had swept over her. She kept thinking, *I'm free! I'm free!*

Sarah dropped the yarn and needles on her lap. The clang of the metal needles brought Mary back to Sarah's jabbering. The old woman recited, "I remember how sick you were at the funeral breakfast. You didn't eat any of that delicious chocolate cake." She turned to the other women and said, "I never saw so much good food in all my life. We had a big feast. Folks brought pastry and roasts for three days. Of course Brother Strang was in low spirits. Elder Praiseworthy delivered the funeral oration."

Mary bit her lower lip nervously. She didn't want to remember anything about that funeral. Melancholy overpowered her. She wanted to leave the dining room. She could say she needed fresh air, but that wouldn't work. One of the women might offer to go with her. Or if she feigned sea sickness, they'd want to help and hold her head over the railing.

Sarah reached over. Mary saw the wrinkled hand move like a slithering snake. The curved fingers stuck out of the black cuffs like fangs. She felt the old lady's icy touch the moment she patted Mary's hand. With a voice that quivered with excitement she asked, "Aren't you proud, my dear? Everyone's talking about how Brother Strang cured Sister Hortense this morning."

Mary smiled weakly and nodded. While the others talked about the faith healing, Mary picked up her shawl and slipped away from the table, glad to escape the strong odor of moth killer on Sarah's clothes.

Mary climbed topside, sat on a bench, and watched the port side of *Zion* glide parallel the length of Beaver Island. Strang's adultery destroyed their marriage. Depression engulfed her as if she'd fallen into a dark hole.

Back in Voree she'd seen women let their husbands slip into seemingly innocent relationships. For instance, they would help a poor widow by repairing her house. The next thing the wife knew, her husband left her for the widow. Mary knew that scheming women lurked in Voree and aboard this ship. She couldn't remember what Strang had yelled at her. The shock of him in bed with some female left her weak. That scene made her feel worse than when she read that note back home about Charlie.

She looked back towards the mainland and wondered when she'd return. Her father had died. Her two brothers had moved away with their wives and left mother to operate the general store. There were times when Strang left for preaching missions. Mary had pleaded, "Let me stay and help mother. Make life easier for her."

Strang had ordered, "Your duty is with me and your children."

Mary watched as the ship approached the island harbor. Paradise Bay looked just like Strang had described. As the ship moved through the smooth emerald water of the horseshoe shaped bay, she expected to see people with their dogs at the dock. James had said islanders greeted everyone who arrived. Today, she saw an empty wood wharf, and not a soul waved a handkerchief.

She looked back at the whitecaps on Lake Michigan, then

to the shoreline, a pure white beach with a background of tall evergreens. A pine odor from the island, carried by the breeze, drifted to the ship. She recalled that James had said an evergreen smell filled the island and got stronger when dampness and evening set in. He had said that fragrance remained as much a part of the island as the sandy street high above the dock in front of the village stores. The woodsy smell would be everywhere—on the juniper bushes, the hills, the cliffs, the fields of corn, the dense forests of maple, and the sand dunes all surrounded by the bright turquoise lake. She thought, *The people expect peace and contentment. It won't be paradise for me.*

The passengers, anxious to see the island, all climbed topside. A gentle breeze blew strands of Mary's brown hair across her face. She brushed it aside and studied the island. They still had a good hour before reaching land.

She walked midway on the ship, and stared below where a wide trail of three waves on each side followed the ship. In the middle, bubbles churned like pure white ostrich plumes, rising up in the air like a fountain. As the people milled about, she returned to sit on a bench. Dr. McCulloch approached her. She recalled how during the trip he had asked about the children several times, and often offered a tonic for seasickness. "No, thank you" had always been her response.

Now he stood before her, tipped his hat and asked, "May I sit with you?"

Mary coldly stated, "No. I prefer to be alone."

"Mrs. Strang, if your children get sick on Beaver please send word. I will come immediately. Brother Strang's family is my great concern." He bowed and walked away.

Mary looked at the long stretch of white beach and the dark evergreens that gradually became larger as they neared the island. She inhaled deeply of the piney odor. The fresh lake breeze whetted her appetite. To become a pioneer on this

strange island did not appeal to Mary. Neither did this ship.
Especially Strang's stateroom that reminded her of his infideli-
ty. She knew he'd be free for more sexual escapades on the
island. She didn't care. Mary knew she had to find a way to
escape.

10

It was nine o'clock that hot Fourth of July when Bill and Virginia drove the buckboard to the picnic grove. The unwanted visit by the Mormon had made them late to the festivities. The team pulled them through the woods for a half a mile, until the couple emerged into bright sunshine. Virginia turned her head and watched the fine dust hang in the air behind the rear wheels to powder the roadside bushes like flour. Sunlight hovered over the tops of giant maple, and slants of brightness gleamed through the tree branches in the dense forest. Other rays of sunshine lay scattered over the ground, like snippets on a patchwork quilt. As they passed a well lit area, Virginia looked down at citron moss, toadstools and acorns.

When their wagon left the woods, they came to the picnic grounds next to a big clearing where a gigantic pine grew in the center. Indians named it the Council Tree. It was so old that many branches had fallen off, making it easy to hoist a large American flag by ropes to the top. Just below the flag grew a few short branches with jade needles, the only indication that the tree was still alive.

Today, the wagons, horses, and people had trampled the ground around the trunk into a dusty circle. As they neared the Council Tree, Virginia pleaded, "Bill, please circle the tree. It's good luck."

"No. Ain't got time," he said, and steered the horses toward the picnic tables.

While their wagon wheels rolled over the tall grass, Virginia saw trees bordering the inland lake. Through openings of birch and pine, she saw young lads swimming and heard their shouts and laughter.

After the couple rode a short distance across the grassy clearing, they arrived at the area where many picnic tables were covered with bright cloths under shady trees. On the opposite side of the field, women sold aprons, sunbonnets and pastries at roughly constructed booths. Four men tossed horseshoes at iron stakes in the hot sun. Clanging metal sounded every so often when a horseshoe hit the stake and a man yelled, "Ringer!" Youngsters ran about laughing and shouting. Throughout the picnic grounds wafts of smoke drifted in the air from a barbecue pit. Virginia looked again at the lake where the boys had built a raft from strong tree branches to dive from. Their yells and splashing water mingled with the sound of horseshoes and an occasional sharp echo of firecrackers exploding in the woods.

Virginia took a deep breath and said to Bill, "I love picnics. Smell the food." She noticed his eyes, slate like Lake Michigan before a storm. "I'm sorry. It was all my fault. I wish I was ready. Then we wouldn't have had to meet Ebenezer and hear about those Mormons."

Bill asked, "Why they gotta come today? They're going to spoil our picnic. Feel it in my bones."

Excitement throbbed away at Virginia just thinking about new people settling here. There'd be more life to the island. New women to meet. Start a bigger sewing bee. She held all these thoughts to herself, not wanting to upset Bill. She had felt like him when she first spotted that ship, but now their arrival seemed different.

She saw how the corners of his mouth drooped when he said, "Every year picnic gets bigger. Too many kids. In the good old days, a man relaxed." He halted the team under a shady clump of birch and climbed down to tie the horses to a tree.

Virginia's lady friends chorused, "You-hoo! Virginia! You're late."

Virginia smiled and waved back. Two women walked toward them. Bill said, "I ain't dropping anchor next to a bunch of females."

"Where you going?"

"Knife target. I'll eat later."

She watched until he stopped and tipped his cap to the women. He continued a few paces, then was almost knocked down by a group of children playing tag. He shook a fist angrily at them. When the women reached her wagon, Virginia lowered the tailgate and climbed inside. She bent over and gasped, "Oh my!"

A woman asked, "What's the matter?"

In a disgusted tone Virginia said, "I knew it."

A young woman, a newcomer called Eloise, asked, "What?"

Virginia held up a cherry pie and cried out, "It's smashed."

The first, a rather plump woman said, "Don't worry. They say the judges go more for taste than looks."

Virginia shook her grey head. "That husband of mine! He's a holy terror. Drives the wagon like sailing the lake." Virginia studied Eloise's pale skin and thought, *Dainty like a bluebell.*

Not a pioneer.

After Virginia's best pie was carried to the judges' table, the women hauled the buckets of flowers to a shady area where a large circle had been staked out using braided sweet grass for the frame. Virginia stepped into the center. Three women, already working on the wreath, wiggled to make room. "Ahhh," Virginia exhaled, "feels good to rest."

A woman reached for yellow daisies and twine. "Rest? I work harder on the Fourth."

"Right," another agreed. "Think of all the work. Bake pies, cakes. Get the kids ready at the crack of dawn."

Eloise added, "Pack the buggy. Unload when we go home tonight. I hate to unload. What a mess!"

Virginia reached for some roses and tied them to the frame. As the women talked she thought, *They don't know about the Mormons. Bill will probably tell the men. They're drinking whiskey. They'll spread the news all wrong. It's my duty to spill the beans.* After the women settled down and stopped chattering Virginia said, "I got some news, ladies."

Bertha looked up with a sly grin. Her thick fingers held roses in one hand, and string in the other. "Juicy gossip?"

Virginia recognized the dare. "No. This is important news." She looked around the circle of eager faces and blurted out, "Mormons are coming."

Bertha kept her head down to work on the flowers. "You call that news? We see Mormons everyday."

A woman sitting across from Virginia asked, "Here? To our picnic?"

It wasn't the reaction Virginia expected. The women looked down as they busily twisted and tied cord on white daisies, pink zinnias, snapdragons, and sunflowers. Virginia explained, "I don't mean to picnic. A new Mormon ship will land today."

A voice behind her asked, "How many?"

Virginia looped twine several times around roses and tied

them to the wreath. "I don't know."

"How long they visiting?"

All the women stopped talking. A crow's "caw-caw," high up in a tree shattered the silence. As it flew away, its screech became fainter. Virginia felt the tension, as if she'd thrown a rock into a pond and watched the ripples spread out and become wider than this floral design. She had started something. News of that Mormon ship would spread wide like ripples on the water. Each woman would repeat what she said. News would travel until everyone knew, even the old trapper too sick to come to the picnic, the Indians on Garden, and the fishermen sailing near the other islands; everyone would pass the word. She said, "Not a visit. They're settling here for good with plenty of folks."

Eloise stopped work and exclaimed, "Oh, no!"

All the women looked up as Eloise continued, "Back home we lived near Mormons. Always had trouble."

Bertha asked, "What kind?"

Eloise held a yellow rose to her nose and sniffed the fragrance. "Bad neighbors. They told us to be quiet on Saturday, their Sabbath. When they didn't fight with us, they fought with each other."

Virginia said, "Mormon families here haven't bothered us."

A woman raised her head and reached for a handful of phlox. She said, "Calm before the storm."

They began to talk all at once. Virginia stood up and placed her hands on hips. "Ladies, for heavens sake! Let's work. Finish the wreath. I'm sorry I told you."

An elderly woman spoke up, "Mormons don't worry me none. I live right near them. They keep close to their hoe."

Virginia stepped out of the circle to get more flowers. When she returned Bertha said, "If Mormons preach to me, my John will close up the store. We'll go back to the mainland."

Virginia set down the bucket and stepped back into her place within the circle. "Bertha, don't be silly."

The heavyset woman bent over, picked up the hem of her dark blue dress, and wiped her perspiring face. Her violet eyes looked at Virginia. "John and me came here to get away from do-gooders. I don't run to church. I'm no hypocrite."

The women murmured and when they stopped Bertha added, "I don't mind when your Catholic missionary comes. You believe your way. I believe mine. But I know Mormons. They will shove their preaching down your throat."

A thin woman with salt and pepper hair and a wrinkled face laughed, "Bertha, it's not that bad. I went to one of their dances back in Ohio. We danced the Virginia Reel. They're fine folks. Real neighborly and fun loving."

Bertha's fair complexion turned ruddy as she faced the speaker. "What about Mormons here? Virginia, Carrie Smith and I knocked on their doors the very next day after they settled. We took fresh bread and jam. Invited them to our sewing bee. Why, you'd think we talked to the crown heads of Europe the way they acted. I hate snobs. When they come to the store, John sells to them. Not me. I never forget when someone treats me like dirt. Mormons live in their own world. Always busy. Makes me tired to watch them."

Eloise turned and asked, "What do you mean?"

Bertha pushed stray flaxen hairs up to the braid around her head. "They moved into some deserted cabins. Picked out the blackest garden dirt on Beaver. Always weeding and singing hymns at the top of their lungs. Too busy to make trouble."

Eloise insisted, "They steal. Call it consecrating. Bet the new ones steal too. Got any more padlocks and chains, Bertha?"

Bertha smiled, "Get your order in. Locks going fast. Might be sold out tomorrow."

A middle-aged woman stopped work and said, "I lived in

a town with gypsies. Had to nail everything down. Even the chickens. I ain't about to go through that again."

Bertha looked around the group. "I hear they have prayer meetings three times a day. If I was to walk in a church, it'd fall down."

Women smiled and laughed at that remark. Virginia said, "We got plenty of food. Some will go to the seagulls. Why don't we take food to their ship when it lands. I bet they got hungry little kids."

Bertha said sharply, "Forget it. We got no place with Mormons before. I wouldn't go to see their ship if I was paid a million dollars."

A young girl in light blue said, "They better not bring extra wives. We ain't putting up with that on Beaver."

Eloise asked, "Polygamy?"

"Ugh!" she replied. "That nasty word. I can never remember it."

Eloise grinned smugly and pushed a thin silver bracelet further up her bare arm, pink with sunburn. "It's easy. Think of the letter P. P stands for pig. I was told they all pig together."

Virginia watched as an elderly woman gasped. She was highly embarrassed at their conversation and put a hand over pale lips, but the other women giggled. One said, "They are quiet folks. Don't bother a soul. Work hard."

Eloise cautioned, "Looks are deceiving. I was taught not to judge a book by its cover."

By noon the group completed the memorial wreath and left it in the shade. Virginia returned to her picnic table. Young lads in old pants cut off at the knees ran bare chested from the lake, then stood with arms folded and shivered in the hot sun. As elderly ladies sat in the shade crocheting, young mothers fed their children at tables, while others sat on blankets spread over the grass. A young girl in a light blue gingham dress and sunbonnet moved through the crowd and sold fudge and popcorn balls from a basket she carried on her arm.

Under a shady clump of trees, musicians sat on benches and tuned up. At the first sound of a scratching fiddle, Virginia watched a row of blue jays, perched in a tall maple, fly away. When the music became louder, several men grabbed their wives and started dancing. The children ran toward the grassy area, and soon everyone left the picnic tables to crowd around the dancers.

Virginia sat on a bench next to a table covered by a red and white checkered cloth with plates for fried chicken and baked beans. She watched a group of men approach from the clearing next to the woods. Bill walked steady, but the others staggered. Virginia felt sorry for women whose husbands bought whiskey from renegades.

As the men walked closer, they raised their liquor bottles high in the air and strutted toward the musicians in an assortment of wild capers. Virginia saw Eloise lift her green skirt above her white ankles and run towards her husband. When she reached the blond young man, she tugged at his arm trying to entice him to dance, but he shook his head and refused. Next Eloise grabbed Bill by the hand to get him to dance, but he snatched his hand free and bolted away. When he joined Virginia he asked, "Did you see that hussy grab me?"

Virginia smiled, "That's Eloise. She's new here."

Bill shook his head. "I'd get a heart attack. I can't polka." He looked at the table where the plates covered the food to keep flies off. He asked, "You eat?"

"No. Waited for you."

He sat down and she dished out the food. While they ate, she studied him. He chewed the chicken faster than usual as his eyes darted nervously about. He looked at the crowd who applauded the musicians after each tune. All this time the older men played horseshoes, oblivious of the music. Bill ate a piece of cherry pie and glanced at the sky and said, "What a day. No sign of rain."

She watched him pull a cherry pit from his mouth. It slipped between his rough fingers and rolled into his grey, short beard. He fumbled about until he found the pit and tossed it away.

Virginia smiled at him sweetly and said, "Sorry about that pit. Bill, when they play a waltz, let's dance."

He took a deep breath, exhaled, and patted his stomach. "Ate too much good food."

"You know I love to waltz."

He looked away as if he hadn't heard. She turned to see what attracted his attention, but only the horses and the wagon were tied to a tree. "I got no time. I'm shoving off for the dock."

"They probably landed by now."

"No. Got a kid up a tree watching the lake." He dug into his pants pocket, took out a watch on an old gold chain, and looked at it. "Ship lands in half an hour. See you later."

Virginia thought, *Why can't he forget Mormons?* She studied his face. Tanned skin stretched over his sunken cheeks and his blue eyes were the shade of Lake Michigan. She asked, "Did anything happen back there?" Her grey brows were separated by deep wrinkles and above, a furrowed brow. "Did you tell them about the Mormons?"

Bill took off the naval cap and scratched at the top of his bald head. "Hell no. They don't give a damn about nothin' but getting drunk today. They're full of whiskey. It wouldn't mean nothing if President Taylor sailed in." A strange, thoughtful look flooded his eyes. He got up from the bench, "See you later."

A feeling of great disappointment swept over Virginia. Now the sensation grew within, and her gay mood disappeared. She didn't want to show melancholy, but felt the corners of her

mouth droop and a lump press midway in her throat. It would
be the first time he refused to waltz with her on the Fourth of
July.

Before long this celebration would end. The kids would get
tired of swimming and chasing the greased pig. The pie and
watermelon eating contests would end, and finally the American flag would be lowered from the Council Tree for the
parade to the dock. Last of all would be the big finale of the
bugler playing taps and the wreath floating on the water.
Virginia asked, "Bill, what can I tell folks?"

He shoved the blue shirt deeper into his brown pants and
gave a quick hitch to the black belt. "Tell them the truth. I'm
sober. I'll protect Beaver from Mormons."

"Please stay. Just for one dance."

He shook his head. "No. I'm shoving off."

"I hate it when you're moody. You act like the lake. Calm
one minute, wild the next. You didn't circle the Council Tree.
You ate too fast. Why don't you think of me for a change
instead of running off? I worked hard. Now you leave me all
alone to go see strangers land." She wiped away tears with the
back of her hand and blurted out, "You're just like your
father. Run to the dock at every ship's whistle."

"I'm going. You're all upset over nothin'." Bill walked
away just as waltz music began.

She followed him to the wagon. After he untied the team
and climbed up into the driver's seat, she asked, "Bill, what
can I tell folks?"

Looking down at her he said in a firm voice, "Ginny, I'll
be back in a little while. Don't worry."

She called out again, "Folks will want to know where
you're at."

"Tell them I got guts to fight and save Beaver. I got to find
out what the new Mormons are up to."

As the wagon slowly rolled away she called after him,

"Wait!" He stopped the horses. She suggested, "Invite the newcomers to our picnic."

"Give Mormons an inch, they'll take a mile."

"Bill, if it was us coming off the lake, hungry, tired and not knowing where our heads rested at night, think how good food and a bed would feel."

"Don't be stupid. Mormons will steal your eye teeth if you give them leeway. I got plans. I'll get rid of Mormons."

11

Zion landed on Beaver Island at mid-afternoon.

The sailors tossed ropes, tied up the ship, and lowered the gangplank. Strang stood on the dock next to the gangplank and directed the unloading of the ship. He ordered, "Crates over here. Ploughs next. Look out! Don't break the furniture."

Sailors rolled barrels down the gangplank. Men lined up single file on the dock to retrieve the cylinders and push them to the wagons. Two young boys held onto horse halters. The animals, excited by the confusion, jerked their heads up, shook their manes from side to side, and snorted. Next all the livestock and crates of chickens came off the ship. Strang tried to keep a long line of crates and barrels in order, but the men carried off the cargo quickly. A tremendous pile of four-poster bed sections, mattresses, tables, chairs, and sacks of grain were all carried to the dock, one heaped upon the other. Strang found it difficult to direct the workers where to stack the cargo on the dock; his voice could hardly be heard above the noise. The only freight to move smoothly was the luggage, sacks of flour, and steamer trunks hauled to Brother Ebenezer's farm. As the men quickly carried the cargo off, the goods became completely piled across the width of the wharf. Strang watched the boxes being stacked higher, and the thick mattresses piled on top of tables. He marvelled that *Zion* had transported so much.

Then he heard music, a melody coming from the village. He walked past the rugged outline of cargo on the dock, past the over-turned chairs, the burlap bags of cornmeal, and iron ploughs. When Strang reached the end of the dock, he saw a procession of people walking slowly towards the harbor. He heard a fiddle, harmonica, bugle, and a drum. A large crowd followed an American flag tied to a tree limb, carried by a young boy in short pants. Children waved small American flags and marched alongside the women who were dressed in bright calico and sunbonnets. Behind them staggered a rough assortment of fishermen and trappers who drank liquor from bottles.

Three men fell down, rolled over on the sandy street, then stood up with their pants covered with sugar sand, a crystal white in the dazzling sunlight. They ran to catch up to the others, then raised their whiskey bottles and yelled, "Whoo-pee! Yahoo!"

When the marchers reached the dock, they stopped and divided ranks. Strang saw a buckboard pulled by a team move forward with a huge wreath of fresh flowers. He had never seen such a floral display. Not even at Nauvoo funerals.

The band suddenly played the "Star Spangled Banner." The men in the crowd pulled off their caps, straightened up and leveled their right hands into frozen salutes. Strang watched a drunk stagger forward from the crowd. This red-faced fellow with bleary eyes stood in front of the drummer, stomped his feet and clapped his hands vigorously. He demanded, "Whatsa matter? Play louder. Louder dammit!"

A woman near the drunk put a finger to her lips and warned, "Shh! We're at the dock."

The man snarled, "So what! It ain't church." He nudged the drummer in the ribs with an elbow and shouted, "Strike up the band."

Strang asked Ebenezer, "What's going on?"

"Fourth of July parade."

"Here? On the dock?"

"That's right."

Strang watched women lift the wreath from the wagon, and carry it slowly in his direction. He pulled his cape together and placed his hands in his pants pockets. "Ebenezer, they're headed this way."

"Do it every year."

Strang looked at the space between the women and the wagon. The sober driver turned the team around and drove off the dock. The Mormon children had been playing on the beach, but now, attracted by the music, they scrambled over the rocks supporting the dock and joined the crowd. Six women carried the wreath and their colorful sunbonnets waggled as they walked in step to the drummer's slow beat. One lady called, "Stop," as they neared the Mormon cargo piled on the dock. The others halted, but the drum continued its mournful dirge. When the drummer stopped, the only sound was that of the gentle waves splashing against the pilings. The woman cried out, "We can't move on. Their stuff's in the way."

The drunk finished a slug of whiskey and yelled, "I'll dump it in the drink."

A chorus of women screamed, "No! No! Don't!"

He shouted, "Just like my old lady. Don't do this. Don't do that. Hellsfire!" He held the bottle tightly in one hand and staggered forward with cautious steps like a baby learning to walk.

Strang asked Ebenezer, "Do they always drink?"

Ebenezer shook his head, "Brother Strang, that ain't nothing. You ought to see them at New Year's. Matter of fact, any holiday. Soused to the gills."

Strang took his hands from his pants pockets. "Disgusting," he remarked. "To think I came to this island of pure air and natural beauty, and I find man contaminated and reveling in dipsomania." He clasped his hands behind his back, looked at the lake and said, "I sincerely wish I'd landed on some other island away from drunks."

"No use."

"Why?"

Ebenezer grinned, "No island's free of liquor. Whiskey Point sells to everybody. Indians too."

"Where's Whiskey Point?"

Ebenezer pointed north, "Over there. Renegades make whiskey. Indians trade fish for fire water."

"That's against the law."

Suddenly the drunk approached the two men. He sat down and leaned against a piling. He took the cork from a bottle, held it up to the men and insisted, "Take a snort."

Ebenezer shook his head and said, "No."

The drunk stared at Strang and demanded, "Drink."

Strang snarled, "I hate liquor."

The tipsy fellow erupted in laughter, "You're a man? Don't drink? Itsa Fourth. Itsa big day."

Strang thought, *What a time to give a sermon on the evil of alcohol to a looney like this. No time. Too much to do.*

The grimy fellow smiled with a mouth full of teeth the shade of horse corn. "I'll drink for youse."

As the drunk raised the bottle to his mouth, Strang thought, *First the death wreath. Now this drunk telling me what to do.*

What a strange welcome.

Ebenezer cautioned Strang, "If we don't move the cargo to one side, they'll shove it in the water. Plenty of men back there. Mean ones. Itching for a fight. We better make way for their parade."

Strang felt extremely tired and didn't want trouble. He waved to the sailors on the first deck, "Come here." When they stood around him he instructed, "Move everything to one side." He pointed, "Over there. Make room for their parade."

The sailors, elders and the young lads carried the heavy grain sacks and the sturdy tables to one side of the wharf. Once again the drum beat a steady cadence as the women picked up the wreath.

The drunk rested against the piling. He slapped his right palm against the wharf planks to keep time to the music. When the American flag came closer, the drunk swung his right hand to his wrinkled brow to salute. He shouted at Strang, "Hey Red. Salute the flag."

Strang hadn't been called "Red" since childhood, when he was the only redhead in school. After his brothers left home to work in the potato fields, the bullies shouted, "Hey Red. Hey carrots." Strang's fist turned raw from fighting. When he came home, his mother cried to see his bloody face. Strang had contempt for the intoxicated. When they called him "Red" his throat burned raw. Strang didn't want this drunk on Beaver and thought, *He's a wastrel. I'll get rid of him and all drunks. The quicker the better.*

Strang stepped up to the befuddled man, and ordered in a loud voice, "Don't call me Red, you low excuse for humanity."

The drunk stood up and stared as if his eyes couldn't focus on the people who hurried past. He bent over to pick up the bottle, wavered and almost fell down. He weaved from one side to the other, but finally managed to straighten up. While

Strang looked at him, the man sighed deeply as if very tired. Then he slumped over.

Not for long. Suddenly the drunk turned wild, smashed the empty bottle against the wood post and sprang to his feet. He lunged at Strang and yelled, "You no good bastard!"

Strang met the drunk head-on. He grabbed the man's wrists until he dropped the glass. The drunk fought back. In the scuffle Ebenezer kicked the bottle into the lake.

When the drunk grew limp from Strang's powerful grip, he fell down and rubbed his wrists. "I'll get you for that."

Strang taunted, "You don't worry me."

Ebenezer ran to the ship. He shouted for help. Several husky sailors rushed down the gangplank. Strang slapped the drunk on the back. The man stumbled forward and weaved from side to side.

The drunk yelled, "I'll fight all youse." He jumped into a crouched position and made fists. One Mormon grabbed him and the drunk twisted and turned under the grasp, but the sailor pinned his arms behind his back.

Ebenezer protested, "Hey, don't hurt him." He pointed at the fishermen and cried out, "There'll be bloodshed."

Strang said, "We'll fight to stay here. We know bloodshed. We've been beaten, tarred and feathered. We're not moving on. No one will interfere with our happiness. We will live peacefully after we hand drunks over to the buffetings of Satan."

Ebenezer hacked and spat into the water. He turned to the drunk and ordered, "Get home." The drunk stumbled several paces, then stopped and glanced back over his shoulder. Ebenezer yelled, "Go on. Get home. Sleep it off."

As the drunk staggered away, Bill Ryan walked along the dock, followed by a crowd of islanders. Bill did not see the commotion with the drunk because the Mormons had formed a circle around him. Bill called out, "Folks, we're here to honor our dead. Some are in the cemetery. Others lost at sea. We honor them with this wreath. Okay boys, give her a heave-ho. Far as you can."

Two men picked up the wreath, swung it back and forth, then tossed it into the lake. First it splashed, then floated on the water as the bugler played taps. Clear, mournful notes sounded across the wide bay from one evergreen shore to the other. Indians on Garden Island, a mile away, heard the sound. The elderly people who remained at the picnic listened as the slow notes echoed over the pines. Then the music resounded further over the lake where later the sunset turned into a spectacular display.

A wave pushed the wreath back to the dock and it hit a piling. One woman groaned, "Oh no! Bad luck! Bad luck!" Then another wave pushed it and the flowers drifted out to sea. The crowd watched quietly as the wreath floated slowly away until it reached whitecaps. There the wreath bobbed, weaved and thrashed between the foaming crests, a giant wheel of roses, daisies, bluebells, marigolds, zinnias and sunflowers. Pushed by an offshore wind towards the mainland, it skimmed over the waves with a tremendous urgency to leave Beaver and eventually sink. Once down in a watery grave, the flowers would separate and scatter here and there, petals of all shapes on the sandy lake bottom where shipwrecks rested with sailors' bones.

After taps ended, a Mormon approached Strang and placed a hand on his shoulder. He asked, "What happened? They say a man tried to kill you."

Strang stepped back and re-arranged his cloak neatly across his broad shoulders. He jerked a thumb at the drunk in the distance and said, "Get that rascal off my island."

Suddenly a fisherman tossed a chair into the water. Women screamed. Two Mormons grabbed the man, but he shoved another chair and it splashed louder. Women kept screaming.

Mormon sailors yelled, "Get back! Get away!" Immediately they bloodied the fisherman with their fists and clubs.

Three fishermen knelt down with hands over their heads and groaned. Mary ran to the sailors and screamed, "Stop! Stop!"

Strang yelled, "Mary, get back." He rushed to her side when she pulled on a sailor's sleeve. "I told you to get away," he demanded.

"It's wrong," Mary cried out.

"Stop," Strang ordered the sailors who pinned the fishermen against the dock, and choked and beat them with their fists. "Let the scoundrels go," he shouted. When his men stopped, Strang yelled at the crowd, "Get out of here!"

The fishermen moaned and staggered away as the Mormons pulled the chairs from the water. The island drummer beat a lively cadance as the settlers retreated. In the melee, the American flag had been torn, but now held aloft, as they marched away helping their injured. Some men limped. Bill Ryan shook a fist and shouted, "You'll be sorry you landed here."

12

*W*hile the islanders marched back to the picnic, Strang
cupped his hands to his mouth and yelled, "Ladies, come
down!"

Women on the top deck carried packages and purses. At
times they dropped things, picked them up, and then clustered
next to the gangplank. Several cried out, "I'm dizzy. I'll fall.
Where's my kids?"

Finally through the bevy of sunbonnets, a young woman in
a dark blue dress said, "I'm not scared. I love solid ground."
She led the way, and others followed single file down the
plank to the wood dock where they got in the sailors' way.

Strang ordered, "Over there, ladies." He pointed to the
beach and said, "Wait inside a shanty. It's nice and cool."

A woman asked, "Brother Strang, where's my kids?"

He called back over all the confusion, "At the beach. Don't
worry." As the group of women ambled toward a fish shack,

Strang shouted, "Men, lower my buggy. Unload before dark. The wolves will be out."

An old woman stopped in her tracks and screamed, "Wolves!"

Strang laughed and said, "Wolves all over Beaver."

She squealed, "How dreadful!" and hurried towards the shanty.

Strang laughed harder. Mary had returned to the ship, and observed all the dock activity from the top deck. She thought, *That's not right to scare an old woman.* Mary eyed the cargo: a machine that shelled corn, ploughs, a dearborn wagon, and bags of flour, cornmeal, sugar and molasses. When the men hoisted Strang's fancy buggy from the ship, they carefully lowered it on the dock. Mary always enjoyed riding in the handsome carriage, shiny black with oil lamps front and back, soft leather seats and a top that folded. She stood and watched all the ship activity, and the women walking to a shanty made of driftwood with a roof of cedar shingles.

When the women entered the shanty, the old floor creaked under their footsteps. They looked at nets hung on rusty nails high up on the wall. The white mesh hung like unstarched curtains. On other walls hung spools of white twine, grappling hooks, sharp knives, fish scrapers, dip nets, and long ropes strung with grey and pock-marked corks.

A woman rolled empty fish kegs against a wall so that others could rest their backs. After they sat one asked, "Where's Sister Hortense?" She patted cheeks as white as a spring trillium, and remarked how cool it was inside. Her perfume drifted across the room and mingled with stale tobacco smoke and a fish odor. She fussed with her dark hair and tucked it under a grey sunbonnet.

An elderly widow replied, "Still in Sister Mary's cabin."

"And Sister Mary?"

"Don't know," the widow said, shrugging thin shoulders.

Another woman said, "I heard she's looking for her kids. Scooted off the ship for the beach."

Sarah looked up from knitting and her big tooth bobbed, "Brother Strang's wife uses every excuse to avoid us."

"What do you mean?" the widow asked.

Sarah said, "Didn't you notice she stayed in her fancy stateroom 'til Sister Hortense got sick?"

"Wish I had a stateroom. I was awful seasick."

Sarah looked up and declared, "No reason for her to act like that. We had a minister's wife do the same thing. No good for the congregation. She didn't last long. Mary Strang should be more like her husband, sociable and talkative."

A chubby, middle-age woman said, "I remember Sister Mary back home. She was a fun loving girl. Smiled all the time when she clerked in the store. I think her family's at fault."

"Why?" Sarah demanded. "I knew her family. Fine, God fearing folks. Never refused to take a soul on their credit books."

The stout woman walked over to Sarah and said, "That's your opinion, Mother Bowers. I never thought much of her father."

"What?"

"That's right. I bought some molasses one day and heard it all. Mary's father said, 'Once that door latch clicks, you'll never put your feet under my table again.' He was solid Baptist and didn't want her to marry a Mormon."

Sarah raised her head in the black sunbonnet, looked out the open door and said confidently, "That ain't got nothing to do with it. Later he gave his consent. Besides, he's dead now. Poor soul." She grinned maliciously, "It's the other that makes Mary melancholy."

"What other?" the widow asked.

Sarah rolled a narrow pointed tongue over her thin upper lip and the tooth. She explained, "Brother Strang's secretary, Charlie. Polygamy will happen here. Joseph Smith gave the revelation for plural wives. We must accept it."

The woman in dark blue asked eagerly, "Does she suspect?" In a more intense tone she asked again, "Does Sister Mary know?"

Sarah replied, "Poor thing. She must. It's so obvious. Glad I don't have her husband to worry about."

The stout matron said sincerely, "Sister Mary won't hear that slander from me."

Old lady Bowers laughed so hard her sunbonnet shook on her grey head. She held onto her knitting with one hand, raised the other and wiggled a finger at the woman. "Slander? You'll see." When she stopped tittering, she grinned with the big tooth clipped over her lower lip. She warned, "Truth shall prevail."

"Stop it!" called out a young woman in green with a sun burned face. She stood up, walked from the rear of the shanty and faced the gathering. "You don't know the real story. Mother Bowers only repeats what Sister Mary's aunt-in-law told her. That's one sided. I like Sister Mary, but she's a loner.

"When I first met her, I wanted to be her dearest friend. But there is something strange about her. You all know women like that. At first she gives the impression of shyness. Little by little you find her different. At first I wondered how such a frail woman could be married to such a powerful leader. Her quiet ways make her seem small, but she has great inner strength.

"Brother Strang enjoys good health. He's proof of why we came here for pure air and spring water. Oh, my dears. So many plans. He wants to operate a fish and lumber business and convert the Indians.

"Sister Mary deceives us like a quiet stream. Remember,

still water runs deep. She has iron in her veins instead of
blood. She's like a volcano too, smoldering and ready to
explode. She's good at lots of things, like the garden, sewing
and cooking. Always busy. I'm sure she has to work hard to
forget Brother Strang's weakness.

"It happened before. We all know. I'm not saying anything
untruthful. He had good reason to visit a woman's house for
a faith healing or a religious conference. But my dears—" She
paused. They bent forward to listen. She lowered her voice,
"It was always sex." She squinted her brows and in a soft, but
forceful inflection said, "He's an oversexed man. You know
what I mean. He covered up his tracks for years. It's different
with Charlie. This time he wants her more than Sister Mary.

"I suppose it's Sister Mary's pride. Hope too that he'll
forget Charlie like the others. I'll tell you one thing. Sister
Mary is not the person I once knew. She looks the same, but
I can tell the difference. She reminds me of a rose whose color
has faded. Yes, Mother Bowers, truth does prevail. But when
it happens, I don't want to be around and see poor Sister Mary
hurt."

13

$\mathcal{T}$he dock confrontation took place mid-afternoon with the sun high. When the shadows grew longer, the men recuperated from their injuries at the picnic grounds, where the women applied ice and liniment to their bruises. The men ate, drank whiskey, and rested in the shade as the horseshoe game resumed. Others threw knives at a bullseye back in the woods.

As if nothing had happened, the women chatted and bought pot holders and knitted mittens. One elderly woman declared, "I'm doing my Christmas shopping in July."

The men continued to drink whiskey and discussed their "Fourth shot to hell." One fellow suggested they follow the Mormons to Ebenezer's cabin. "I know they'll end up there. Passed by this morning. They had cooking fires outside. That boatload will feast there."

Suddenly from the roadway two horses galloped into the picnic grove. The riders had faces painted like Indians. One carried a stout branch. When he raced next to the pastry display on a table, he knocked all the baked goods to the ground. Virginia's cherry pies, other women's cakes frosted pink, chocolate and white, lemon meringue pies, raspberry tarts, and a long jelly roll all were smashed. Hours of baking ruined. The women screamed the moment it happened, but the intruder spurred his horse past the booths, the horseshoe game, and the Council Tree. He disappeared down the road leaving only a cloud of dust.

The other "Indian" rode up to the long clothes line where quilts hung. They had been judged and pinned with large blue and red ribbons for first and second prizes. He grabbed the line as his horse raced nearby. One patchwork quilt fell over the horse's rump, and the other quilts followed horse and rider, dragged behind like colorful kite tails.

The pastries were picked up from the ground and thrown away. The quilts, dirty and torn, were found a half mile away on the roadway. While the men vowed to get even, Virginia said, "Bill, I know their leader has a wife. I'll go talk to her."

"No. Let me handle it."

Virginia insisted, "The men are drunk. If they try to get even, someone will get killed."

"I got a plan, Ginny. You just wait. I'll take care of Mormons."

14

*M*ary awoke at seven o'clock as bright sunlight flooded the bedroom through unbleached muslin curtains. At first she thought she was back on the ship. She shut her eyes and groaned the instant her stomach cramped. She regretted eating so much at last night's feast. When the Mormons had arrived at Ebenezer's cabin, there were caldrons of boiled soups and vegetables, as well as oven-roasted beef, pork, and wild turkey. She ate and listened to people chatter while depression slipped into her heart.

She drank warm cider and maintained a fixed, pleasant expression. Mary acted as if she enjoyed the feast by laughing at little jokes, while a sensation of terror spread internally. She had felt suffocation from the noisy crowd, the closeness of bodies pushing about, voices shouting back and forth, and trays of food shoved at her. "Eat this, Sister Mary. Try this. Hot cocoa or cider? More custard pie."

She had waited until after dinner when others talked in

groups or pairs, then walked past them unnoticed. She sat outside and breathed the evergreen-scented air, until her children joined her. They were her best excuse to leave. She told Strang, "They're tired. They want to sleep outside. I'll go tuck them in."

As she lay in bed recalling the events of the previous night, the melody and words of a song the brethren sang at the campfire began over and over in her mind like some big wagon wheel that she couldn't stop:

> *"There's a good time coming, boys*
> *A good time coming*
> *The people shall be temperate,*
> *And shall love instead of hate*
> *In the good time coming."*

Just as the memory of the refrain faded away, she heard the door squeak. Mary kept her eyes closed. Whoever had peeked let in loud voices and the greasy odor of bacon. The smell nauseated Mary. Like her children, many people slept under the stars last night, while Mary slept in this small bedroom. Her husband had supervised unloading the wagons after the feast. She didn't know where he had slept.

Beaver Island had looked wild from the ship with evergreens and bushes along the shoreline. A large colony of gulls dipped their wings, dived at the water, then rested on the waves, bobbing like corks. Other gulls flew towards Luney's Point and the round lighthouse at the harbor entrance.

Once *Zion* landed, Myraette and William had followed the Fourth of July parade. Afraid that Strang would blame her, Mary and two teenage girls hunted for the children around the fish shacks and the village. Finally an elderly woman walked out of the woods with the two little redheads. The villager introduced herself as Virginia Ryan and said she'd visit Mary later.

Mary told her, "I don't know where I'll live."

Virginia had smiled, "I'll find you. I know every inch of Beaver."

While she laid in bed, Mary recalled the trouble at the dock, then their ride to Brother Ebenezer's cabin, ten miles up and down rolling hills. They rode through dark maple forests with the road damp from swampy ground on either side. Next, they emerged from that long stretch of woods into daylight, and traveled on a sandy road past dunes where juniper bushes grew in wide clumps. The lake stayed on their left, a deeper blue as the sun lowered in the west. She recalled more forests and hills, and a steep cliff that hung over the lake. At times the land was such a study of contrasts that it seemed like Wisconsin. Everything had been scrambled in their haste to leave the dock. What if her clothes were lost? Or the good china smashed?

The island Mormons prepared a hot meal. Kettles steamed and hissed in the kitchen while under the trees long tables were piled high with roast turkey, greens, smoked fish, preserves, relish, fresh bread, cakes, and pies. Pitchers of cold milk were kept filled and rows of thick candles glowed late into the night.

Voices this morning sounded louder outside. Mary got out of bed. While she dressed, she studied the small bedroom. There was a hooked rug on the floor and a single bed. She hoped her future cabin would be larger than this. She picked up her leather purse at the end of the bed, opened it, took out a small jar of face cream and used a cloth to cleanse her face.

Door hinges squeaked again and two dark eyes peeked into the room. A heavyset woman, Harriet, walked in and said, "My goodness, you sleep late, Sister Mary. I fed your kids."

"Thank you. I'll be outside shortly."

Harriet frowned as if hurt by Mary's abrupt statement. "Yes, Sister Mary." She left the room and closed the door softly.

Mary went to the outhouse, then joined the women. The first person to see her was Sarah, who called out, "Good morning Sister Mary."

The other women seated at the long table nodded. Harriet asked, "How do you want your eggs?"

"No eggs."

"Oatmeal?"

"Never eat breakfast. Drink milk." The sight of the greasy bacon and the thick gruel brought a salty taste to Mary's mouth. She clenched her teeth. If she became sick in front of these gossips, they'd know she was pregnant. They'd look at her stomach every day. She swallowed and forced the bitter liquid down her dry throat. When the bile was gone she asked, "Where is everybody?"

Sarah said, "Children at the beach. Men at the ship." She patted a space on the bench and demanded, "Sit here."

The widow reminded Mary of Strang's Aunt Rachel, the same height and dressed in black. Sarah's voice droned steadily to slip into the past, like a sunset lowering into the horizon. She manipulated any conversation and dramatized her experiences. Her eyes shifted back and forth, never looked directly at a listener and her tongue forced a raspy sound against the front tusk.

"I don't care to sit," Mary retorted. "Walking early is good for the constitutional."

Harriet brought the milk. Mary took the mug from her and drank slowly. When finished, she wiped her mouth with a white handkerchief. She felt her stomach quiver from the cold drink. She didn't enjoy being with these women or listening to their trite, ignorant conversation. Listening to them now reminded her of Wisconsin when they had complained daily. They bothered Mary with tales of what man had been caught and punished for adultery, who drank whiskey, who needed food from the supply house, and what family hadn't paid weekly tithes.

After being with them for ten minutes, Mary heard wagon wheels sounding from the woods. The men arrived in several buckboards stacked high with goods. Strang led the procession in a buggy pulled by his black horse, Ezekiel.

The women left the table and greeted their husbands. As Strang climbed down from his buggy Sarah called out, "Brother Strang, was there trouble back there?"

Mary watched how he took off his wide brimmed black hat, smoothed his red hair and said in a vexed tone, "No." He put his hat on and ordered, "Women, get your kids. Cabins are ready." He turned to Mary and demanded, "Get Myraette and William. After the toil of a hot morning, I want to roll."

When Mary returned, Sarah and the others had departed. Mary boosted each child up into the buggy. Strang held the reins. After Mary climbed up and sat down, he turned the horse around. Mary waved and called out, "Good-bye. Thank you, Sister Harriet."

Her husband curtly reprimanded Mary, "Don't thank her. She's supposed to be hospitable."

Mary put William on her lap. Myraette sat between her parents. The buggy wheels moved easily over the path, which was wide enough for two wagons to pass. Ezekiel trotted at a steady clip-clop over the dusty roadway and Mary thought, *Now I'll ask him about Charlie.*

William stirred. Mary resettled him from one side of her lap to the other. The boy's red head bobbed and it was difficult for her to see her husband's face and evaluate his mood. She had to find out if this was the right time to talk to him.

Myraette tugged at her father's sleeve. "What's that?" She pointed to the side of the road where a row of short bushes loaded with red cherries followed the trail.

Strang glanced down and smiled at Myraette, "Want a

bellyache?"

Myraette shook her henna head and pouted, "No, papa."

He insisted, "Don't eat wild berries. You'll get sick and die."

William's body jerked forward. Mary held him tighter. "Sit still," she demanded impatiently.

Strang said, "Don't fuss at the lad. He's tired."

Mary said, "He almost fell out."

William looked up at his father and said, "I wanna rabbit."

Myraette clasped her hands together and begged, "Please, papa. Please."

Strang looked fondly at her. Mary saw a benevolent smile spread over his face. He answered, "I'll trap you each a rabbit. Biggest rabbits here."

Myraette clapped her dainty hands, "Oh goody. Goody." She turned to William and said, "Our own rabbits."

Strang winked at Mary and said with a smile, "Two rabbits will be a hundred."

Mary warned, "James, watch what you say in front of them." He laughed harder.

Myraette asked, "What's papa laughing at?"

Mary said, "Never mind, dear."

The tired children settled down, and the four rode in silence. After ten minutes, they reached a two-story log cabin. All their possessions had been unloaded in front. The sofa and dining room suite had been set on the front porch.

The log cabin faced the road and was surrounded by open fields. The original owner had constructed a rustic log fence to keep out deer from the garden and apple orchard. Behind the cabin, whitecaps were visible on Lake Michigan. On all sides behind the clearing grew cedar, maple, birch, and pine. Mary wondered if every time the women traveled to the village, they'd stop for water and bring gossip. They hadn't bothered her aboard ship, but she knew eventually they'd bring slander to her door.

A wide, crude chimney built of smooth lake limestone faced north, and the roof had been well shingled with tree bark. On either side of the front door, the windows contained twelve small squares of glass. There were two more windows on the south side. The porch steps needed repair. Overhead an awning made from thin, wood planks was supported by four thick knotty pine posts.

Mary turned to her husband and nodded confidently, "It's nice."

He said, "My next house will overlook the harbor. It will be a castle. Ships from Chicago to Mackinac will know it's mine."

"When?"

He smiled faintly, a deceptive grin as if he had something in mind, not to be shared with Mary. She had noticed that certain look often lately. Were his thoughts about Charlie or that hussy in his cabin on the trip?

"Not long," he said.

Strang climbed down, tied the reins to a porch post, then boosted down Myraette and William. Myraette asked, "Can we go play?"

Mary said, "Yes. Not far. Be careful."

The two scampered towards the orchard as Mary carefully walked up the uneven porch steps. The wood shook underfoot. She said, "This must be fixed."

Strang avoided the steps. He leaped up to the porch, and squeezed between the furniture. Mary followed him to the front door. It was open and revealed floors blackened by the weather. At one end she saw a big kitchen with a stone fireplace. At the opposite side, a fairly large bedroom contained a smaller fireplace. A strong, musty odor permeated the cabin. A narrow ladder led to the second floor loft. In the kitchen she saw an open trap door to a fruit cellar. The wood

cover had been dragged to one side. She bent over the opening
and saw a ladder. While Strang climbed up the loft, Mary
decided to explore the cellar. As she descended a few rungs,
she smelled dampness. After several steps, her eyes became
accustomed to the darkness, and she made out wood shelves
and plenty of space to store apples and potatoes for winter.
When Strang climbed down the loft ladder, Mary came up
from the cellar.

They inspected all the rooms, then walked out to the front
porch. Mary yelled to the children, "Look out for poison ivy!"

"Let them be," Strang ordered in an annoyed tone. "You're
too protective."

"I must. I'm the one who's up all night when they're sick."

His attitude provoked her. He hardly talked on the buggy
ride, as if she were a housekeeper, not his wife. Her head
became dizzy, and she wished she had eaten breakfast. She
finally decided that this was the time to talk about Charlie.
Strang walked to the buggy. Mary followed. He reached for
the reins and untied them. Before he climbed up Mary said, "I
have something to tell you."

"What? I have much to do."

Her throat turned dry and a knot formed in the middle. This
wasn't how she planned to speak about Charlie. But she had to
see it through. She took a deep breath, but the lump in her
throat hurt more. "Back home, a rock was tossed at our
house."

"Mary! Are you daft?" He scowled, "You bother me with
idle talk. I must escort brethren to more cabins." He took out
a small map from his breast pocket and unfolded it.

Mary watched as he studied the paper, preoccupied as if she
didn't exist. She protested, "Will you please listen? I'm not
finished."

"Hurry up!" he insisted, and kept reading the map.

Her faced warmed as she raised her voice, "You never pay

attention. I sit in church when you preach for hours."

Strang raised his head and glared as he folded the chart, "The prophet's wife better harken to his sermons."

Mary felt her lips tremble. She bit her lower lip and asked sullenly, "Can't you listen to me for one moment?"

"What's so important? I told you. I have to settle brethren before dark."

Mary replied in a low voice, "Nothing."

He climbed into the buggy and without a farewell, he whacked the whip on the horse's hide. The animal took off at a quick trot. As Ezekiel's hooves sounded fainter down the roadway, she heard a burst of childish laughter in the orchard. Myraette had climbed high up in a tree.

Mary walked to the orchard and screamed, "Get down! You'll fall and break an arm. That's all I need. I have work to do."

"Mama, we're playing nice," her daughter called back.

Mary yelled, "Get down. Get out of that tree!"

After Myraette descended safely, Mary walked slowly back to the cabin and sat down on the sofa on the front porch. She smelled the pinery, studied her belongings and thought, *All these boxes and barrels. What a mess. I don't want to unpack. I want to leave this miserable island.*

15

It was daybreak, chilly and quiet, when Mary got up from the floor where she slept on blankets with the children. She pulled a grey cotton dress over a muslin petticoat, slipped bare feet into leather slippers, and walked quietly past her husband stretched out on the couch.

When Mary returned from the outhouse, Strang had dressed and hitched the horse to the black buggy. As Mary walked toward him, she felt a heavy dew wet her ankles. The scene reminded her of Voree, when the early sun glistened on the grass, and cast a silver shine on the top of a split rail fence. Today, she looked at a buckboard covered by a damp canvas, and wondered if her possessions would fit inside the log cabin. She asked, "When will you unload this?"

He said, "I'll be back at noon. Clean up the cabin. My men will haul things inside."

"I'll scrub. The place is filthy."

When he climbed up into the buggy seat he said, "I'll bring milk."

She looked up and asked, "When can I shop? I saw stores in the village. I'd like to go shopping."

He reached down and patted her head. Strang smiled and said, "Later. Hard work for the Lord comes first." He picked up the reins, hit the horse with the whip and the buggy rolled away. She walked back to the cabin. After the children awoke, she fed them bread and jam.

Myraette complained, "I want milk."

"Drink water. Papa will bring milk."

"Can we play at the beach?" Myraette asked.

"No. Play here. I got work to do. Can't worry about you kids drowning. Bring me the broom."

After Myraette returned from the front porch with the broom, Mary swept the log cabin. Myraette asked, "Mama, can I get our toys?"

"All right, but don't touch anything else. Just your toy box."

"Yes, mama."

After a short while Mary stopped sweeping, looked out the door and saw the children carrying the box to the front porch. As she mopped the floor, she heard Myraette bouncing a ball. Next she heard William yell, "Pow-pow-pow!" as he played with toy soldiers.

When Mary finished mopping, she wrapped an old towel around the broom, dampened it in the bucket of sudsy lye soap, and wiped cobwebs from the cabin walls. As she cleaned the windows with a cloth, she noticed the children were nowhere in sight. She rushed out the open door and looked for them. The porch where they had played had toy soldiers scattered about, but the two were missing.

Mary shouted, "Myraette! William!" The countryside stillness pushed at her ears. She called over and over. No answer. The only sounds were from a bumble bee who buzzed near the bottom step, and deer flies who droned and bumped against the front windows.

Maybe they're in the orchard, Mary thought. She ran through the dry weeds. As she ran she called out in a loud, determined voice, "Myraette! Myraette! William! Where are you?"

When she reached the orchard, she expected to find the children playing hide and seek. Any moment one would pop out from behind the thick trunk of a snow apple. The more she walked, the more provoked she became not to be cleaning the cabin. She circled the cluster of trees, looked up, and wondered if the children were hiding there. She saw a raspberry bush growing tall and wild in high weeds. Despite the appealing red berries, she could not stop and pick. The kids had to be found before their father returned. She became very frustrated hunting for them and her throat felt sore from yelling their names.

She left the orchard and walked toward the roadway. In the distance she saw smoke hanging in the air from a fire. Last night at Harriet's cabin the men had talked at length about cleared land. A fear came to Mary. What if Myraette and William had been attracted to a fire? She rushed across an open field toward the smoke. She walked so fast that at times she had to stop, rest and start up again. Her dress hem became tangled with small brown burrs, but she had no time to stop and pick them off. As she ran through a forest of maple, she yelled the children's names, but only bluejays high in the trees shrieked back at Mary.

After she trampled through a soft cushion of dry leaves near a smoky field, she shouted again, "Myraette! William!" A crow screeched a loud, "caw-caw." She looked at the land where a pile of newly cut trees had been stacked for future cabins. Behind it was cleared land, another apple orchard and four large heaps of smoldering brush.

Mary walked towards the orchard and thought, *They must be there*. Suddenly her slippers sank into a soft piece of ground. Smoldering wood burned the top of her bare right foot. She screamed in pain. It made her sick to her stomach to see a round black spot, as if the skin was burned by a poker tip.

Tears rolled down Mary's cheeks as she ran through the weeds back to the road. As the pain became more intense, she began to hobble favoring her left leg. When she felt the strain on that leg, she tried to straighten up, but the pain became unbearable. She thought she'd faint. At last she came out of the field and forest to the road. Her cabin seemed miles away. On her right she saw the blue water of Lake Michigan. She tried to determine the shortest path. On one hand she wanted water to cool the burn. On the other, home meant comfort.

Mary continued to stumble along the gravel road, the pain becoming more intense with each step. When she heard a wagon rattle behind, she turned and saw the lone figure of a woman in the driver's seat. The two chestnut horses pulled to a stop next to Mary, and she recognized the elderly lady she had met yesterday. Mary's foot throbbed a steady, fiery pain. She gasped, "Help! Help me! Burned my foot!"

Virginia had left home for a ride. She was curious to see what empty cabins the Mormons would move into. She climbed out the wagon as quickly as possible and helped Mary up into the front seat. Without a word, she whipped the horses, and they took off at a fast trot towards Mary's cabin.

The moment they reached it, Virginia said, "Stay put. I'll fetch water." Mary took off her slipper and stayed in the wagon. Virginia climbed down, then ran toward the pump. She returned with a bucket of water and said, "Soak it good. Water takes out the heat. Got any salve?"

"No," Mary said as she plunged her bare foot into the

bucket. Immediately she felt relief. She eased her foot out and saw how the black had washed off and left a raw spot as red as a ripe watermellon.

"Keep it in. I'll go home for salve," Virginia said.

Mary reached over and placed her hand on Virginia's blue gingham sleeve. Mary said, "I'm much obliged, but I'm worried about my kids. I was hunting for them. That's how I burned my foot."

"We'll find them. Don't worry. I gotta get my salve."

"My foot feels better already. I'll look for them."

"Oh no. You keep that foot in water. I knew a man had his whole leg cut off from a burn smaller than that. Burned to the bone. I'll help you to the house."

"The cabin is a mess. I was cleaning up when the kids took off."

Virginia carried the bucket and supported Mary who limped towards the cabin. Once inside Mary kept soaking her burned foot. A few minutes later, Myraette and William came home wearing sea gull feathers tucked in their hair. Each child clutched a handful of feathers.

"Look mama," William cried out, holding a feathery bouquet.

Mary shouted, "You were at the beach! Myraette, you know better. I told you not to go there."

Myraette hung her head, then turned and looked at Virginia for sympathy.

Mary yelled, "Get in the loft! Stay there. I'll punish you kids good." In a louder voice she screamed, "I ought to take a switch!" The children darted to the ladder and their heavy leather shoes pounded against the rungs as they climbed up still holding the feathers.

Virginia said, "I'm going home for salve and bandage. Keep your foot in water. Air hurts a burn." She walked to the door, stopped and turned around. Her white hair glistened in the sunlight as she said, "I'll bring lunch."

"Thanks. That's kind of you," Mary said in a calmer voice. "I appreciate your help."

Virginia left the house and drove the team out the yard to the roadway. After a few minutes Myraette called down, "I'm sorry, mama."

"Shut up!" Mary yelled. Her voice echoed in the empty cabin.

The youngsters cried as they sat in their loft. They continued crying until Mary screamed, "Stop it! Come down here." They stopped crying and descended the ladder. Mary pulled her foot out of the bucket of water. "See what you did to mama? I burned my foot looking for you."

Myraette put her arms around Mary's neck and said, "I'm sorry, mama. I'll be good." Mary noticed how the girl's pink cheeks were wet with tears.

She looked at her son. His red hair had turned damp with perspiration from the warm loft. It made his hair dark red like his father's. William said, "I'll be good."

Mary shook a finger at them, "Don't ever, ever run away again. You hear?"

"Yes, mama," they recited together.

"Play on the porch. Just the porch. If I find you any place else, I'll take a switch to you."

After the children walked outside, the throbbing in her foot became worse, and spread up her leg towards her knee. A half an hour later Virginia returned with the salve in a small glass jar. She smoothed it on Mary's burn and bandaged the foot. Virginia walked to the wagon and returned carrying a picnic basket of bread, cheese, jam, pound cake, and a jug of cold milk. The children ate hungrily. After they finished eating Virginia said, "Stretch out on the sofa and rest."

Mary laid down and elevated her foot. She looked at Virginia's team tied to a large maple. The sun had climbed high and she figured it was noon. James would return soon. She wondered, *What will he say about my injury and this Gentile woman?* Mary went to sleep. When she awoke from the nap she heard Virginia moving about. Mary called out, "Mrs. Ryan, what are you doing?"

Virginia stood in the doorway and said, "I cleaned up." She folded her arms over her thin breast, covered by rows of pleats on the blue gingham dress, and said, "Call me Virginia. Feel too old when folks say missus."

"The women call me Sister Mary, but I'd rather you just call me Mary." She sat up from the sofa and exclaimed, "You even folded the bedding."

"I opened those two windows, too. There's a good lake breeze."

"Thanks. I appreciate it."

"Your buckboard is still loaded."

"The men will be here soon."

"I'm heading home," Virginia said and picked up the empty picnic basket. She walked towards the open front door. "I'll stop by tomorrow and look at that burn. We'll chat a bit."

Mary smiled at her and said, "That's real neighborly of you."

Virginia climbed into the wagon. The children shouted, "Good-bye." Mary waved from the porch. As the last sound of the wagon wheels disappeared in the distance Mary thought, *I'll have to tell James about Virginia.*

In the following days a large water blister popped up over the burn. Strang said, "I'll get Doctor McCullough. That Gentile woman could poison you with her salve."

Mary protested, "No. It's all right. Feels fine."

Strang said, "I hope so. The doctor leaves on *Zion* tomorrow. He will help seasick passengers sailing here from Voree. I'll send the good church ladies to help you."

Mary insisted, "No. I want to nap, not have a bunch of

women fussing over me. They'd snoop about and click knitting needles in front of me all day. I had enough of that back in Voree."

He stood over her and looked deeply into her eyes. "I'll have the elders come and pray over your foot."

Mary said in a cool manner, "No thank you, James. As soon as the blister breaks, my foot will be better."

He turned, stopped at the doorway and said, "Don't say I didn't try to help you."

She didn't mind his surly attitude. It pleased Mary that the gap between them grew wider.

When her foot healed, the island solitude and its natural beauty helped to ease the pain in Mary's heart. She took the children on daily hikes. Keeping busy helped Mary forget the adultery episode aboard the ship. Strang didn't sleep with Mary. Every night he shut her bedroom door and slept on the couch. The children called down from their loft, "Good-night, mama. Good-night, papa." Hearing their voices caused tears to gush down Mary's cheeks before she went to sleep. They were her only treasure. They had to leave the island with her when the time came.

16

Two weeks after *Zion* landed at Beaver, Strang printed the first island newspaper, the *Northern Islander*. The press was installed in a two-story white frame house, located a short walk from the harbor on a corner near the stores. An old fisherman had lived there alone and died in the house. After his few belongings had been shipped East to a relative, the villagers never set foot inside.

Today, Strang stood on the front porch and heard *Zion* blast three long and two short whistles before sailing for the mainland.

Strang was about to tour the island, his daily custom, when Frank Bowers came to the front porch. The former actor asked, "How's Mrs. Strang's foot?"

Strang replied, "Blister popped. Almost healed. And your mother?"

Frank shook his head, "Melancholy and homesick." He

bent over and brushed dust from his black pants. When he straightened up he asked, "When's Charlie coming?"

Strang looked steadily at Frank with hazel eyes, "Soon."

Frank grinned and shook his head. Next he held both palms open in front as he exclaimed, "What a classic deception! How long before Sister Mary finds out?"

"When the Lord tells me the opportune moment," Strang replied and put on a black plug hat.

"This triangle's like a theatrical plot," Frank said with a slight grin. "You got a cabin for Elvira?"

Strang quickly admonished him, "Charlie. Not Elvira."

"Find her a place?"

"I'll tell you when the Lord instructs me."

Frank rubbed a hand over his pock-marked chin, lowered his voice and said, "Six months ago I asked Charlie to marry you."

Strang reached into a side pocket, pulled out a gold watch, unsnapped the cover and glanced at it. He said, "I will marry her soon."

"It's hard to understand. You with two wives."

"Nothing is impossible with the Lord. He instructed me on spiritual wifery in the most important of revelations."

"But you always preached against polygamy."

Strang rubbed a finger over his serpent ring, "My views are unchanged and unchangeable about polygamy. I am but an instrument of the Lord. I am not ready to talk about His revelation of multiple wives, until He commands the day and the hour. Only you know about my plans, because the Almighty said to me, 'Take heed of a friend.'"

Frank said, "We've been friends for years. I'll go to my grave with your secret about Charlie. I'll never forget that day I took her the marriage proposal. She just got back to her boarding house from teaching school. A clear day. She asked me to sit in the front parlor. When I popped the question, she could hardly believe you wanted to marry her."

Strang smiled, "I'm sure you acted the part most eloquently. No one is ready for my new revelation. Especially not my lawful wife, Mary."

Frank asked, "Where's the trunk? It better be locked. My mother likes to snoop."

Strang and Frank walked inside the print shop. Strang handed Frank a large set of keys. Frank took them, knelt down, and unlocked the trunk. After he opened the lid, he got up and stepped back. Strang bent over and took out a red velvet robe. He stood and pulled it over his black suit. The robe had three rows of glittering metallic braid down the front and around the ends of the wide sleeves. Strang reached into the trunk and unwrapped a crown from white paper. He asked, "How do you like this?"

Frank puckered his lips and whistled. He took the crown, held it up and exclaimed, "Magnificent. I never wore one this good on stage."

Strang smiled pleasantly at his remark. "Of course not. These are real jewels."

Frank held the crown closer for inspection, "It's heavy."

"When I preached in the East, the good ladies of the Church donated diamonds, gold and emeralds. That large ruby in the center came after my special healing. I cured a woman with erysipelas."

Strang grinned. "I had the crown designed in New York. The nosy jeweler wanted to know who it was for. I told him it was for a friend of mine. The jeweler had a bald head and a mustache like a pencil line. He twitched his little mustache as if he just sniffed snuff. His hands shook when I said it was for a king. He asked, 'What country?'"

Frank handed back the crown and asked, "What did you tell him?"

Strang set the crown level on his head, walked up to a wall

mirror, stared into it and said, "I told him the king was in exile."

Frank laughed, and studied Strang's face in the mirror. His henna beard jutted over the neckline of the crimson robe. The beard's split ends bristled in the sunlight as if on fire. A streak of blinding sunlight shot through the window and illuminated his hair and the crown.

Strang turned around and called out, "Look! An omen from the Lord! Heaven approves my kingly figure."

Frank bowed and clapped hands several times. He cried out, "Bravo, Your Highness. King Strang! King of Beaver Island!"

Strang turned back to the mirror, studied his hazel eyes and thought of Elvira. A slow grin settled on his lips as he thought, *Elvira has the same color eyes.* He wondered what she was doing on the mainland. *Elvira, sweet girl. Soon I will call you by your real name, instead of Charlie. Elvira is not like Mary.*

Mary reminded him of a beautiful chestnut filly he once owned. When the animal became a mare, it lost the luster of its hide, became listless and wouldn't respond to the whip or jog faster. Mary's body soon would grow heavy on the hips like other middle-aged women. Flesh would sag under her chin, dark circles would remain under her eyes. Even now he noticed how she walked slower. And lately she had acted sickly. All of her youthful vitality had disappeared. He grinned and reminded himself, *Why put up with an old mare, when I can have a pretty young filly like Elvira?*

Sunlight flooded the room and warmed his face. Strang's body tingled as he recalled how he held Elvira firmly against his broad chest and kissed her eyelids, cheeks and finally her mouth. "Elvira, my sweet," he told her, "I love you more than any woman in the world."

She responded, "I love you, but I'm afraid to be your second wife."

He reassured her. "You have nobody to fear. I will protect

you, always. All the brethren will honor you greatly as my celestial wife."

Elvira protested, "What if there's trouble with Mary? I can't live in a house with a woman who hates me."

"Mary is a very simple person. There's not a bit of mystery about her. Not like you, my love."

He tossled her short, boyish hair with his hand, and liked the feel of the silky strands. The two traveled on an Eastern speaking tour for the church. "Win Souls For Christ" had been the title and theme. But all that was forgotten when Elvira slept with him. She was spunky and laughed over the deception to be his "nephew Charlie."

Suddenly Strang laughed. Frank asked, "What's so funny?"

Strang replied, "Nothing." *Frank wouldn't understand. He's tied to his mother's apron strings. He can't get near a woman.* Strang removed the crown and handed it to Frank.

The actor wrapped it up. After he helped Strang out of his robe, he neatly folded it, placed it in the trunk and turned the key in the lock. He handed Strang the key and said, "Mother spoke proudly about you today."

Strang wished Frank had come alone to Beaver, but his mother always followed him. She had traveled with him to Europe with his Shakesperean troupe. His mother liked to repeat village gossip that happened years ago.

Frank said, "She reminded me how you burned the midnight oil studying law books."

"I like to be busy."

"I like your famous quotation."

Strang studied Frank's face covered with pit marks from smallpox. "Which one?"

Frank jingled coins in his pocket, "Irons in the fire."

Strang clasped his hands behind his back, rocked on his heels and recited slowly, "There is not a more abominable saying than, 'Not too many irons in the fire.' The more the

better, I say, provided they are not forgotten. While cooling
the first, hammer the second and heat the third. Regularity and
attention are necessary, then none will burn."

Frank listened intently and smiled. He said, "Ah, that's the
one. I like it. Why don't you print copies?"

"I will."

Frank walked to the door. "I've got to get home. Mother
worries about me." He stopped, turned around, and pointed to
the steamer trunk. "I'll protect your royal vestment and
crown."

They carried the trunk to Frank's horse and wagon. After
they boosted it inside Strang said, "Don't let your mother see
it."

"She won't. I'll keep it locked. When's mailcall?"

"Tomorrow."

"I'll go with you."

"No," Strang insisted in a forceful tone. "Too many
brethren bite the dust from renegades. Brother Ebenezer
warned me. I'm taking Mrs. Strang. They won't do anything
rowdy when there's a lady present."

After Frank climbed into his wagon, he picked up the reins
and the horse pulled him homeward. Strang returned to the
print shop and sat down in a cane chair on the front porch. He
watched Frank's wagon disappear down the roadway, and
thought about Frank's mother. He hoped she didn't snoop into
the trunk. His coronation had to be a surprise for the brethren.

Every time old lady Bowers talked about the past, she
reminded Strang of a black coach that tried to run over him.
He wanted to forget about his past and the family. Even the
fresh lake smell didn't purify his mind of all the miserable
years back in New York. His family was poor and Strang
worked all summer in the bean and potato fields to buy new
school clothes and books. But the family always demanded his
earnings.

In September he started school in a hand-me-down tweed suit, patched in the seat, knees and elbows. When he complained his mother chided, "You want to be a dandy like Uncle Pat." His Uncle Pat dressed in fine clothes and traveled about the country with a medicine show. Uncle Pat had been Strang's hero at an early age.

Strang's most depressing memory at school was the fourth grade when he suffered as "the new boy," the shortest fellow and the only one with red hair. He felt like a rabbit in the center of a pack of wolves. One pair of boy's eyes after another stared at him. He wished he was home or could escape through a crack in the floorboard. He recalled how the teacher's voice had droned with the lesson. When the instructor's chalk stabbed and squeaked as she wrote on the blackboard, he saw how the eyes signaled each other. Next, they made winks and hand motions that meant they planned to gang up on the "new boy" at recess. It had happened at the last school.

Strang's father had worked all his life as a hired hand and loved the open air. Instead of "moving on," the elder Strang took a new job at the sap works to please his wife who wanted to "get roots" in a New York town.

There were times when his father hiked the woods and taught his son to set traps and shoot deer. In winter they had walked over new fallen snow on snowshoes and rode sleds down the steepest hills. All that ended when his father took a new job. Long hours shut up inside the factory turned Strang's father into an alcoholic.

Strang heard someone pound a hammer in the Beaver village. It reminded him of heavy footsteps when his father staggered upstairs. As a child Strang laid in bed and shook with fear under the blankets knowing his father was drunk again. Strang's mother took in washing and ironing to keep food on the table as his father's health declined and he couldn't work. One of Strang's brothers worked in a sawmill in the next town, and his sister had married and moved away. When Strang was fourteen years old, his father died, but James Strang was still called, "son of the town drunk."

Strang wanted to be important and rich as a king. He daydreamed about showing up all his schoolmates who had called him "red" and "carrot top." Most of all, he'd like to forget all those cold winters.

It seemed like yesterday when at twilight he had looked over a snowy field at the trees, with bark the color of coal. He studied the contrast of black and white. The gnarled branches turned skyward as if pleading to the heavens for the return of their leaves for warmth. Strang had often wondered who was wrong? Mother, tired of moving about? Or the old man who couldn't tolerate being a factory worker?

Many times Strang had stared at miles of snow as darkness edged over a long line of trees and misery swept over him. He kept a vow, *I'll not be like my father and take to drink. I hate grog shops.* It disgusted him to walk past an establishment that sold liquor, hearing men's loud voices and coarse laughter.

Just last winter he had passed such a place where sawdust had been tracked outside, and mixed with the slushy snow like a path of tobacco juice. The odor of the beer had drifted outside too, and conjested Strang's nostrils. He grinned as he thought of all the groggeries where he had spat at their front doorways. He'd see to it that liquor barrels on Whiskey Point would be blown to pieces. He studied the peaceful harbor and remembered the drunk who had insulted him that first day. He thought, *I will rid Beaver Island of drunks and liquor. The quicker the better.*

17

$\mathcal{A}$t daybreak a westward wind swept over the island at fifty knots. The breeze blew fresh and cool, and formed high waves. Frosty breakers pounded the shoreline and rocked the fishing boats tied in the harbor.

Lead gray clouds hung low over the quay. About ten o'clock the sky changed to a charcoal ceiling pushed steadily by the wind.

The sky became darker when the cloud approached. Instead of rain, the air turned cold and a fine black mist descended. As it passed over the harbor, the water stilled. After the haze departed, a colony of seagulls stood motionless, as if adoring a sea-god who had just calmed the lake and smoothed their feathers.

Mary had washed clothes early in the morning. Strang insisted, "We're going to Whiskey Point to get the mail." She had studied the sky and paused to hang up the laundry until the strange dark mist moved towards the mainland. When the weather turned pleasant, she stood beneath the tall pines and hung up a litany of dresses and shirts, evidence that a couple and two small children lived here.

She faced the line. A sack of clothes pins hung over one shoulder. She tasted a bitter wood pin clenched between her teeth. Her jaws hurt from gripping it, until she pinned it on a towel. She didn't want to go with James.

The very thought of going to Whiskey Point, where all the renegades hung out, disgusted her. Ebenezer had warned Strang, "Roughnecks hang out there. Great sport to beat up Mormons."

Another time at the general store she heard a woman say, "Poor Lydia! Whiskey Point criminal kidnapped her. Rowed her to a fishing camp on Hog Island. Lucky our men folks saved her in time."

Mary didn't want to ride there. All the mail came from Strang's secretary. She dreaded Strang's "nephew's" arrival on Beaver. "He's a nervous fellow," Strang had explained. "I want to cure Charlie. Island air will do him good. Settle him down."

Mary gazed past the clump of lilac bushes on the right, then beyond low spreading junipers to the lake. She had to hurry. James had been eager to make the trip all morning, even though an elder had pleaded, "I beg you, Brother Strang. Please send someone else. They hit me. Shoved my face in the dirt. Don't go to Whiskey Point. They're a rotten bunch. Broke a man's crutches. Laughed when he crawled. Poor fellow laid on the main road over two hours for a wagon ride home."

Even Shanahan the storekeeper warned, "They're desperados. Escaped jail at Mackinac. Postman feeds them 'til they shove off."

"Get rid of the postman," Strang demanded.

"Can't. His brother is state representative."

Strang said, "They'll give me mail. That's U.S. government business. I'm a lawyer. I'm taking Mrs. Strang. We're going in fine style in my carriage. Class puts ruffians at a disadvantage. Mrs. Strang is my witness."

After she hung up the last towel on the washline, she carried the basket inside the cabin and heard James' stern voice, "Hurry up." He had just returned from taking Myraette and William to stay with a neighbor woman.

She walked to the front room where he faced the oval wall mirror, a tall man in a black Sabbath suit and well polished boots. She smelled the clover pomade as he brushed his red hair back from his broad forehead. When he stepped aside, his eyes ignored her. Now she faced the mirror and tied a sunbonnet over her dark brown hair, braided and pinned into two side loops.

He stood at the doorway and asked impatiently, "Ready?"

"Yes," she said and followed him outside. He pulled the door shut and walked briskly to the opposite side of the carriage. She struggled to climb up to the buggy seat. After he sat down next to Mary, he picked up the straps and hit the reins against the horse's hide until the animal trotted.

Carriage wheels crunching into the gravel reminded Mary of another ride on the mainland. Back then they had traveled over corkscrew roads that curved uphill to a village. At the top they marveled at the spectacular view of corn and wheat planted in squares like a patchwork quilt. Cows grazed like toy figures penned in by tiny wood fences, and windmills built on farms rotated at a fast pace on breezy summer days.

She had not thought of that village for a long time, how the road descended and curved as houses multiplied on either side shaded by elm and maple. The main street, midway on the large hill, had bustled with people on foot and in buggies. Wagons spilled corn kernels until the roadways seemed to be paved with gold. There had been a millhouse, a butcher, two dry goods, an apothecary, and a general store. The homes spread out from the town in all directions with the school house just three blocks from the courthouse, where Strang had studied law and joined a debate club.

That particular crossroad for travelers had changed their lives. European immigrants stopped for supplies and water before moving west. They talked about a new religion, Mormonism. Strang became a convert and an elder within six months.

As the horse trotted steadily on the forest-framed road, they passed the wind blown dunes and several inland lakes where white birch grew next to the water. Mormons waved at them from cabins. She waved back. Strang did not slow down. There was an urgency in the way he gripped the reins, and the horse seemed to sense his master's determination for haste.

At the village, Strang slowed the horse, and he studied a Chicago lake steamer tied at the wide dock. Large ice blocks dragged from the island ice house were stacked on the wide dock to be lugged aboard. As the sun's rays reflected on the ice, they shone like diamonds, and the glare hurt Mary's eyes. They traveled past the harbor until they reached a sandy road where a roughly printed sign with a black arrow pointed the way to the post office. Strang did not talk. Silence set in, hard and cold as the ice blocks.

After several rods the dirt became deeper and the horse slowed down, straining to pull the carriage. Finally the carriage reached hard soil for another half mile, until they came to small shacks, blackened from winter storms. Here the road dead ended at Whiskey Point.

No trees. No flowers. Wind blown sand drifted about and choked the stunted snake grass. Scraps of filthy cloth, once curtains, fluttered at broken windows. The largest building was an old rooming house with rocking chairs on a sand tracked veranda. Above the long front steps hung a sign of faded black letters on a knotty pine board, U.S. POST OFFICE.

Strang helped Mary down from the carriage. She felt watched as she stood and waited for him to tie the horse to the porch railing. They climbed up the stairs, and the old boards creaked. Strang pushed open the door, and a small bell tinkled overhead. It was dim inside until Mary's eyes adjusted and she saw shelves lined with Indian baskets, a few rolled up blankets, and lanterns. An assortment of tobacco pouches and round tins of snuff were locked inside a greasy glass counter. Towards the rear of the store a semi-circle of surly faced renegades propped muddy boots on the fender of an unlit potbelly stove. The six bearded men wore mud crusted pants and stained leather vests over dark shirts.

Mary felt ashamed to be inside this groggery where a strong odor of whiskey permeated the room. She detected straight back chairs against a wall where more men sat. There wasn't a sound after the bell until one man cleared his throat with a loud disgusting hack. The others turned their heads to lean over and watch the fellow spit. The moment his saliva hit the center of an old spitoon, a lusty voice shouted, "Bulls-eye!"

The men laughed. When they stopped, Strang called out, "I'm James Strang. I want my mail."

Mary saw how the men gawked at her. She hated that. To ignore them she studied a wasp building a nest on a wall. After Strang spoke, there was quiet. She prayed. *Please Lord, don't let anything bad happen. Please protect us.*

A short man, cleaner than the others, stepped forward. He looked directly at Strang and said in a good natured tone, "Howdy. Ed Smith. U.S. Postmaster. Step over to my office. You too, little lady." He bowed low at the waist and smiled slyly at Mary. He winked. All the men laughed.

The postman's familiarity annoyed Mary. The titters and low murmurings made her uneasy. The mailman limped across the room. Strang grabbed her suddenly by the elbow and they followed the man to a sign, POST OFFICE, printed unevenly in white paint overhead. After he walked behind the counter, the man bent over and picked up a grimy canvas bag from the floor. He raised it high and dumped letters on the dusty counter top. As the papers fell out, several long legged spiders tumbled over the mail and scooted away. The man pushed the letters about with his hand. "Let's see," the postman said. "Got a Donovan, Gallagher, O'Malley. What's your name, pal?"

In an annoyed voice Strang replied, "Strang. Prophet James Strang."

The man said, "Prophet, eh? Never met one of them." The renegades laughed. The postman pushed the envelopes around. At last he said, "Here ya are. Four letters."

Strang reached, but the postman jerked them back and demanded, "Not so fast pal. Pay postage."

"I will not! They're stamped."

The chorus snickered. Mary turned her head so that her sunbonnet brim obliterated the leer of a man who had slowly shuffled and edged his way close to her. He was short and stared at her with bleary eyes. As he moved closer, a shaft of sunlight invaded the place and lit up the outlaw's hair, as red as Strang's. The man moved so close that Mary smelled his body stench and whiskey while his gaze penetrated her flesh and dug at her bones. He made her sick to her stomach.

"How much?" Strang asked.

"You're getting off easy, mister. Winter—it's more. Use dog team. Risk my life in storms for scraps of paper. This here's July. Hmm—." He rested his hand against bushy whiskers and looked up at the rafters.

The men laughed. One yelled, "Give the sucker a break, Ed. Done brung a cutie with him."

Mary bit her lip and her face burned with embarrassment.

Foot stomping and laughter erupted from the spectators. The postman looked at Strang and demanded in a harsh voice, "Five bucks."

Strang bellowed, "That's robbery! Stamps been used for three years. Law says I don't pay one cent for U.S. mail. The sender paid five cents for a Ben Franklin. Ten cents for a George Washington stamp." He turned to Mary, but she remained silent and lowered her head. She was mortified to be called "cutie." *Why didn't James speak up and defend my honor? Why do those letters mean more than me?*

"Take it or leave it," the man snarled, and with both hands shuffled the four letters like playing cards. Strang reached into his wallet and threw a bill on the counter, "Give me a receipt."

"Don't Ed. That bird's a lawyer. He'll sue you."

After the postman took the bill, he handed Strang the letters. Strang glanced at the letters with a grin of anticipation. Mary recognized Charlie's distinct verticle handwriting.

From the back of the room a man screamed in a falsetto, "He's a prophet! He can tell your future. Ain't that something? Knows where to catch fish." His taunts didn't annoy Strang. Not even when the crowd laughed uproariously.

Suddenly the smelly man next to Mary shouted as if she was deaf, "Hey girlee! Don't bring your old man next time!"

His loud voice infuriated her, as if this despicable old renegade controlled her mind, and those words continued ringing in her ears, "Hey girlee—hey girlee!"

"James, do something," she pleaded.

"Do what?"

"That man insulted me."

"Let's go."

She felt like vomiting as the outlaw leaned closer and breathed a strong whiskey breath into her face when he said intimately, "I'll wait for you, honey."

Angry at this additional insult and because Strang refused to defend her, Mary turned and faced the redhead. She pulled back her right hand and slapped the man hard on his leather-like cheek above his scarlet beard. The slap echoed like the sharp crack of a buggy whip. The moment her palm smarted against his face, she watched the outlaw's eyes squint. She screamed, "Don't call me girlee." Then she strained her throat and shouted, "Don't call me honey."

He stared surprised, then grinned with crooked horse corn teeth and yelled, "You're a high spirited gal." He puckered up fat, worm-like lips and pleaded, "Kiss me, honey."

All his renegade friends laughed. One raspy voice yelled, "You old bastard. Not just a kiss."

Mary's face turned hot. She wanted to run, but felt weak. Strang pulled her by the arm and they walked quickly out the front door, as the overhead bell jingled. She gasped, "You heard! Why, why didn't you do something?"

"Do what?" he asked and stared blankly at her. "Start a ruckus? Get beat up? My face rubbed in the dirt?"

She cried out, "Why didn't you defend my honor? You heard that filthy language."

"All your fault," he declared in a disgusted tone. "You lowered yourself."

"What? Lowered myself?"

He frowned, "A lady would ignore them."

"I'm always a lady. Why did you bring me to this horrible place? Look at this miserable village. I'm sure those rough-necks spilled blood right here where we're standing. Why did you degrade me by bringing me here? I've never been so humiliated in all my life."

Strang roughly grabbed and pulled her by the arm to the buggy. "We're getting out of here. It doesn't matter what happened back there. I got my mail. You won't come next time."

"Who will? Charlie?"

"None of your business."

"What you and Charlie do is my business."

He scowled and his mouth tightened in a thin line. She felt his strong hand on her cotton sleeve when he said, "Pull yourself together. Stop making a scene."

When he let go of her arm, she lowered her head and walked towards the buggy. As she climbed up into the seat, Strang untied the reins. After he swung up into the driver's side he cautioned, "Don't tell anyone I paid for mail."

As the horse trotted homeward, Strang remained silent. When they reached the village, the ship hauling ice had sailed away. She thought of that ice, buried in sawdust in the ship's hold, and her hands were clasped together just as cold. Before this trip she had anticipated forgiving Strang, but not now. Melancholy swept over Mary to recall Strang's face when he recognized Charlie's handwriting on the envelopes. To realize Strang loved another woman broke her heart more than the foul mouth, drunken renegade's shouts, "Hey girlee—kiss me honey."

Strang's actions on this trip certainly proved again he no longer loved her. Now she was more determined to leave him. The quicker the better. She had to reach the mainland before rough weather kept her a prisoner on this island all winter or forever.

18

$\mathcal{T}$wo days after Mary's trip to Whiskey Point, Virginia arrived by horse and wagon. After she stopped the horses under a shady maple, she tied them to the fence. She walked over to Mary, who stood outside the cabin, and said, "Strawberries are still ripe. Let's go pick."

"I'll go when the kids get back."

"Where are they?"

"Beach. Promised not to go in the water. I'll tan their hides if they do."

Virginia followed Mary inside the cabin and sat down on the couch. Mary poured her a glass of milk and said, "Just baked pound cake." She cut a golden slice, put it on a plate, and handed it to her friend.

Virginia said, "Thanks. Looks good. Every time I see you, it's like you're my child. All grown up into a pretty young lady. Not in that grave in the woods where the birds chirp and rabbits and squirrels play over the tombstone. You got the same dark hair, blue eyes and gentleness. I bet you'd never harm a living thing. The first time I saw you, it tore at my heart, as if the Almighty had played a trick on me and any second you'd drift away like a ghost."

While they ate, Mary said her husband didn't want Virginia to visit anymore. With great determination, Mary said, "He won't stop our friendship." Next, she told Virginia everything that took place at Whiskey Point.

Virginia asked, "Is your mind made up?"

Mary looked through the open doorway where the sun shined on tall weeds bent a velvety green by the wind. "Yes. It's hard to walk away from my marriage, but I must, to have a peaceful mind."

Virginia said, "If that was Bill he'd of cursed out those post office renegades. He's too old to fist fight, so he uses his mouth. I watched your face. Saw you cry. I'm talking to you like a mother. It's your marriage. Your decision. Your husband. Think it over good. Do what will make you happy. Only you can decide what's best for you and your children."

"I don't want to live in polygamy; I heard that a bishop in Nauvoo came and told a man he should marry again. The wife took her broom handle and beat the bishop on the head and shoulders. She chased him down the street, and screamed that he'd better not darken her door again."

Virginia said, "I heard the most scandalous things from Mormon women. They tell me because I never leave Beaver to spread the dirt. They said a man beat up on his first wife when he found her putting the young servant girl's clothes out of the house. The husband planned to marry the servant. After he gave the wife a black eye and terrible bruises on her body he said, 'I'm determined to live my religion if it kills me.'"

Mary said, "I'm sure they told you the truth. At campfire on our wagon trail, headed this way, I had to eat with the women. They were glad when I told them James promised no polygamy. Despite their common ways, I'm a woman and I sympathize with them. I heard about a very sick woman. When her daughter asked the father to come and visit the mother, the second wife said, 'She had her week with him. She should be satisfied.'

"When the daughter asked the father again, he said, 'I can't. I have to go to the ward-party tonight. If she's not better tomorrow, let me know. I'll have the Bishop lay hands on her.'"

Virginia said, "I heard the women explain about 'the week.' It's a downright shame it affects the children—the little ones know what's going on and say, 'Father's week at the other house.'"

"My children will never go through that disgrace," Mary insisted. "I would die before I'd live that sort of life. I'd kill myself first."

Virginia cried out, "Don't say that!"

"I'm sorry." Mary stood up, walked over, and once again put an arm around Virginia's shoulders. "I didn't mean it. The words just slipped out. I'd never do that. I love my children. Please don't cry."

Virginia took out a small white handkerchief and dabbed at her eyes. She said, "All this Mormon talk has upset me. It has always depressed me to know what Mormon women and their kids go through. They live a life of hell. Most won't admit it. I wish I was smart with a good education. I'd go to the Lansing legislature. I'd tell folks what's going on. It's a rotten shame Mormon women accept what their husbands say, that polygamy comes from God. They told me that Brigham Young said, 'If women would not submit to polygamy, they should be eternally dammed.' Isn't that awful? We are human beings. We have rights just like a man. One thing about my Bill, he has always treated me decently. I heard that Mormon apostles out West starved their wives and beat them. They step on their wives' hearts as if they walk on stones."

Mary agreed and explained the reason she didn't accuse her husband in public was that no one would believe her. They consider him a holy man. "I can't get nervous because of my baby. You are the first to know. I haven't told James."

"You with a baby? When?"

"Late January."

"You should tell him. What if he wants to sleep with you?" She blushed and added, "You know what I mean."

"He never comes near me. He has kept separate sleeping habits for some time." Without a trace of embarrassment, Mary looked directly at Virginia and said, "He sleeps with other women. I'm sure that naked hussy in the stateroom wasn't the first time. He's had an eye for pretty women ever since we were married. I'm more disgusted than jealous."

"Your baby doesn't show. How many months?"

"Two. I never get big. James wasn't home when I had morning sickness. I was fine on the wagon train, but it was rough. We cooked and ate over open campfires. All day I heard men snapping whips at the horses. Cows followed. Chickens were in crates. Kids crying. I told you James is a lawyer. Before the trip he kept busy closing land sales and telling folks what to bring here."

"How many Mormons coming?"

"Over two thousand. Back home folks worked all summer. Winters were always rough. James told us rabbit, wild turkey and pheasant are all over the island. Deer too."

"That's right. But tell me, why didn't you talk to him? He's a minister. Surely he'd listen to his wife's complaints."

"You don't know him like I do. He's different around me. Nothing will change. It will only get worse. Before we left Voree, I teased and tried to act like when we were newlyweds. I told him to have a good log cabin picked out, that I'm not a pioneer. At the time I was being extra nice, but it was no use. He's an over-sexed man. I don't interest him anymore. He says he needs many irons in the fire to be an editor of his newspaper, preacher, lawyer, and businessman. He's like that with women too. The more women, the better for him."

Mary's eyes glared angrily, her lips trembled, and she twisted her hands as she talked. "Back in Voree, someone tossed a note on my front porch. The words were printed so I'd never know who wrote it. I'll never forget those words. I'd give anything to forget them."

"What did the note say?" Virginia asked.

Mary slowly recited, "Mr. Strang's secretary ain't his nephew. Charlie is a girl."

"Do you know who wrote it?"

"No. I burned the note. Never told James. Look how red and rough my hands are." She showed Virginia the palms of her hands. "I do all my washing. There isn't a Mormon woman I want to help me. They all know about Charlie. They're laughing and gossiping behind my back. The sooner I leave this place the better. Virginia, please help me to escape."

"If that's what you want, I'll help you. Bill and I can take you to meet the Indians. They're my friends. I'll ask them to take you to the mainland."

19

$\mathcal{T}$he plan to visit the Indians on Garden Island came sooner than Mary expected. First, Virginia convinced Bill to be hospitable to Mary by promising, "She'll let me know every move Strang makes." Then, she explained that Mary wanted to leave Beaver, and only the Indians could transport her back to the mainland. Bill agreed to help.

The day of the trip to Garden took place when Strang told Mary he'd take the children with him all day at the village. No explanation. But Mary knew he wanted them to get better acquainted with Charlie without Mary along.

The next morning after Strang and the children left, the Ryans arrived in their wagon pulled by two chestnut horses. Upon seeing them, Mary closed the heavy cabin door and walked over a path of weeds now flattened by footsteps. As she neared the road she called out, "Shall I bring a lunch?"

"No," Virginia said. She wore a dark blue dress and

matching sunbonnet. "We'll be back before noon."

When she came close to the wagon, Mary said, "Good morning, Captain Ryan."

Bill tipped his naval cap and replied, "Howdy." Mary could tell his tone wasn't too friendly. She recalled how Virginia had told her, "Bill is slow to warm up to newcomers."

Mary struggled to climb inside. Virginia said, "Let me help." She bent over and took Mary strongly by the arm to steady her up into the front seat. After Mary sat down, Bill shook the whip and the horses moved. The wagon rolled forward over a dry, rutted path that separated miles of pasture, until they entered a dense forest followed by hills and valleys. When the cobbled road stretched down one long ravine, pebbles hit underneath like hail on a tin roof.

In places where the trees thinned out, Mary saw the sparkling blue of Lake Michigan. Patches of sunlight fell across the trail and streaked into the forest to reflect on the grey bark of maple like silver poles. Finally, they traveled next to the lake where the wagon wheels moved more quietly on the sandy road. Mary asked, "How far to your boat?"

"Just a little farther, but we need to make a quick stop on the way," Virginia said.

After they passed a row of sand dunes near the lake, they reached a fork in the road where Bill guided the horses to the right, over a path of high weeds. Virginia pointed to the path and said, "Cemetery Lane. No one uses this trail."

Ahead in another forest of shady maple, Mary saw the large angel statue. Bill slowed the horses and they stopped in front of a picket fence around Leonora Ryan's grave. Mary saw how the emerald forest washed over the whole area. No birds chirped or wild flowers bloomed. The cool forest air rushed at her. Dankness permeated the place. After Mary climbed out of the wagon, she heard dry leaves crunch underfoot.

Virginia asked, "Isn't the angel pretty?"

"Yes," Mary replied, still awestruck. The angel was carved out of white stone and had blank eyes, a cap of shoulder length curls and wide wings. The hands pressed together had tapering fingers pointed skyward in prayer while the wings were extended from the long chisled robe with wide sleeves and a scoop neckline. There was a tombstone below the angel with the inscription: LEONORA MARY RYAN 1813-1829.

"Why, my goodness. She died at sixteen. Her middle name is the same as mine."

Virginia explained, "Leonora went ice skating at Font Lake. Fell through thin ice. Spring time and ice started to melt. We warned her. She promised to be careful. She wanted to skate one more time. Almost froze to death. We did everything. Couldn't save her."

"What a shame. So young. I'm so sorry," Mary said compassionately.

"God's will," Virginia sighed. "I'll get the flowers from the wagon." She wiped her damp eyes with the back of her hand and walked to the wagon.

Bill said, "Only child we had. I guess every woman craves a daughter." He reached inside his pants pocket, took out a cloth, and blew his nose. "Took three years saving fishing money to buy her angel. Ship hauled it from Chicago. Not a scratch on it. Indians as far as the Manitous paddled birch canoes and followed. Got the statue three years after my little girl died. We was all broke up. So many folks and Indians came to see the angel, it made me feel better. Just to see that angel riding into Paradise Bay, high in the stern with bright sunshine on it made me feel that Leonora came back. Every time I think of her dead, my insides burn raw. We know she's an angel in heaven." He shook his head, "I can still see the Ottawas, big gang of them paddling canoes like crazy behind the ship right into Beaver. No one ever seen such a grand statue. They forget now. Only Ginny and I visit Leonora's grave."

Virginia returned with a bouquet of red roses. She walked up to the grave and set the flowers on the granite marker. Bill ambled over and they stood in silence. Mary walked back to the wagon. Shortly afterwards they joined her, then they all climbed in the wagon and the wheels rolled away from the grave. Mary turned and looked back. She watched as the angel became smaller. Finally, only the tip of one wing glowed white between the trees like a distant whitecap on Lake Michigan.

They were gone an hour, but already it seemed like a full day. The bouncing wagon tired Mary when the ruts in the road became deeper. With every jolt she thought the rough ride might hurt the baby in her womb. She held her arms across her stomach. Virginia asked, "You all right?"

"I'm fine," Mary said confidently. "I just hope I don't get seasick in your boat."

"All in the mind," Bill cautioned. He looked straight ahead as he steered the team on the narrow path and tapped a finger on his forehead and repeated, "All in the mind. You won't get sick. Lake's calm. Besides," he added with a grin, "I'm the best sailor from Chicago to Mackinac." They rode in silence for a mile until Bill said, "Here we are."

The road dead ended at the lake. An overgrowth of sumac bushes and wild fern among the pine and birch grew on each side of the road. For a moment it reminded Mary of Whiskey Point where the vines grew thick. Here too, wild grape vines climbed up the sides of the trees and choked back patches of sunlight. The odor of wintergreen hung in the air.

Bill warned, "Stick to the trail. Poison ivy and sumac everywhere."

He tied up the horses while the women walked to the lake. Beyond the gravelly beach Mary saw large smooth limestone in the clear, shallow water. A rowboat was pulled up and

secured to a narrow birch that leaned over the water's edge.
Beyond the birchbark, a long line of cedar protruded over the
shoreline like flag poles dipped in salute. Virginia walked over
to the birch and tried to untie the thick rope, while Bill walked
the team to a shady area.

When he returned to the skiff he said, "I'll do it." He
worked ruddy fingers until he unraveled the knot, then held
onto the rope to keep the boat in the shallow water. "Get in.
I'll climb in after I shove off." He took off his boots and socks
and threw them in the bow. The women got in and sat down
next to each other on the wide stern seat. Bill rolled up his
pants to the knees and waded in the water, gingerly stepping
over the rocks, as if they were hot. Once the boat drifted into
deeper water, he threw one bare leg over the side and got
aboard. When he sat on the center seat, he picked up an oar
and dug it into the sand to push the craft away from shore.
Then he rowed toward Garden Island, with his back to their
destination. He'd stop and let the boat drift as he rested. Other
times, he glanced over his shoulder at the island, and kept
pulling on the oars.

When they reached Garden, Bill rowed to a narrow wood
dock. Mary thought the Indians lived in tents. Instead she saw
shanties and log cabins. Dogs ran about on wide, sandy streets,
and half-naked children, wet from swimming, ran with bright
blankets pulled over their dark skin. Mary saw all the children
had coal black hair. Some played on the beach and toddlers
thrashed naked in the shallow water like muskrats. A tall
Indian maiden yelled at the children. She had long black braids
that reached the waist of her buckskin dress. Upon hearing
her, the children ran out of the lake and scampered to the
village as the sun glistened on their naked buttocks.

Mary and Virginia waited for Bill to tie the boat to the
dock. After he finished, the three walked to the Indian village.
Mary felt a pang of guilt. She stopped and looked back at

Beaver and hoped the visit wouldn't take too long. She feared James might come home and find her gone. Then what would she tell him?

The trio entered the Indian village and walked next to a row of roughly built shacks, shaded by tall maples whose thick leaves hid the sun. They passed huts built of driftwood from wrecked ships, then reached the end of the dirt street where they stopped in front of a large log cabin.

Chief Sogimaw watched them approach. His face had been fleshy, but now the skin hung from the cheeks with deep vertical lines at either side of his thin lips. He wore buckskin decorated with bright beads on the front and the sleeves. As the three walked into the yard, he struggled to his feet by using a wood cane to support his thin body.

He was on his feet when Bill said, "Greetings, Chief Sogimaw." Bill motioned his hand towards Mary and said, "Mrs. Strang. New on Beaver."

The Chief bowed his white head slightly and his black eyes pierced Mary's. Sogimaw held out a trembling hand and grasped Bill's in a firm grip. He asked, "You fishing?"

After the Chief let go of Bill's hand Bill said, "Every day or I get cabin fever."

"I know," the Ottawa nodded solemnly.

"Where's Enewah?" Virginia asked.

"My woman pick dandelion and choke cherry. Dye baskets," the Chief explained. "Neoma here."

Mary stared at a tall post with all the bark removed. It had been painted a variety of colors and stood firmly in the ground in front of the Chief's cabin. He asked Mary, "Like it?"

"Yes. It's pretty. Why all the colors?"

Sogimaw replied, "My lake pole. Fifty-five souls saved. Red means Indian; white, white man; yellow, woman; green, papoose."

She asked, "What about people who drown?"

The Chief tapped his cane tip on the ground several times and said, "In lake. Washed on beach. We bury them."

Virginia looked about the deserted village and wondered if the braves had gone hunting or fishing. A group of squaws sat in the shade of a large tree, a few rods from the Chief's cabin. One young maiden in sepia buckskin walked past. She carried her wash in a large woven hamper that she balanced on one hip and headed for a stream. On one side of the log cabin the Indians had stacked wooden buckets to collect maple syrup in the spring.

Last year Virginia saw buckets everywhere, hanging on small, wooden pegs driven deep into the sugar trees. When the squaws were late collecting the sap, it overflowed on the ground with a soft "drip-drip" on dry leaves to sound like a gentle rain.

Sogimaw turned his head just as his daughter, Neoma, walked up. The girl of medium frame appeared to be about eighteen years old and had smooth tanned skin. Her raven braids were neatly plaited down her back to a slim waist. She wore a pale buckskin dress with many beads in front.

Virginia said, "Neoma; my friend, Mary. I want to show her the island."

Neoma smiled at Mary and asked in a soft voice, "Idol?"

"Yes," Virginia said. She turned to Bill and asked, "You coming?"

"Hell, no. I seen that gul-durn thing a dozen times. I'll set a spell and chew the fat with the Chief. Find out when his braves are going to the mainland."

The women followed Neoma past a group of elderly squaws weaving baskets. As Neoma walked near, she held up a hand to greet them, but the squaws kept working and didn't say a word. As they walked past the weavers, Mary smelled the sweet grass, dyed for the baskets and hung to dry. When the roadway narrowed down to a path in the woods, the three walked single file.

Being here again brought back old memories for Virginia. It seemed like only yesterday that she had spent a month on Garden as a young girl. Her oldest sister had married and left Beaver. Her father was related to some Ottawas, and wanted Virginia to experience her Indian heritage. She had lived with an Indian family in one of these shacks. All were dead now, buried not far from Leonora's grave.

Virginia had been fourteen then, and had dressed in buckskin like all the Indian maidens. They taught her how to identify weeds for cures and how to weave baskets. She showed them how to knit. There had been more Ottawa living on Garden back then. Gradually many moved to the mainland. The old ones traveled from Garden to Pine River once a year for the government's Treaty Payment.

Virginia recalled cleaning fish on the beach; how the scales flew in the air and formed a crust on her hands and arms. Memories flashed to mind like when the long line of braves returned from fishing. They marched single file back to the village and carried canoes over their heads. Seagulls fought over fish scraps at the beach, and every sunset, a beautiful sight.

Neoma led the way. When she stopped, Mary called out, "How far to the idol?"

Virginia said, "A few more rods."

"My feet hurt," Mary said. Several times she had stopped, then walked faster to catch up to the other two.

Bushes and tree limbs stretched over the path. Virginia and Neoma held branches so that Mary would not be hit in the face after they passed through. Virginia could see the bright colors of the Indian idol between the sugar trees. As she held aside a large willow branch for Mary, she looked at the clearing. The tall idol had been carved like a totem pole. It towered fifteen feet high and had a fierce animal face at the top. The rest of the pole had part animal and bird figures with wing spreads of three feet attached to each side. It was painted with more colors than the lake pole in the village. The idol had been decorated with beads and dyed seagull feathers.

Mary said, "It's pretty. What's it for?"

Virginia pointed at a face with a hawk-like beak and said, "Some Indians worship it. See the beads? They throw them up to the idol. Look here at the worn path. They dance a million war dances around this idol."

Mary asked Neoma, "Do you worship it?"

Neoma shook her black hair and said emphatically, "No. Devil worship. Not me. Not my father."

Mary walked towards a large stone slab nearby covered with bloodstains. She asked, "What's this?"

Neoma said, "Sacrifices."

"By whom?" Mary asked.

"Pagan Indians," Virginia said quickly. "Not these Ottawas. Chief's tribe are Christian."

Mary looked at Virginia and said, "I don't understand. What do they sacrifice?"

Neoma said, "Little animals. Rabbits and dogs. Good Indians. Don't hurt a soul."

Mary looked up at the fading sun, "I got to get home. My husband might come home early."

Virginia shrugged a shoulder and said, "We just got here. I got to get my sugar." She turned to Neoma and said, "I'll never forget years ago. I'd sit on the beach and look at the moonlight from Garden to L'Arbre Croche. I'd hear the call of the whippoorwill. The Ottawas told me stories like: 'Why the Pine Tree Weeps,' 'The Joke of the Choke Cherries,' and all about 'Na-na-bo-jo, the Ottawa Wonder-Worker.'"

Virginia continued to talk about the past as the three returned through the woods to the village where Chief Sogi-maw and Bill sat on the fur rug, just as the women had left them. Virginia looked around and then asked the Chief, "Where's your braves?"

Bill took his pipe from his mouth and said, "Chief Sogimaw says they're hunting Waugoosh."

"Who?" Virginia asked.

"Waugoosh, The Fox," Bill said.

Chief Sogimaw shook his head with disgust and said, "Bad Indian. Kill white man."

"Where is he?" Mary asked.

Bill exhaled a puff of pipe smoke, "Don't know. They'll find him. Takes an Indian to catch an Indian, eh, Chief?" He nudged the Chief slightly in the ribs.

Chief Sogimaw nodded. A slight grin spread over his thin lips. He said, "Get him before full moon." His face turned sober and the skin quivered on his sunken cheeks. "Bad Indian. Drink firewater. Go crazy."

When they headed back to Beaver, two buckets of maple sugar were at Virginia's feet inside the boat. After a period of silence, they moved closer to Beaver and Mary asked, "Will that Indian come to Beaver?"

Virginia shook her head and said, "No. Not a bad Indian on Beaver in years. The Fox shot a white man at Mackinac. He'll head for Cross Village or Pine River."

"What about Whiskey Point?" Bill asked.

"Don't scare Mary. You set that bunch straight last year. Remember?"

"Yes. Some left. New rats ship in. You never know when a devil like Waugoosh will land. He'd live at Whiskey Point for a long time. Yes sir," he paused and added thoughtfully, "A long time."

Virginia turned to Mary. "Don't pay any mind to Bill. I'm not worried about The Fox."

Mary watched the oar tips dig into the calm lake. Her forehead felt warm, but she thought it was the afternoon sun.

Mary said, "I can't let the Indians take me to the mainland."
"Why not?" Virginia asked.
"I'm afraid to sail in their small boat. I know my kids
would get sick."
"What will you do?"
"I'll go back the way I came. On the Mormon ship."
"When?"
"I'll let you know my plans." Mary held a palm against her
cheek.
Virginia asked, "You all right?"
"It's nothing. Just the sun. I'll feel better when I get home
and rest."

20

*L*ater, when they left the rowboat and rode home in the wagon, the sun began to weaken and lower behind the forest. The warmth in Mary's body persisted and spread from her face down her arms. She knew she had a fever, but didn't tell Virginia. After the Ryans left her at home, Mary fired up the stove and put on a pot of potatoes. She laid down to rest, and woke up when she heard Myraette and William yelling, "Mommy! Mommy! Look what we got." They ran inside Mary's bedroom, each carrying a handful of licorice and peppermint sticks.

Mary got up when she heard Ezekiel whinny outside. Through the open doorway she saw James seated in the buggy headed back to the village. She asked, "Where's papa going?"

Myraette said, "I don't know."

Mary took the candy away from them and placed it on a high kitchen shelf. As she expected, the two weren't very hungry. *Too many sweets*, she thought. She warmed up a pot of leftover stew. At the table as the children nibbled on the stew Mary asked, "Did anyone act mean to your papa? Any trouble at the stores? Who'd he talk with?"

Myraette kept saying, "I don't know." Finally she said, "We saw Charlie. He's fun. We like him. He bought us candy."

"Did you kiss Charlie good-bye?" Mary asked.

"No momma. Charlie's at papa's print house."

Mary had dreaded the day when Charlie would arrive. *James didn't have the decency to come inside and tell me he'd miss dinner*, she thought. *He had to be with Charlie right now. He'll keep ignoring me as long as he has Charlie to run to.*

The fever became worse. She felt warmth at every blink of her eyes. She asked Myraette, "Where will Charlie eat?" She felt foolish asking Myraette that question, but she had to know. Myraette had been with them. She had heard what went on.

Myraette said, "Papa told Charlie to eat breakfast at the sawmill with him. Supper with Mrs. Smith."

Mary knew why James had taken the children today. He wanted Charlie to know them better. After she put the two to bed, she laid awake and tried to keep from crying, but the tears flowed. She stared for hours at the rough log ceiling lit by the bright moon. Outside, strange noises sounded in the field, and in the distant woods an owl hooted.

She couldn't sleep. The wind picked up and rustled the tall pine branches outside her window. She heard waves pounding the shoreline. At last the owl stopped, and she closed her eyes hoping to sleep. She dreamed of the angel statue at the foot of her bed. When she woke up, she felt the dream had been a terrible omen.

When Strang didn't return, she knew he slept with Charlie somewhere. The next morning the children didn't ask for papa. Mary thought, *Someday my dears, you will think back. I will not have to say one word. You will remember and judge how your father treated me.* After a breakfast of hot oatmeal, she let Myraette and William go to the beach. That's when Mary became very sick.

At first she felt a sudden elation. A strange giddiness joined the fever. She staggered weakly to a chair as blood trickled down her legs. Next, she cried to see the bloody mess that reminded her of a small animal run over by wagon wheels. With reverence she carried the warm, bloody discharge in a linen cloth to find a burial place. She craddled it in one arm next to her heart, and dragged a shovel to dig the grave. The fever burned hotter. Her legs trembled and at times she stopped because of stomach cramps. More blood trickled down her bare legs and into her slippers. She hated the sensation of walking in her own blood. It squished in her shoes, as she moved slowly over a thorny path to find a special burial place.

At last she stumbled towards a large weeping willow where the ground looked fairly soft. She laid the cloth on a nearby log and used all her failing strength to dig a hole for the little grave. Tears blurred the ground. At times she stopped digging. She was so weak. She tenderly placed the cloth package in the hole, but before she covered it with dirt, she prayed for the little soul. She found a limestone and dragged it over to mark the grave. Just to inch the rock a little at a time made her faint. When finished, Mary knelt and prayed again for the child she'd never know.

She was glad her husband stayed away. The next day she still remained weak with more stomach cramps, and used a clean cloth to soak up the bleeding between her legs. When she faced the stove, it was a tremendous challenge. Her legs were shaky and her hands hardly had strength to lift a small skillet. Several times a day, she looked into the mirror and pinched her cheeks for color.

Three days passed slowly while she recuperated, resting all

day in bed while Myraette and William played outside. When Strang returned, he never looked closely at Mary, but busied himself with paperwork at the table. Mary vowed not to tell him about the miscarriage.

Alone at twilight Mary felt a certain presence, just like when she dreamed of the angel statue. It was as if the dead child hovered nearby, engulfing Mary with a pleasant but vacant feeling. Mary didn't know if she lost a boy or a girl. Not knowing added to the emptiness, as if a part of her had drifted away in Lake Michigan.

When stronger, she walked in the woods and thought the faceless child, like a ghost, stalked her from tree to tree like an elusive spirit. When no one was around, she picked wild flowers and placed them on the limestone, longing to write something on the smooth rock to commemorate her baby's gravesite. Everytime she visited the grave she left a bouquet of wild buttercups, tiger lilies and bluebells. She felt a part of her had died with that miscarriage. It brought her more misery than Strang's unfaithfulness.

The realization came swiftly one day as she placed another bouquet on the grave. *It's a sign. My marriage is dead, too.*

21

The sun had not set. It hung low, a soft tangerine over the lake as dampness from the woods filtered into the village. Zenas Caldwell walked quickly along the village path toward Strang's print shop. He had been summoned there by a messenger. Zenas felt a certain excitement like aboard ship when Strang had cured his wife, Hortense. After landing at Beaver, Strang busied himself about the island, and the two never met. Zenas had vowed to help Strang, "day or night," but so far Strang had not contacted him.

When Zenas climbed up the steps to the print shop, he saw a single lamp glowing inside. Before he had a chance to knock, the door opened, and he faced a group of rough looking men. Zenas asked, "Where's Brother Strang? Said he'd meet me."

No one answered. Two men grabbed Zenas, tore off his shirt and pushed him out the door. When he protested, they

accused him of talking too much at the general store to a
Gentile. They said Zenas told the man all the Mormon plans
to get wealthy cutting timber. Zenas said he'd help Strang steal
boats and nets from Beaver fishermen. "We heard you, big
mouth. You get forty stripes, save one."

They dragged Zenas down the steps and fifty feet away
behind the building, where they tied him to a thick pine post.
Using a rawhide horsewhip four men took turns flogging him
thirty-nine times with beech switches toughened by heating and
twisting.

When they finished whipping Zenas, they cut the ropes
from his hands and legs. Zenas fell to the ground. One burly
fellow straddled his legs over him and snarled, "Ought to cut
out your tongue. You talk too much."

They finished flogging Zenas shortly after sunset. When Dr.
McCulloch arrived in his wagon, he saw a group of men in
front of the print shop. The men moved away from a buckboard when the doctor drove up.

McCulloch climbed down from his wagon. He walked over
to the buckboard and saw a man laying face down. The man
was bare to the waist with welts on his back. The marks, the
shade of ripe watermelon, were raised, like a stick that had
been dragged across damp sand. The cuts bled and the swelling
marked his skin as if the blows were inflicted to deliberately
create a criss-cross design.

"My God!" McCulloch exclaimed. He looked at the nearest
man and demanded, "Get my bag." The fellow stared and
didn't move. "Go! Hurry up!" McCulloch shouted.

The man ran to the doctor's wagon. The victim turned his
head and moaned. "Zenas!" The doctor said in a compas-
sionate tone.

Zenas stared up at the doctor with feverish, swollen eyes,
the whites bloody and the skin on his cheeks scratched and
embedded with dirt. He mumbled incoherently.

The doctor asked, "Who did it?"

"Gang. Tied me to post. Back in woods." His words were almost indistinguishable as he lay with face turned. He took a deep breath, turned his head and clenched his teeth in agony. "Put something on me, Doc. Burns like hell. Can't tolerate no more. No more."

McCulloch turned from Zenas and faced the group of curious onlookers. "Get me a cup of water," he demanded. An old man hurried to an outdoor pump where a tin cup always hung. The doctor opened his black case, and took out a bottle of white pills. The man returned and handed the doctor the tin cup of water. The doctor said, "Sit up. Swallow this before I dress your wounds." Zenas managed to push himself up and swallowed the water and pill. Then he eased himself down in the buckboard.

Dr. McCulloch opened a jar of ointment and set to work to dress the lacerations. Zenas said, "They told me I had the honor to be the first. First almost killed at Strang's new whipping post. Ain't that something?"

The doctor stopped spreading the ointment, raised his head and asked the crowd, "Who saw the flogging?"

No one would admit they saw what took place. They all had excuses for being elsewhere at the time.

Zenas' skin remained hot to the doctor's touch. McCulloch spread the salve gently and felt the flesh quiver like a dozen small nerves set in motion. Next he took out a wide bandage and asked Zenas, "Can you sit up?"

Zenas said in a drowsy voice, "I dunno."

"Try."

Zenas slowly pushed up with the palms of his hands. The doctor helped him into a sitting position. Then, McCulloch wrapped the gauze around his wounds. After that he helped Zenas slowly inch his body towards the tailgate where he draped his legs over the edge. "Step down," McCulloch said, supporting Zenas as he walked on wobbly legs. The doctor took him to his wagon. "Somebody double up a blanket in my wagon," the doctor called out.

A Mormon shouted, "Don't do it. Shun him."

"I'll shun every bastard in this crowd when you're sick," McCulloch yelled in a loud voice. A short man rushed to the doctor's wagon, spread the blanket, then helped the doctor lift the injured Zenas. They carried him to the doctor's wagon where they gently placed him on his stomach for the ride home.

Zenas Caldwell, drugged from the pill, lay in the wagon behind the doctor. When McCulloch came near the grocery, he saw Strang's black horse tied to the store's front post. The doctor stopped the wagon, tied up the horse and walked to the building.

Strang stood in the doorway and watched the doctor approach. McCulloch demanded, "I got Zenas in my wagon. Why was he whipped?"

"I did not whip him. I only dictated what punishment was to be given. It was to be over with quickly."

"Why? You cured his wife on the ship."

"That's got nothing to do with it. He talks too much. No one slanders James Strang. The whole island, Mormon and Gentile alike, will know about the whipping post. There is a vigilante group to enforce law and order. I have men I trust."

McCulloch said, "I believe in your prophetic calling and your faith healing, but how can you order this man or any human being to be whipped?"

"My book, *The Law Of The Lord*, orders chastisement."

"Why a whipping?"

"For serious offenses. My people must be obedient."

The doctor said, "I won't live here and treat men whipped for no good reason. I'll leave."

Strang pointed towards the lake and asked, "How, doctor?

Not on my ship. I'll not allow it. Your services are needed. You'll stay until I let you leave."

"I'll find a way to go."

Strang laughed, "It's a long haul rowing to the mainland. Haven't you noticed how rough the lake is getting lately?"

McCulloch turned and headed for his wagon. He knew he wouldn't be duped to stay here. He'd join forces with Zenas or anyone else who wanted to get away from Strang and his whipping post. Whatever the cost.

22

The men yelled, "Captain Ryan, town meeting!" Bill walked faster with a sailor gait, past the gathering of women and up the steps of Shanahan's General Store. It reminded him of the time they had all banded together against the rough gang at Whiskey Point.

He stood on Shanahan's porch and faced the crowd. A middle-age woman wearing a blue cotton dress with matching sunbonnet shook a finger at him and yelled, "I told you Captain Ryan. No. You didn't listen."

"About what?" he hollered back.

She screamed, "Mormons! I can't go nowhere. They're a bunch of crazy, shooting fools. Burn land. Their younguns stripped birchbark for miles."

"She's right," another woman agreed. "I can't pick strawberries. Scared I'll get shot. My kids found a dead fawn. Mormons shot it. Buzzards feasted on it."

The large crowd of settlers talked all at once until Bill raised his arms high in the air and cried out over the confusion, "Folks, listen to me."

A lean trapper in a grey shirt and pants pushed through the crowd until he was up front. He yelled, "I eat what I shoot. Those Mormons shoot what moves. Worst one that Zenas Caldwell." He turned around and warned the crowd, "He might kill you."

Another man yelled at Bill, "Why aren't they coming from Gull, Seuil Choix and The Cross? You said they would."

Bill said, "I sent word. Mackinac came."

"Hah!" the man scoffed. "They ran scared. Thought we'd have a little fight and a big celebration. Took one look at Mormons and shipped out."

Bill said, "Folks, I don't know what to do. We never had this trouble before."

A young dark haired woman said, "Empty cabin is next to me. Got back from the picnic. Mormons moved in. My kids played in that cabin on rainy days. Ever since old lady Reilly died. It's mine. Ain't it?"

Another woman said, "She's right. I live near it too. Keep my winter stuff inside. Mormons threw everything out. Dumped it on the road."

"Did you tell them not to?" Bill asked.

"No. They got a bad dog. I can't go near."

A twelve-year-old boy climbed up the stairs and tugged at Bill's sleeve. The boy said, "Me and Butch picked berries. Mormon kids came. I said, 'This here's ourn.' They grabbed our berries and yelled, 'Get outta here.'"

"Did you fight 'em?" Bill asked.

"Naw. We scrammed. Too many again' me and Butch."

An elderly woman cried out, "I washed yesterday morning. Back hurt from scrub-board. Hung up whites. Mormons whipped teams of horses dragging logs. All my wash was covered with dirt. They done it just to be mean. I yelled at them. They laughed. I know they done it on purpose. I'm packing. I'll leave this week."

A tanned elderly man with a frizzy white beard and bald head yelled, "Don't leave. We'll kick the damn Mormons out."

A woman next to him said, "The first bunch ain't so bad."

The man replied sarcastically, "Sure. Peaceful at first. Now they're same as them newcomers."

From the rear of the crowd a young mother cried out, "My kids can't swim at Font Lake. They keep baptizing."

A thin matron with a face wrinkled like a dried apple stood next to her and called out, "Been here all my life. Can't live nowhere else. I hate Mormons. With all my heart and soul I hate them." She buried her face in a handkerchief and sobbed. When she stopped she screeched, "I'll have to leave too."

Next to her an old trapper in grease stained buckskin shouted, "Sheriff won't help. Mormons got more guns and men. They'll blow us all to kingdom come with their cannon. I'm shipping out too."

"They swiped all my nets," a fisherman said. "Scuttled my boat. I'm not hanging around. We're out-numbered. I'm going, but I'll be back with plenty of men. We'll pay off those damned Mormons."

Turbulent shouts of agreement erupted among the crowd until they heard the sound of loud wagon wheels rolling into the village. Strang sat in the front seat of a buckboard driven by a young lad. Seated behind Strang on either side of the buckboard were the Mormon Church Elders dressed in heavy dark blue work clothes. They sported long dark beards and looked bad-tempered as if itching for a fight.

The people quieted down and moved closer to the store front. The wagon stopped a few yards from the crowd. Strang climbed down. He wore a light blue workshirt and a buckskin vest. Brown riding pants were neatly tucked into black leather boots. When he took off a wide brim black hat, the sun lit up his red hair. He stomped up the steps, wiped at his damp forehead with a white handkerchief and put the hat squarely on his head.

Bill said, "Mister, you're here in the nick of time. Let's talk."

Strang said, "Time's valuable. I can't waste it on you, old man." He opened the door and walked inside. The bell tinkled overhead.

"Captain Ryan, make him listen," a man yelled.

Bill opened the door and followed Strang inside while curious onlookers climbed up the steps. Inside, Strang glanced about and appraised the shelf goods. He asked the storekeeper, "How much is bean seed going for a pound, my man?"

Bill called over, "Hey, mister. I want to talk."

Strang turned and faced Bill. His hazel eyes glowed like a cornered bobcat. Strang said, "I haven't time to waste. What do you want?"

"You Mormons shoot guns too much."

"Stay away from gunshots."

Bill replied in a louder tone, "Mormons shoot at anything that moves. Awful dangerous. You will kill some poor soul."

"Who's killed?"

"Nobody. But—"

"Stop worrying."

A trapper who followed Bill inside yelled, "Quit clearing land. You're gonna burn down Beaver."

Strang faced the man and said, "The earth's the Lord's and the fullness thereof. Any land we claim is ours by right of conquest. What we take will be filed in the United States Claims Office."

A man shouted, "Ain't no such thing."

"You're ignorant about laws of land registration. It's on the

Lansing books."

The trapper declared confidently, "We own what we live on."

"Ha! That's what you think," Strang said.

"We settled here first," Bill declared.

Strang smirked, "Won't hold water in court."

The bell over the door sounded a series of light jingles as two Mormon Elders entered. They leaned against the front counter as Strang walked about and eyed the shelf merchandise. When he stopped, he asked the storekeeper again, "How much for bean seed?"

Shanahan sat on a high wood stool behind the counter and figured his credit books, unconcerned about the dispute. Bill demanded, "Shanahan, don't sell them nothing."

The storekeeper ignored Bill, looked over at Strang and said, "Nickle a pound."

Strang faced Bill and said, "Old man, I'm not looking for trouble. You are. Why don't you—" He jerked a thumb at the islanders. "And your fellow rascals get out. Leave me alone."

Years ago when Bill was young he had slugged it out with any guy who crossed him. Strang's attitude brought back that feeling. Bill's face flushed with anger, but he had to restrain himself. This fellow was bigger, younger, and a lawyer. Bill said, "I ain't done nothing. You folks started trouble. Moved in cabins, swiped strawberries, shot animals for sport, dragged logs smack on top a poor woman's wash. You got no right to do them things."

Strang grinned, "I'm a peaceful man."

A trapper yelled, "Quit shooting up the woods. You damn fools will kill somebody."

"Forests are for everyone."

"I got news for you mister," Bill warned. "Beaver ain't big enough for you and me. My battle lines are tight. Don't step on our land. We got guns too."

"Tell him, Bill," a man yelled back in the store.

Shanahan looked at Strang and repeated, "Beans is five cents."

The day before Shanahan had told Bill, "If I don't sell to Mormons, they'll aim their cannon at my store. I can't live scared. I'll sell the shelves bare. Then I'm getting the hell out of here."

Shanahan picked up a pencil and his hands trembled. He asked, "How many beans?"

Bill left the store. Outside he addressed the crowd, "Folks, they got no damn business taking fish and wood. Don't anybody leave Beaver. Things will get better. It's our island. We can get a court order. Let's all work together."

"How? With what?" a man asked. "Mormons dumped our gun powder in the lake. Bill, can you look your neighbors in the face? The folks Mormons beat up and shot? Don't forget those injuries. Rifle ball flattened a hip bone. Flesh wounds. Hole in a man's left arm. Those men all fought for their fishing grounds and nets. Strang won't let his doctor treat our people. Soon as I can, I'm leaving."

Others in the crowd agreed and cried out, "Me too. I'm shipping out. I'm going."

A trapper called over to Bill, "Are you leaving? Will you get on the first ship sailing to Pine River?"

Bill said, "Don't know. I'll talk with Virginia."

23

*B*ill didn't tell Virginia about the large group of settlers who planned to leave Beaver. He was determined to hold his ground and not abandon ship. It was mid-day on Sunday when Bill walked up to the cabin front door, past the hollyhocks. The plants had ceased blooming, and the tall stalks sagged limply against the log cabin. When he stepped through the open doorway, Virginia asked, "What's the matter? Why the long face?"

"Hear it?"

"What?"

"Dadburn Mormon fools yelling timber. Drives me nuts. All that noise. Chopping and sawing. Won't be a tree left."

"If you stay out of the woods, it won't bother you," Virginia advised.

"I got to know what they're doing. They're taking over Beaver day and night."

"Yes. Wagon wheels woke me up last night."

"I felt you tossing and turning. It ain't right making us lose sleep."

"Oh Bill! You got manure on your boots again. It stinks!"

He sheepishly lifted up his right boot and looked at the sole. "Nothing. It just smells. I'm leaving. Be back later. Want to come?"

"No. Supper's cooking."

After he left the cabin, Bill heard loud noises as he sat in the wagon and the horses trotted along an island trail. The road passed close to Mormon smoke houses built near fish shacks on the beach. They had stacked huge piles of corn cobs and pine bark to smoke trout and whitefish. Today, the Mormons used this fuel to cook the fish, laid over wire frames. The Mormons' boisterous laughter and shouts filled the air along with wafts of smoke. The smudge drifted towards the village. Bill knew the women would complain again about smoke in their cabins and clothes.

Further up the trail he saw husky Mormons chop down trees. Others yelled and whipped at teams of horses that dragged logs towards the sawmill. Bill thought, *Why can't they rest on the Lord's day?* When he passed the sawmill, he observed all their activity to make lumber. The woods became quieter after he passed the stream where logs floated to the sawmill. When he rode near Mormon cabins deep in the forest, he saw washlines filled with clothes, and women and children chopping at garden weeds.

He hit the horses with a long buggy whip to speed them away from the scene. It disgusted him that the Mormons didn't honor Sunday. He thought of how quiet it had been before Mormons came here. When he got up early, and walked to the harbor, he seldom met anyone. If he did, he recognized the person by a tune whistled at dawn. Now Mormon wagon wheels awoke him long before daybreak, and rumbled towards the pier making all the village dogs bark.

Today, he saw where giant maple, pine and birch had been chopped down. Only burning stumps were left after Mormons hauled the trees to a sawmill. He passed one smoldering area after another. Patches of dry weeds crackled flames that shot up in spurts and tried to spread. Bill determined the fire wasn't out of control because the Mormons had dug a deep ditch around the burning land.

Bill had seen how the Mormons cut trees with one pine thrashing against another until it fell and hit the ground with a final thud. Now as he rode in the woods he thought about Indians and pioneers who had seen these same trees and chopped sparingly for a cabin of pine logs, or used stumps from the beach coated with sticky pitch to make a hot fire, instead of chopping down virgin maple. When Bill needed firewood, he always picked a tree growing too close to another with branches entwined fighting for the sunlight, or uprooted and dead after storms. Instead, the Mormons looked for the largest trees to cut. The cry, "timber," sounded daily.

On Monday morning about eleven o'clock, after the fishermen had washed down their boats and iced their fish, they met at Bill's shanty. One man said, "Dammit to hell. All these years we took turns cutting wood for the lake steamers and shared profits. Now we can't sell cordwood."

Bill took out the pipe from his mouth and said, "So what if they built a dock? No ships landed there yet."

A burly fisherman said, "They will. They spot that big hunk of dock, they'll land. Buy cordwood cheaper from Mormons."

A short man said, "Bet you guys my next haul of trout, Mormons get ships lined up stem to stern buying wood. We'll be out of business. My old lady will raise hell. No more money for shopping trips."

Bill said, "The dock is for *Zion*. It don't tie up here. Ain't that a relief?"

"No," the big man replied. "When *Zion* dropped anchor, we counted Mormons. Now we can't set foot on their dock."

A tall man in dark work clothes and a moth-eaten wool cap said, "They ain't shooting in the woods so much."

Bill said, "Course not. Afraid to kill their own."

Suddenly, a young man ran from the village toward the group. He yelled, "I been robbed! My ice is gone!"

The heavy set fisherman laughed quickly, "Told you bury it deep in sawdust. Sun melts it."

"Sun, hell! Damn Mormon marauders stole it," the angry man replied. "They're selling fish. Need ice. They ain't got ice. Stole mine. What can I do?"

Bill said, "I'll get the sheriff at Mackinac."

"Dynamite their dock," the young man cried out. "Blow it to kingdom come."

Bill said, "No. They'd build again. Need the law. Beat them at their own game."

Later that week Bill heard about an Indian on Garden who planned to sail to Mackinac to visit a sick brother. Bill sent word with him for the sheriff to come to Beaver.

When the sheriff arrived several days later, his ship coasted into Paradise Bay and tied up at the Beaver dock. Sheriff O'Brien, a heavyset man, trudged down the gangplank. He wore a blue serge uniform, white shirt, black tie. The silver star on his chest shone in the sunlight. He shook hands with Bill and said, "Hello Captain Ryan."

Bill looked at a group of Indians who leaned over the ship's railing. They hardly blinked their steely eyes in the warm August sun. "Why all them redskins?" Bill asked.

"My posse," the sheriff answered proudly. "What you want with me?"

"Mormons are stealing our winter ice and government trees. Selling lumber. Sawmill runs day and night. Look at that new dock. See what I mean. Good maple planks all stacked and ready to sell. Cordwood too."

The sheriff said in a matter-of-fact tone, "No law against that. You been cutting trees for years."

"They ain't got a right. We lived here first. Won't be a tree left or fish in the lake. We want things to stay the same."

O'Brien said, "You got a thin case. If I arrest them, judge might not see things my way. False charges. I represent Mackinac. I'd look bad in Detroit. Mackinac's got good trade with Detroit. I can't get Mackinac in bad with Detroit over a few trees, fish and ice. I got nothing against free enterprise. Besides, you don't own this land."

Bill yelled, "What you talking about? My old man mapped out every foot of Beaver!"

"It's open for public sale," the sheriff said. "Times change." He glanced up at the pensive Ottawas aboard ship who waited for him and added, "My Indian posse will find that bad redskin."

"Damn it! Don't change the subject. I need help. Beaver needs law and order. Mormons got us outnumbered."

"Look Ryan, if you were me would you arrest a man for cutting trees and making a few dollars?"

"Yes," Bill said with conviction. "You don't live here. You don't know what's going on."

The sheriff shook his head, "Ryan, I'm heading for the Manitous."

"You don't want to listen. You think I'm wrong, eh?"

"No." The sheriff looked at Bill and said, "Your complaint is nothing compared to me finding a killer Indian."

Bill shook a finger at his face, "You mark my words. I'll give these Mormons less than a year. They'll put Mackinac out of business." He turned and walked a few paces from the sheriff, then whipped around. He faced him, pointed a finger and cried out, "You won't get re-elected."

The sheriff yelled back, "Hold on. Don't threaten me."

"I ain't. Facts is facts. What I gotta do? Hold a gun to your head. Then will you enforce the law on Beaver?"

The sheriff's face flushed. "No, Ryan. You don't have to hold a gun to my head. You ain't the only one who hates Mormons. If I was you, I'd find another place to live. Get off Beaver."

24

W hen Mary walked inside the general store, she saw Thomas Bedford talking to a Gentile. Upon seeing her, Bedford tipped his hat and said, "Good morning Mrs. Strang."

Mary nodded and walked about the store. It smelled just like her father's store in Voree; a combination of apples, pickles and freshly ground coffee. Mary saw dill pickles in a large wooden barrel with milky brine floating on top, boxes of apples, and sprouting potatoes. Bolts of yard goods were stacked behind the counter against a wall almost up to the ceiling. A glass showcase revealed rows of credit books arranged alphabetically.

Mary stopped in front of a coffee grinder with a sign in front. "Hero Coffee, 11½ cents per pound." Alongside it were two tall glass jars, one filled with red and white peppermint sticks and the other containing licorice. The main difference between her parents' store and this Beaver establishment was articles for survival on this remote island. Snowshoes hung from the rafters alongside metal animal traps and iron sugar kettles. On low shelves were stacked candles, Indian blankets and leather boots. Inside a glass case next to snuff and tobacco, all sizes of knives were displayed.

While she walked around the store, a blue velvet string purse dangled from one wrist. Mary heard two women talk to the storekeeper. They stopped and looked down at her black leather slippers, then at her blue linen dress with white lace trim. When she walked near the front counter a second time, the owner asked gruffly, "What you want, lady?"

Mary had the impression from his tone that he expected a quick answer, as if she should reply with a list of articles, like flour, molasses and sugar. Strang had brought all those supplies. She looked at Shanahan. He was freshly shaven with sleepy dark eyes. Again he asked, "What you want?"

Mary thought of Voree where they always let the customers browse around the merchandise. Now she had a strange feeling that he expected her to buy something.

She answered, "I'm just looking."

"You a Mormon?" he demanded sharply.

It wasn't the first time she had been asked. "Why?" she asked. Mary wondered if Brigham Young's polygamous exploits had reached this island.

"No reason," Shanahan said. "What you need?"

The women in the store looked hard at Mary when she said, "I just came to window shop."

As Mary walked to the front door she noticed Thomas Bedford still talking to the islander. After she opened the door and stepped outside a wave of depression swept over her. She didn't want to come here again. The store reminded her too much of her life in Voree. She couldn't allow sadness. If she weakened, she'd never have the courage to leave Beaver Island.

25

Strang wrote in the *Northern Islander*, "The First Church Conference at Font Lake is for the purpose of returning thanks to God for averting calamities on this island."

The morning of the conference Mary fired the stove early and cooked breakfast. Whenever her husband stayed home, Mary concealed her true feelings. By now her strength had returned after the miscarriage. After she told Virginia about it, her friend made another trip to Garden Island for some special Indian tonic. Mary kept it hidden, not wanting Strang to know. Not only did the tonic make her feel stronger, but she felt her spirits uplifted. She could concentrate on the day when opportunity would come her way and she'd be on the ship headed back home to her mother. She had to wait for *Zion* to leave next time for Racine. Then, she'd take the children aboard even if it was just with the clothes on their backs. She stood at the stove where bacon sizzled in an iron skillet and said to Strang, "Hot today. Lake Michigan's misty." Strang sat at the table with his head bent over paper and wrote with a pencil. Mary said, "I'm used to island weather. Ring around the moon. It will rain. Gulls flying inland means a bad storm coming."

Suddenly Strang threw down the pencil. It bounced off the table and rolled across the floor. He yelled, "Mary! Don't chatter. I'm writing my speech."

"I'm sorry," she said. She walked back to the stove and turned over the bacon slices. Then she sliced bread and meat for lunch at the conference.

By ten thirty they rode in the buggy with their children to a grassy area next to Font Lake. All the church members would attend. Mormon fishermen returned to shore early and spread nets to dry. The farmers dropped their plows. When a carpenter working on a house stopped using a plane, the small particles of wood no longer flew into the air. Children had finished their chores of hauling buckets of water and cordwood to the cabins. The shoemaker stopped hammering on soles and heels. Women, weeding gardens to the steady clink of hoes that hit pebbles mixed into the dirt, were glad to quit and head for the grove. Every Mormon brought a lunch, for the service started at eleven and continued far into the late afternoon. While they waited for Strang, women sat on blankets, knitting and crocheting. Children skipped stones at the lake, and men threw knives at a white bulls-eye painted on a wide oak trunk.

When Strang's buggy pulled up, many people rushed over to greet him. He wore a dark blue suit and vest, a white shirt and a black tie. Before he stepped down, Strang took out a gold pocket watch, glanced at it and put it back in his vest pocket. When he removed a tall silk hat, his bright red hair glowed in the early morning sunlight. After he climbed down he addressed the crowd, "Greetings, brethren. Peace be with you. Let us gather at the lake."

Strang walked over to where Mary sat and steadied her arm
as she stepped down from the buggy. Next, he lifted out
Myraette and William. The two scrambled away to join
playmates at the edge of the woods. A man unhitched Ezekiel
and led the horse to graze. As the crowd approached the lake,
the children stopped tossing rocks in the water and ran to join
other youngsters.

Strang called out, "Join me in singing *Arise O Glorious
Zion.*" When the song ended he shouted, "Let us pray."
Strang's voice reverberated over the evergreens that circled the
lake. Bearded men in dark work clothes and the women in
their best cotton dresses and sunbonnets bowed their heads.

Mary thought, *Just like him. Use a long prayer like you
would on the Sabbath. So strict when it's the least expected.
Like this morning, mad at me.* His attitude at breakfast had
spoiled her morning, but she set a pleasant look on her face.
Inside her heart sagged with despair. Every day she felt
trapped until she engaged in fantasies about sailing back home
with her children.

During the next half hour Strang's voice echoed through the
woodland. When the long sermon ended, a loud "Amen" came
from the congregation. Mary spread a blanket and rested her
back against a strong maple. Like Voree, first came the song,
then the opening prayer, and now the grievances against the
Gentiles.

A weather-beaten picnic table had been set in front of
Strang covered by a white cloth. He called out, "Let's
proceed. First report is from Brother Henry. Come up front
Brother Henry."

A tall, thin man, sixty years old and dressed in dark
coveralls walked slowly to the table and faced the people. He
said, "President Strang, if this was a meeting hall back home,
I'd be tongue-tied. Here in the open air with my brethren, it
ain't so hard. I brung my cow from Ohio to Wisconsin to

Beaver. You folks seen her. Only brown cow here. I grazed her. One evening I went to milk. No cow. I had staked her same way every day, with a deep post and a chain. I looked high and low and was ready to give up. Then I heard cow bells along the shore. I ran there fast and found my Jersey with a herd of cows."

Strang raised his right hand to quiet the group, then lowered it. He said, "Brother Henry, I'll question you like in court to understand both sides of the case. Is there another Jersey on Beaver like yours?"

He shook his head, "No sir. My brand is on my Jersey."

Strang said, "A Gentile claims it is his. Swears you branded his cow."

Brother Henry took a few steps forward and hit the table hard with his right fist and yelled, "He lies! It's my cow!" He turned to the Mormons, shook a fist angrily in the air and demanded, "You folks saw me lead that Jersey down the gangplank."

Strang said in a sympathetic tone, "Don't get excited, brother. We believe you. We saw the Jersey. Not your brand."

"Do I gotta show proof?" Cried Brother Henry. "I'm married, but I don't show my marriage license."

The women tittered and Henry's wife, a fat woman with an expressionless, pale face like a cabbage, lowered her sunbonnet.

"I'm just telling you what they'll say," Strang said. "We can march to that Gentile's cabin and take your Jersey by force. Instead of bloodshed, I'd rather fight Gentiles with the law."

A man stood up and yelled, "Law's no good at Voree. Houses burned. My brother tarred and feathered. It will happen here."

Strang replied in a loud voice, "If we are marked for destruction, we will not huddle up like frightened sheep and turn our backs to be destroyed by a chance blow. Brother Edgar, we cannot live in the past. There aren't many Gentiles left on Beaver. We outnumber them."

"Do we turn the other cheek?" the man asked.

Strang held his right hand up in the air and thundered, "No. Keep away from them. Two flints will not make a fire if they are not struck together."

Strang stood up, reached over the table and placed a hand on Henry's shoulder. He said in a solicitous tone, "I know you miss milk from that Jersey."

Henry pouted, "Miss all that good cream too."

Strang said, "I realize it's a great loss for you and your family. I'll see that you receive a goodly supply of cream and milk from our brethren until I win the case. You must admit your family eats well since homesteading on Beaver."

Henry replied, "President Strang, we never ate such good food. If I had that cow, I'd be a happy man."

"Be patient," Strang advised. "I predict you will have your cow back before next weekend. Trust in the Lord as I do and He will help. He is on the side of the righteous."

Mary noticed at the start of the meeting that Charlie sat next to her husband and wrote notes. Mary avoided Charlie today just like she did in the village yesterday when Charlie walked towards the print shop dressed in the same gentleman's black suit.

Mary now studied the secretary's face, more emaciated with dark circles under the eyes. She watched the secretary's right hand dip the pen often into the ink pot to copy Strang's words during the conference. Charlie's silk hat had been placed at the end of the table next to Strang's. Each brim was weighted down by a lake stone because of the breeze.

Mary listened carefully to the controversy about the cow. *I hate to sit with my back against this rough tree bark*, she thought. *My legs are almost asleep, and my stomach is growling with hunger. I envy Charlie sitting near James at the table.*

An arm covered by a black sleeve with white lace at the wrist waved in the air. A slight groan of disapproval erupted from some men in the crowd. Strang asked, "What is it, Mother Bowers?"

Sarah Bowers called out, "How often will we meet like this?"

"As often as I think it necessary," Strang replied.

"When will the newspaper be printed?"

"The *Northern Islander* will be published weekly to keep our brethren informed. Boys will deliver it. Won't matter if you live at the south tip or near the sawmill. Everybody gets a copy."

"What about the tabernacle?" Sarah asked.

Strang said, "I will discuss that in my next talk. If you don't mind, Mother Bowers, I want to continue with our current business. Brother Ebenezer is next."

Ebenezer Wright approached the table. His black hair shined with goose grease. His teeth gleamed brightly and his small eyes scanned the crowd as he faced them. He said, "I been here a year. My trouble is mail. Only way I sent President Strang letters was by Indians. I gave them plenty of cornmeal.

"Cutthroats run the post office. They were kicked off Mackinac and some escaped jail. I got my rights more than them. It ain't fair. They pushed me around and kept my mail from me because I'm a Mormon."

Strang stood up and asked, "Brother Ebenezer, what proof do you have those men are convicts?"

Mary knew the seriousness of that question. The main reason Strang came to Beaver was to live in complete peace. If he admitted a bad element lived on the island, the brethren might panic and want to move again.

Ebenezer said, "I got it straight from my Indian. He told me about renegades on wanted posters. He saw them on the mainland during the free money time."

"Indian Treaty Payment," Strang corrected.

"Yeah. Free money and goods from the Great White Father in Washington. That's what the Indians say."

Strang turned to the crowd and said, "I didn't know renegades lived here."

Mary listened to Strang lie. He knew about renegades long before coming to Beaver. She watched as he pulled letters from his jacket pocket and said, "Here's my mail. I had no trouble obtaining it at the Post Office." He called out, "Sister Mary was with me." He leveled his gaze at her and asked, "Didn't the postman gladly hand over my mail?"

Mary felt uneasy as the people stared at her. She pondered what to say. How easy to cry out, "No. You're wrong. I was insulted by renegades. You paid for mail." What revenge she'd have for the ill treatment at that miserable place. She'd get even this very moment while Charlie sat next to him. She felt Strang's eyes tear into hers that short distance in the grove, as he waited for her reply. She stood up, faced him and said in a low, flat voice, "You had no trouble getting your letters."

Strang turned and dictated to Charlie, "The truthful statement that mail at Whiskey Point had been easily accessible to me was confirmed by my wife, Sister Mary, who safely accompanied me before this conference."

After Mary sat down, Ebenezer protested, "Brother Strang, women's safety worries me."

Strang said, "Brother Ebenezer, I'm not afriad of a few roughnecks."

Ebenezer said, "Ain't a few. I counted forty on Whiskey Point. More outlaws make booze at Whiskey Island. First thing you know, they'll gang up on us. That starts, I'm leaving."

Strang glared at him and asked, "With your tail between

your legs? Are you going to run and not fight with your brethren?"

"I got my wife and kids to protect," Ebenezer cried out. His face paled during his exchange with Strang.

Strang raised his voice to a tremendous roar, "You listen to me. I don't want any missing links to destroy our strength. If you want to go, leave now."

Ebenezer protested, "I didn't come here to fight. I want to live in peace."

"We all want peace. The only way to keep it is by lawful process. Those who want to go back, get off Beaver. You can walk away right now and go the next time *Zion* sails."

Mary thought, *That's me. I'll be on that ship the next time it sails.* The crowd began to murmur and Mary wondered if anyone would get up, but they all stayed. Brother Ebenezer sat down and talked to his wife. She nodded, but neither got up and walked away.

Strang turned to Charlie and said, "Write that we have no dissenters. All agree to stay on Beaver Island." Charlie dipped the pen in ink and began to write quickly while Strang watched in a pleased manner. Finally the secretary stopped writing and gazed fondly at Strang. Mary saw the look. She bit her lower lip and snapped a piece of tree bark in two, then she continued to tear it apart angrily into tiny pieces. She thought, *I hate that Charlie. With all my heart I hate that person.*

"Brethren," Strang said, "I've received many letters to sell fish and lumber. One's from Scott Fisheries, another's from Mohawk Lumber. I'll read them to you.

John W. Scott
Scott Fisheries, Inc.
208 S. La Salle Street
Chicago, Illinois

May 15, 1850

Mr. James Jesse Strang c/o Post Office General Delivery Beaver Island, Michigan

Dear Mr. Strang:
In reply to your letter of May 10, we are writing you at Beaver Island as you requested.

We acknowledge your proposal to sell us whitefish and lake trout, and will be most anxious to commission our ships to stop at your island.

For years we have tried to interest Messrs. Brian W. Gallagher and William Ryan of Beaver Island in just such an enterprise, but they always were reluctant to do business.

Please advise us if you can supply us on weekly or bi-monthly sales. At such time we will proceed to set up a time-table for our ship. In your area our buyer will be Mr. Arthur Wilson.

We hope your trip to Beaver Island was most pleasant.
Yours truly,
John W. Scott, Pres.
Scott Fisheries, Inc.

"The next letter is about lumber.

John R. Cunningham, President
Mohawk Lumber Company
122 Woodward Avenue
Detroit, Michigan

May 18, 1850

Mr. James Jesse Strang c/o Post Office General Delivery Beaver Island, Michigan

Dear Mr. Strang:
The Mohawk Company is interested in purchasing first rate lumber.
Of course you realize we cannot pay as much as in central Michigan. We have to calculate the overhead of ship and crew. Also, our buyer must inspect the lumber quality. If your sawmill will process pine and maple, we might offer a better price.
I am sure stowing the cargo aboard ship will not be difficult. You claim you have enough men.
Hoping to hear from you in the near future I remain,
Respectfully yours,
John R. Cunningham,
President

"The Michigan Land Office wrote me too. When you sold your farms, I promised you free land. Beaver will be thrown open for public claim. Stake your land where you live and keep farming. It's yours. I'll print more news about this in the newspaper. About selling fish and lumber, when arrangements are completed, we will know exactly how much fish to pack in ice, and what days the buyers will be here. Brother Amos, how many boats are built for fishing?"

A man's baritone voice at one side of the crowd called out, "Two, Brother Strang."

Strang shook his head dejectedly and reproached him, "More. We need many boats. I thought your crew would work faster. What's the matter?"

"Not enough men and lumber," Brother Amos explained.

Strang called out, "You men at the sawmill. Forget about lumber for houses. Let's build ships. We need six right away."

Sarah Bowers stood up and asked, "Mr. Strang, why don't you use *Zion* for fishing?"

"Mother Bowers, that's a passenger ship. Why don't you knit, my dear woman. Leave men's work to men," Strang said in a callous tone.

"I'm sorry," the old woman apologized. "I need a new house. My roof leaks. I thought my new place would be built by now instead of boats."

"Your roof will be patched. Frank, take care of your mother. The sawmill must run day and night to make lumber for boat construction. We have to establish our fishing business now." Strang doubled up his right fist and pounded on the table to emphasize the last word. Then he warned, "Don't discuss our fishing with anyone. Especially you women. The fish buyer will meet with me soon. We'll store lumber until the man from Mohawk Lumber arrives. Meanwhile, I must get my house built."

A tall man with a bushy, black beard and hair down to his shoulders stood. He wore a wide leather belt with a knife sheath. He asked, "Brother Strang, aren't you rushing us? We just got here. You want us to sell fish and lumber and build your house."

Strang said, "Brother Philip, I admire your inquiring mind, but we must move fast. Winter's coming. Work hard everyday. We need fishing boats before the lake freezes. After that we have to fish through the ice."

The man said, "I know you need a house in the village to be close to the harbor and the print shop, but why another dock? Why build a second one?"

"Ah," Strang drawled with a smile. "Privacy is important for *Zion*. Every time it lands, Gentiles swarm on the wharf and eye the cargo. Last week Sister Bessie Henderson had silverware stolen. Too many Gentiles around. No security. I don't want Gentiles to see what we own, or count noses every time Mormons arrive."

Brother Philip called out, "That's a heap of work to build that dock."

Strang boasted proudly, "Eighteen rods long."

The crowd began to talk all at once. Above the chatter a man yelled, "How wide?"

Strang answered, "Big enough to turn a team round."

The people kept jabbering until Strang pounded on the table with his silver mallet. He said, "If you want to know the new dock's location, Brother Eustis dumped logs on shore across from the print shop." He said to the women in a friendly tone, "Ladies, treat those horses kindly. Feed them if the old man's too tired at night."

The women looked at each other and tittered. Strang continued, "Let us thank the Lord for fish and lumber buyers. I made personal visits to other companies, but all in vain. They all told me the same thing, 'Write me from Beaver Island.' But the Lord revealed to me to act immediately, not to wait until I arrived on this island. Now, we can settle down to the business of praising the Almighty and thanking Him with hard work in field, forest and lake."

"Amen, Brother Strang!" a woman's voice cried out. Others joined and shouted, "Amen! Amen! Praise the Lord. Hallelujah!"

Strang's silver mallet gleamed in the bright sunshine as he pounded the table and called for order. "Brethren, we will meet here every Saturday, our Sabbath. We will raise our voices in thanksgiving and song. Folks asked me this past week as I toured, 'When will the tabernacle be finished?' It will be completed after my house and the new dock. The Lord wants us to get our business established. We can gather and praise the Lord in the fresh air. I'm like you. I want to see a

church built that we are proud of. It will be round, a symbol
of our unity with each other and the Lord. There will be an
opening in the center roof for our prayers to ascend to heaven.
Mother VanDusen is in charge of making my church vest-
ments. Any ladies who want to help, see her. However, many
of you will be busy sewing on your new dress pattern."

Several women sitting on blankets wiggled and tried to find
a more comfortable position. Strang rubbed a hand over his
red beard and smiled, "You know, I can spot my brothers at
a great distance by their coveralls, but you ladies blend into
the Gentile society with your pinched waist, petticoats and puff
sleeves. I have a new revelation from the Lord. First, the Lord
says you must wear a new dress style for your health and for
freedom of movement to work in gardens and in cabins."

Mary watched Strang reach for a large sheet of paper that
Charlie handed to him. She noticed how the two exchanged
glances, and their hands touched as he took the paper. Mary
felt a surge of depression sweep over her heart. He had never
told her about a new dress style. She stared at the large
drawing of a short dress with trousers of the same material.
The women gasped. Strang said, "It's a pantalet uniform."

Several women cried out, "Bloomers! It's bloomers!"

Strang ignored them and said proudly, "Modest and
practical. A matching sunbonnet will look nice," he suggested.

One young woman seated on the grass at the back yelled,
"You copied it from Amelia Bloomer. I hate it. I won't wear
bloomers."

Dr. McCulloch, Alex Wentworth and Thomas Bedford sat
at one side with their wives. The men yelled, "No! Bloomers
are looney. No bloomers for women!"

Dr. McCulloch yelled, "I saw that style in *The Lily*."

Strang shouted back at him, "Amelia Bloomer's magazine
is for temperance. I know nothing about her dress styles. This
is my revelation. No more hoop skirts or laced-in waists to

injure health. Women will get hereditary diseases and won't live long."

Strang looked at the crowd and said, "If a Mormon woman does not wear the pantalet uniform, she is not a respectable lady. She will be shunned." He took his "blue hen's egg" out of his pocket and began to swing a cord threaded through a hole in the lead. "You, Bedford, were flogged for adultery. Better keep a civil tongue in your mouth."

"Lies. All lies. I'm faithful to Ruth." He helped his wife up from the grass and said, "Come, Ruthie." They walked away.

Strang ignored their departure and said, "The Lord has decreed this as the official Mormon uniform for all women. I will order bolts of dress material. Then ladies, sew your new uniform immediately. Little girls must wear it too. Now, there is a second and most important revelation from the Lord. As of this day at this First Church Conference, everyone abstains from tea, coffee, liquor and tobacco."

The crowd grumbled loudly all at once. "No tea. What can I drink?" "I need wine for poor circulation." "No tobacco? I smoked since I was ten." "I don't like it. Ain't fair. I won't wear bloomers."

Strang hit the table over and over with the mallet. When the multitude quieted down, he walked away from the table and faced them. He said, "The Lord God saved the Israelites at the Red Sea. Like them we have reached our Promised Land. The law of God shall be kept on Beaver, or men shall walk over my dead body. We must sacrifice to show our gratitude. Abstain and we make progress. Don't try to fool me. I know exactly what you're talking about if you speak of tartantula juice, strychnine, red-eye, Jersey lightening, leg-stretcher or tangle-leg. I've been around the block more than once.

"Tomorrow the press will print these new rules. I want them posted inside each cabin door so when you walk in or out, you are reminded. Remember, we are superior to the

Brighamites out West. Give up those vices and the Lord will
bless your garden with more produce than you can pick.

"Fishermen, throw away the pipe and that cud of chewing
tobacco. I predict your nets will break from the weight of fish.
You loggers, forget about stashing away corn juice in the
bushes. You work a dangerous job. You need a clear head to
fall trees. Ladies, cook good meals and your husbands will
come home on time eager to sup. To sacrifice is to give
thanks. The Lord blesses us and continues to do so. Our
strength to build up Beaver Island comes from Him alone."

Strang raised his arms to the heavens and in an extremely
loud voice prayed, "Lord, give us strength. Don't let Beaver
become another Nauvoo. This is our paradise. We do all in
Your name. Help us, O Lord! Help us!"

He fell to his knees and the people watched in silence. After
several moments he got up slowly as tears washed down his
cheeks. He took out a handkerchief, wiped his face, then
brushed away dust from his pants.

"Please kneel for the blessing," Strang said. The people
knelt down, bowed their heads, and clasped their hands
together at their waists. Strang stood straight and raised his
hazel eyes to the sky. He called out in a sonorous voice,
"Lord, hear the prayer of your humble servant. Bless these
people gathered before You. Help them to do Your Holy Will.
Save them from sickness and injury at work; deliver them
from storms and bless all their crops. Bless too our fish and
wood enterprise. Give these good brethren courage to build.
Make holy all You have blessed us with. Amen."

After the conference ended, Strang left with Charlie before
Mary could talk to him. Mary asked a neighbor woman, "Will
you please give me a ride home? Brother Strang has urgent
business at the print shop."

26

*A*t daybreak Mary stayed in bed and listened to a neighbor's rooster crow. Next, a horse clip-clopped past the cabin until the sound became fainter in the distance. Mary knew it was a Mormon going to the lake to set nets. After that, Brother Matthew's horse and wagon dragged a rattling chain to the lumber mill. Cows mooed and a collie barked on their way to the pasture. Finally, when all became quiet, a cricket chirped inside the cabin.

Strang always left early to eat breakfast with the sawmill workers. After he rode away, Mary waited for the sun to warm up the bedroom. She got up and stood in her nightgown at the door and marveled at the peaceful country. No one traveled now on the roadway. She looked at the yard where tall grass beaten flat became paths. She had enjoyed the quiet, but soon she'd move to the village. Strang had built a new frame house not far from the village overlooking the harbor.

It pleased Mary to be near *Zion* and know when it would sail.

Yesterday, a wagon slowed down and the driver gawked at the cabin. Mary asked Strang, "Who's moving in?"

"Brother Silas. No hurry to move. His family won't be here for a month."

Mary said, "That wasn't Silas. It was a stranger."

"Don't worry. You are always safe. No one dares to harm my wife."

On a Wednesday Mary moved out. As she rode away in the buggy, she glanced back and said to Strang, "Family after family will live in that cabin and abuse it. Once deserted the storms will blow down the door and wild animals will wander inside to keep warm. Finally, a few logs will fall off, but the roof will remain with half the brick chimney. Maybe, a hundred years from now, people will trample through the high weeds and the tall buttercups and wonder who lived here."

Strang said, "Don't be so sentimental. It's just an old log cabin."

Mary looked back where the clothes line had stretched from tree to tree. On windy days when the wash dried fast the sweet breeze filled the towels. She had smelled wild clover when she dried the laundry. All those memories were gone.

After Mary moved into the new house, Virginia saw less of her. "I lost my best friend," Virginia complained to Bill.

"She don't need you. Busy with her own."

A week later Mary knocked at Virginia's door and apologized, "Sorry. I couldn't come sooner because of James. He's at the sawmill now. I must warn you. Lock up all the time. Mormons will steal. I even fear for your safety. You're the only real friends I have. I don't want anything to happen to you."

"We've lived here all our lives," Virginia said.

"My heart goes out to you," Mary answered. "I thought Mormons would live in peace. I didn't expect James to hurt people. I tried to reason with him, but he's strong willed. I wish I could help, but he says he will baptize every Gentile family. If not, they will get off Beaver in ten days. He printed posters. They're nailed to trees everywhere."

"I saw one. Don't mean nothing to me," Bill said. "I heard Mormons put Josh Conroy aboard *Zion*."

"Why? Where they taking him?" Virginia asked.

Bill said, "I bet they toss him overboard like an alley cat."

"Oh no!" Mary cried out. "They wouldn't do that."

"I know, but what about the roughnecks at Whiskey Point? What about them?"

Mary said, "He knows they're mean and armed. I heard he's waiting for some Mormons coming here from Ohio."

"I got guns and bullets. Mormons try to kick me off, I'll fight," Bill said.

"No use, Bill. We're outnumbered. Look up and down the street. Folks shipped out left and right, day and night," Virginia said.

Bill cried out, "I'll tell the government. Folks can't get kicked off Beaver. They'll lose everything. Homes. Crops."

Mary said, "James has powerful friends in the Lansing legislature. They want Mormons to rule Beaver. If you leave now, you'll get free passage to the mainland."

Bill said, "I ain't going. I'm staying. That's final."

When the two women walked to the gate Mary said, "Tomorrow James will be crowned King of Beaver Island. I have to be there. I'll see you as soon as I can sneak away."

"We heard he'd be crowned king," Virginia said. "Bill says we have to go to Garden Island. He doesn't want to be on Beaver when your husband is made king. I'll wait for you when I come home. Take care of yourself."

27

On Strang's coronation day, Mary watched the multitude gather at Font Lake. Twenty adults waiting to be baptized walked around in long, white robes. One man dipped a hand in the lake and complained, "It's cold."

His baptism had been delayed for a week. Roughnecks kept Strang from baptizing. The rowdies came from Whiskey Point, stood on the opposite shore and shouted in drunken voices, "You-hoo! Hey Mormons! Watch me baptize."

Strang had commanded, "Women, turn your heads." But Mary caught sight of a naked man before he jumped into the lake. His arms splashed crazily about. Five other men pulled off all their clothes and paraded up and down the shore for ten minutes before they dove into the lake.

Mary recalled Strang's anger. His face had turned a deep pink as he shouted, "Go home, women. Get out of here. Don't look!" The ladies packed their picnic baskets and left the area.

Mormon men wanted to pull the renegades out of Font
Lake, reserved as their baptistry. Strang had insisted, "It's not
time for us to engage in violent acts. When we do, they will
regret this."

Today, no Whiskey Point outlaws ventured near the lake
because too many Mormons arrived for Strang's coronation as
King of the Island. Bill and Virginia rowed to Garden, and the
other settlers had vowed to ignore the Mormon festivity, called
King's Day. The afternoon turned exceptionally bright and
warm. The tall pines and cedar hardly moved in the soft
breeze, and a tangy odor of wintergreen filled the air. Mary
did not become excited over the celebration. She couldn't
forget Strang and that woman in his stateroom. His adultery
remained branded in her memory, as permanent as the distant
horizon. *Let them crown him king*, she thought. *I don't want
to be queen of the island.*

Food was heaped on the picnic tables, enough food for a
week. Men and women talked in groups while children ran
around playing tag. Girls had filled baskets with flower petals
of roses, buttercup and bluebells to throw in Strang's path after
his coronation.

Sunlight gleamed brightly on the musical instruments. Four
musicians tuned up silver trumpets, preparing to herald
Strang's arrival on stage. The practice notes sent a chill
through Mary's body. She estimated the crowd at three
hundred. Many new Mormons didn't know her as they bumped
against her without an apology. Some women had set up a
quilting frame, and two little girls sat underneath to push back
the big needles. Young mothers sat in the shade with their
backs against the trees as they nursed their infants. When the
youngsters' tag game became too rough, a woman shouted,
"You young'uns, stop it!" Little girls with younger brothers
and sisters in hand walked to the lake's edge. A woman
screamed, "Get back here!" Another standing near Mary

shouted in a high pitch, "Susie, don't get your dress dirty."

A platform, large enough to hold ten people, had been built from planks hauled from the sawmill. Constructed in front of a row of six pine trees, a purple curtain had been nailed on the trees. White birchbark logs formed steps that led up to the stage. At times the curtain moved because of people working behind it. There were three chairs on stage. The largest in the center had red velvet upholstery on the seat, back and the wide wood arms. The other two were half that size and made of plain wood. Mary hadn't seen Strang since her arrival, but she knew he must be backstage with Elder Bowers.

Earlier Frank Bowers carried a notebook and talked with the people and the trumpet players dressed in black suits and blue velvet capes that came to their waists. Frank instructed the people to be baptized to sit up front on the wood benches that had been built for this occasion. His mother sat in the center of the baptismal crowd. Her black dress and bonnet contrasted sharply with the white baptismal robes.

Frank walked up to Mary and said, "When Brother Strang calls your name, come up on the stage. Take the chair on his left." She had protested, but Frank insisted, "He says you must be up there. He wants to introduce you to the newly arrived brethren."

Earlier that day Mary walked up to the curtain concealing the stage, but one of the elders said, "No, Mrs. Strang. We have orders. No one goes back there. Brother Strang does not want to be disturbed."

Mary scowled and said, "I'm his wife. Why can't I see him?"

The elder said, "Sorry. I have my orders." He grinned at her strangely. The man's expression reminded Mary of the way women had stared at her on the wagon trail and aboard *Zion*. Could she identify that look as amused or arrogant? No. It was more secretive, as if they all knew something that she didn't. She smoothed down her blue silk pantalet costume. All the women today wore the new Mormon uniform in gingham, cotton or rayon. Beyond the crowd, Mary saw her children playing hide and seek. As she sat down at the end of a bench, a new woman said curtly, "This is saved."

Mary stood up, but Harriet, sitting nearby said, "Mrs. Strang, take my place."

The strange female placed a hand on Mary's arm and apologized, "I'm sorry. I didn't know you were Brother Strang's wife. Sit here."

Mary said, "No thank you." She walked towards a clump of young birch and thought, *I must be going daft. I saw the same look on that woman's face, Harriet's and the elder at the stage. Why do they all look strangely at me? I must be tired and nervous.* She sat down under a spreading maple.

At last the musicians climbed up the log steps onto the stage. They faced the crowd and raised their silver trumpets to their lips. The sharp musical notes echoed over the clearing to the lake. People stopped talking in groups and moved towards the platform. Women stopped quilting and hurried up front. They spread their blankets on the ground to sit before the musicans while other people sat on the benches.

When the last trumpet echoed over Font Lake, the curtain parted and Frank Bowers stepped forward in his black velvet suit. At a distance his pock-marked face seemed smooth. He bowed from the waist and Mary watched as he moved about the stage, waved his arms dramatically, and paced the platform to address the audience who listened politely. His voice resounded over the crowd, as he spoke of Brother Strang, "A man called by God to lead you here." His voice droned on.

Mary had heard Frank speak before. She recalled that back in Voree Frank had been a toastmaster at a Christmas party and at a Church conference. She knew his words almost by heart, as he reviewed Strang's life from baptism and ordination to the priesthood by the Mormon founder, Joseph Smith. She closed her eyes and heard him recite, "Reverend James Jesse Strang is a man of hard work. He spends long hours as editor, yea, even printing, working by the sweat of his brow, dirtying his priestly hands so that you get a newspaper with Mormon principals and island news."

Mary looked ahead where Mother Bowers sat erect. Her black bonnet didn't move as she posed immovable with the group in white baptismal gowns like a black stump frozen in an icy lake.

Frank continued, "I recall this joke by President Strang. He was accused of stealing. The charges were dropped when President Strang said, 'It's like the man accused of taking a mill. That night he went back for the water.'"

The multitude laughed heartily. When they stopped, Frank recited dramatically, "There is no greater lawyer or debater ready to defend our Mormon faith. He brought back Brother Henry's cow, stolen by Gentiles. He registered our land deeds on the mainland." His voice became louder as he announced, "My brethren, it makes me extremely happy to be chosen the elder who will crown James Jesse Strang as the King of Beaver Island."

Immediately the four trumpets sounded with a triumphant peal of notes. The crowd cheered and applauded. The stage curtain parted. A young lad about ten years old dressed in a white suit held a white velvet pillow with a gold tassel dangling at each corner. On it sat a gold crown sparkling with jewels.

Strang strode majestically on the stage. He wore a long red velvet robe and held his head high with kingly pride. His red hair and beard were neatly brushed, and highlighted by rays of sunshine that descended through the trees. The people stood up, cheered loudly, and clapped their hands enthusiastically.

After several minutes of strong applause, Strang raised his

arms high in the air to quiet the crowd, then motioned for
them to be seated.

To see him in such glory reminded Mary of yesterday when
she had asked to go with him for a buggy ride to this grove
and see the stage. Instead he'd said, "No, I got business to
handle."

"Please, James. I'd like to see what it looks like."

He had lowered his head and slapped a black hat over henna
hair. He shut her out when he said, "I travel faster alone.
Besides, I'm meeting men."

"When will you be back?"

"I don't know. Don't keep supper waiting. If I don't come
back, I'll stay at Frank's." As he walked away he said,
"Brother Ebenezer and his missus will bring you to the
ceremony."

She had begged, "Come home tonight. Myraette and
William want to ride with you to the coronation." He didn't
answer, just stomped his boots heavily down the steps and
headed for his horse and buggy.

The trumpets blasted a fanfare. After they stopped, Frank
called out, "Everyone kneel."

Mary knelt on the grass with the people. Strang walked
across the stage and sat in the large chair. Frank and the young
boy were the only ones in the crowd standing. When Frank
took the crown from the pillow, the lad stepped back and knelt
down. Behind the lavender curtain, a high soprano sang loudly
accompanied by two violins. The woman sang, "Hosanna,
hosanna, hosanna in the highest." After a short pause her voice
pierced the air, "Blessed be our king, James, forever." She
held the last note as long as she could and her shrill tone
echoed over the tall trees. When she stopped, Frank Bowers,
who had held the gold crown over Strang's head while the
woman sang, now proclaimed, "I, Elder Frank Bowers, crown
thee, James Jesse Strang, King of Beaver Island."

The musicians on stage faced the crowd and blew a long salute with the trumpet notes sounding higher and higher. When they finished, they bowed to Strang. The people stood up and cheered. Strang got up from the red velvet chair, and held out his arms for quiet. He commanded, "Kneel down." The musicians walked down the log steps at the stage, and knelt in the grass facing him. Strang said, "My first act as King is to bless you."

He raised his arms straight up at the hard, blue sky, and the sun lit up the jewels on the crown resting squarely on his red hair. He called out in a forceful voice, "Lord, grant me the wisdom and strength to rule Your people. Bless them with Your infinite, bountiful goodness. Keep them well in soul, mind and body. Counsel them to obey Your commandments as written in the Bible. Help us God, as You did the prophets of old. You brought us safely to Beaver Island. We will praise and honor You with hard work and sacrifice and glorify You always. In Your holy name, I envoke Your blessing on all the brethren here today. Bless too, the ones I will baptize that they will follow Your rules under Your humble servant, James Jesse Strang."

Strang's arms fell limp at his sides. He hung his head, then in a loud voice proclaimed, "Lord, God almighty, I know You are present with us. Hear my humble plea. Grant Your divine blessing on all brethren here." Strang knelt down with his hands clasped at his breast and remained silent, with his head lowered, for several moments. When he got up he dictated, "Before I baptize, I will introduce my wife, Sister Mary. Many of you are new and have not met her."

Mary felt her cheeks turn warm when Mormons nearby turned and smiled. When she stood up and walked to the stage as Frank had earlier instructed, she heard polite applause. She was glad her children were away playing, because she would not like them hanging onto her bloomer dress now. When she reached the stage, Strang bowed politely, and gestured towards a wood chair.

Mary sat down and clasped her hands over the blue pantalet dress. At times she looked up and studied a few dark clouds that threatened to rain. To avoid the multitude of faces, she looked down as Strang talked. She wished he'd finish. There remained the ordeal of the baptismal ceremony. The picnic would be last. The women had all cooperated. Each tried to out-do the other with fancy cakes and pies.

"Revelation!" Strang shouted. "My views are unchangeable, but I must bend to the Lord's will. His revelation to me is the most important one. Increase and multiply!"

Mary wondered what he was talking about. Back at Voree he had preached for three hours. She hoped he'd not do that today.

He called out, "That is why I embrace the Lord's new revelation. Increase and multiply. It is only acceptable if a man can support another wife. I am the first! I set the example!"

The crowd murmured. Mary felt the back of the chair hurt her spine as she pushed against it, shocked at his words. Strang shouted, "I am forced to follow the Lord's new revelation. Prophets and kings in the Old Testament believed in spiritual wifery. I too, must obey the Lord's law. Today, I bring forth Sister Elvira Field, my first spiritual wife."

Mary's whole body stiffened. Her mouth turned dry. She watched as Strang walked center stage, and pulled the curtain aside. He escorted a young girl on stage by holding her hand. Mary stared at Charlie, transformed from a "nephew" in a black suit to a young lady in a white taffeta short dress and pantalets. A white bonnet with rows of tiny lace covered her bobbed hair and she carried a bouquet of red roses and wild fern with a wide, white velvet bow, and from it hung six long narrow streamers of ribbon.

Mary's hands and feet turned cold, and her body trembled.

She knew it might happen someday, but never like this in
public with such great humiliation. She couldn't stop shaking.
Her pulse beat faster and her eyes stared. She almost fainted
at the disgraceful scene.

She heard Elvira move forward and the taffeta rustled like
a wild animal in the bushes ready to attack. Mary did not look
directly at Elvira, but was only aware of Strang in red and
Elvira in white. Mary wanted to cry, to have her tears blur the
couple. Instead she strained her eyes and watched Strang smile
at Elvira. With his hand in Elvira's, he promonaded with a
kingly stride to lead his new bride to Mary.

The two stepped up to Mary and he said proudly with a
confident grin, "We three will live in harmony, doing God's
will." He gazed deeply into Mary's eyes and said, "Mary, my
dear, meet your new sister, Elvira."

Mary felt numb. His second wife! So much humiliation! It
was like reliving Whiskey Point in front of renegades. Now
she was degraded before all of these Mormons. Her head
became lighter. No past or future. Only the present with this
monumental disgrace before this crowd. One moment his
lawful wife. Queen of the Island. Now nothing. He had tricked
her.

The way people had looked at her earlier came to mind.
They all knew about Elvira and the new house where two
wives could easily live without seeing each other. Elvira's
smug face angered Mary so intensely that she felt a warmth
spread from her fingers, past her bare arms and up to her face,
as if she suddenly experienced sunburn. She took a deep breath
to scream, but no sound escaped from a dry mouth.

Elvira looked at Mary in a way that seemed to say, "He
loves me. Not you."

That glance triggered the only response Mary could think
of. She rushed at the young woman, tore the bouquet of red
roses from her hands and with all the strength she could

muster, Mary hit Elvira again and again across the face.

The shocked crowd gasped as Mary slapped Elvira hard. Red flower petals flew in all directions like blood spurting from the neck stub of a freshly killed chicken.

Strang lurched forward towards Mary. She threw down the ruined bouquet and ran nimbly down the log steps past the musicians, the little girls with baskets of flowers, the crowd, and tables of food. Tears flowed, converting the whole scene into a kaleidoscopic blur as she ran faster and faster.

No one followed Mary along the road next to the clearing. Her heart pounded from running and fast breathing cut her windpipe. She tripped and fell down, gasping for air as more hot tears rolled down her cheeks.

Mary rested a few moments, then got up and ran further down the roadway. She ran until her head ached and throat became dry. She panted and gulped hungrily for air. *Where am I going? What will I do?* She asked herself.

She screeched at the blue sky, "I'm going mad! Devils drive me insane."

A terrible hallucination came to mind. One moment she visualized Charlie in the black suit, then Elvira in a white bridal dress. Mary tripped again over a tree root and the apparition disappeared. When her palms hit the ground, it broke the impact of her fall, but made her hands ache. She saw dirt imbedded in long bloody cuts in the skin. She got up and staggered along the path, hoping to find a peaceful refuge somewhere on this trail that took her away from Font Lake.

Warm tears blurred the trees and the path into a haze of green and sepia. The route stretched along Lake Michigan, lonely and untraveled. Everyone was attending the coronation. When she stopped crying, it was quiet with only the slow waves touching the shore murmuring, "go home—go home." When she laid down under a maple she heard the faint rasp of a fiddle back at the coronation. The people were dancing.

She got up and walked along the cobbly shoreline until she came to a place where her leather boots sank into the wet sand. She sat down and took off her boots. Nearby a dead fish bobbled in the water. Neither lake nor land wanted the trout. The waves pushed it back and forth, an outcast like Mary. She hurried away from the fishy stench to a sandbar, sat down and stared at the wide lake. Not a canoe or ship was in sight.

Mary dipped her hands in the lake until the dirt washed out of the cuts. All the while her head ached from the top of her head to her neck. She tried to reason it out, *Why did he treat me like that? I've always been a faithful wife, a hard-working mother.* A large shadow from the sage pines bordering the lake moved toward her, and the turquoise water turned grey from the clouds overhead to remind her of dead bodies and ship-wrecks. The sun disappeared behind the clouds. Paradise had ended.

At last she stood up, splashed water on her puffy eyes, cupped water in both hands and drank. Next, she squeezed the water out of her clothes. Back on the beach she pulled off her stockings, dress and pantalets and laid them on the sand to dry. She laid down and deer flies buzzed overhead and tormented Mary. Water dried slowly on her skin and caused an itchy sensation, like sand fleas.

As the air chilled, she shook the sand from the clothes, dressed and walked back to the roadway. The stillness of the forest and its dark interior frightened Mary. She knew if she knocked on a Mormon cabin, they'd shun her. It was too far to walk back to the village and Virginia. Mary hiked along a familiar side road toward her first log cabin. As the trees melted into a blotch of grey from the charcoal sky, she ran faster. When she reached a clearing, she cried. Her wails caused a forest animal to howl a long, mournful cry. Mary became afraid and ran headlong toward the deserted log cabin.

28

The Ryans visited with their Indian friends all day on Garden Island and returned at sunset. A cherry-red sun hung low over the pines. Bill stopped the horses at the gate, climbed down, and tied them to the hitching post. While Virginia got out, he pushed the gate open and walked on the limestone path up to the front door. Virginia watched as he took his keys from a side pocket, unlatched the lock and opened the door.

When Virginia walked inside, she felt the warmth. Bill moved about and opened all the windows. Virginia saw how the crimson sky reflected on the bleached floors. At the open doorway a shaft of brick-red light slanted towards the fireplace and dust motes danced in the ruby gleam. She looked at Bill. His eyes had a glassy surface, like peeled grapes. Sunlight shined on them to give off strange rays, like tiny bolts of lightning.

Virginia said, "All the way home, I kept thinking the same

thing over and over. The wagon wheels pushed it around in
my mind. I know for sure, Bill. We got to leave Beaver." She
looked out the open door where the sunset turned the yard into
a spectacular fiery scene, highlighting the stone path and the
stately white birch.

Bill groaned, "Ginny, your talk makes me weak. Once I
had cholera. So damn sick I thought I'd die. If I lived, thought
for sure I'd be too weak to lift a net or oar. I'd feel like that
if I left Beaver." He reached for a chair at the table, pulled it
out and stumbled over a braided rug.

Bill sat down in the chair. Tears filled his blue eyes as he
blurted, "Where can we go? I can't lift and carry furniture.
My God, Ginny. My old man will turn over in his grave if I
ship out."

She shook a finger at Bill and warned, "Don't talk like that.
We've lived with nothing but trouble since the Mormons
came."

"Are you daft?" he asked. "We worked hard all our lives.
You think I'm gonna walk away? Leave everything to strangers? I'll stay here 'til I croak."

"You think they care?" she asked. "They'll make it tough
on you 'til you draw your last breath."

"I got ideas popping into my mind like bubbles behind a
rudder." He lowered and shook his head, "I can't leave. It's
too late."

Virginia frowned. The vertical lines above the bridge of her
nose deepened. She implored, "Please, Bill. It's never too
late."

He took his hand from his head, stared at her, and pointed
at the floor. He said, "Look at this rug. You made it from
scraps. Scraps from your old dresses, my pants and shirts.
Leonora's dresses too. It's a fine carpet. Did you ever look at
it spread all over the fence when you beat sand out with a
broom, and think of our years here together? All the memories

of our life caught up in pieces of this pretty rug."

Virginia reached over, patted him on the shoulder, and said, "It won't be so bad, Bill. Life will be the same for us no matter where we live. We got each other."

He lowered his head, "I don't know. I'm an old man. My brain feels like a leaking bilge with water sloshing back and forth. Never thought I'd leave Beaver. Look around this cabin. We worked hard all our lives. Can't leave my horses and boat. I'm too old to pioneer again. You too."

She insisted in a persuasive voice, "We got to leave. I'm afraid to stay. I know our lives aren't worth a plugged nickel. Lake will get rough. We got a chance to go now."

"No!" he cried out. "You're upset. I'm not going to do something we'll both be sorry for." In a low, sad voice he said, "Remember our promise. We knelt together. Held hands. We vowed at our little girl's grave, we'd never leave her."

Virginia nodded and the flesh sagged under her high cheek bones as she replied quietly, "I remember, but our life has changed. Now you listen to me. I can't stand living like this—wondering what harm will come our way. I say we go."

Virginia knelt down next to Bill. She hugged his waist and leaned her grey head with the circle of braids against his heart as she pleaded, "Bill, there's no other way. We got to leave. We still have each other."

In that brief moment as she waited for his reply, lonliness stabbed Virginia and a feeling of great melancholy spread misery over her body. She had experienced this before when Bill went hunting or to the mainland. It had come to her swiftly in the daytime, when she had looked out the window and had seen husband and wife riding by in an open buggy sitting close together, laughing and enjoying themselves. Other couples would have children with them in a wagon on their way to picnic or families passed on foot with baskets to pick berries. Seeing those contented groups always made her lonely.

She had begged Bill not to be gone so long, but he had laughed at her and took off, seeking companionship with trappers and fishermen. Now all those men had sailed from Beaver. They feared their lives. Virginia began to cry.

Bill put an arm around her shoulders and said in a comforting tone, "Now Ginny. Don't take on so. If you want to leave that bad, I'll go. Guess we can start over. I know fishermen at Pine River. We'd have to ship out before September squalls."

"I'm sorry. I'm afraid to live here." She dabbed at her eyes with the hem of her skirt.

"Guess you're right. Things is starting to pop. Life's gone sour. Never told you, but I was shot at in the woods. They took my fishing nets in the lake. Things is probably going to get worse before they get better. I'm just fooling myself to stay here." He squeezed her shoulder as she cried softly. Then he bent over and kissed her tanned, wrinkled cheek. "Now you pull yourself together. We'll come back someday."

All of a sudden they heard a wagon roll along the deserted street, driven by a fisherman named Malone, who halted his team in front of their cabin. He called out excitedly, "Hey! Captain Ryan. Beaver's got a king!"

A neighbor woman hurried outside upon hearing the commotion. Her husband followed and cursed at his barking dog to shut up. With only work pants on, the man yawned and scratched at his bare, hairy chest.

Malone cried out, "King! Strang made himself king. What you think of that?"

The half-naked neighbor exclaimed, "I'll throw his royal ass in the lake."

Bill stood in the open doorway and asked Malone to step inside. Malone pushed open the gate, climbed up the front steps, and entered the cabin. Bill asked Virginia, "Got a hunk of pie?" Bill went to the kitchen shelf and brought a saucer to the table. Virginia walked to the sideboard for the pie. She brought it to the table, cut a large slice and put it on Malone's plate.

"No fork," Malone said when Virginia reached into a glass of spoons and forks in the center of the table.

Bill asked, "Wash it down with milk?"

"No. This will tide me over 'til supper."

Bill asked, "What happened?"

Malone replied, "I seen it all. Strang baptized ten or more in Font Lake. They wore white outfits. Got soaking wet. He dunked 'em underwater one at a time."

"I don't care a fudge about that," Bill said impatiently. He sat down opposite Malone and demanded, "Who in hell crowned the son-of-a-bitch?"

Malone said, "They had a stage fixed up. Strang wore a long king's outfit. Some tall Mormon put the crown on his head. Bugles blew. Did you hear the music?"

"No," Bill snapped. Sweat broke out on his forehead. "We can't stop Mormons anymore. Too late now. We should of stopped them right away. First day. Damn fool. He'll make Beaver the laughing stock of Lake Michigan."

Malone bit into the pie, chewed and turned to Virginia, who sat on his right. He said, "She ran away."

Virginia raised her grey eyebrows and asked, "Who?"

Malone said, "Strang's wife."

"Where is she?"

"Don't know. She tore into another woman." He laughed, "She beat the living Jesus out that female. Smacked her in the mouth with flowers. That Mary's spunky." He stopped grinning and said soberly, "I gotta get home." He shoved the last piece of pie in his mouth, licked his fingers and said, "Looks like a bad storm. My old lady is awful scared of thunder." He got up and moved toward the door.

"Wait, Mr. Malone," Virginia said. "Why did Mary run away?"

A grin spread across Malone's ruddy face, "Because Strang got two wives now."

"Two wives!" Bill exclaimed. "What you mean?"

"Two wives," Malone repeated. "I saw it. His first, Mary, sat in a chair on the stage. Then he brought out this other woman. A young girl."

"Who is she?" Virginia demanded.

"Indian or half-breed?" Bill asked.

"No," Malone replied.

Virginia looked at Bill and said, "Can't be a local woman. They're all married. Gotta be a Mormon woman."

"Sure," Malone agreed.

Virginia asked, "What did Mary say? What did she do?"

Malone shrugged his broad shoulders, "I didn't hear everything. I was too far back. But that Strang talks with a big mouth. I heard him loud and clear. He said the new one is wife number two and the Lord told him to marry her."

Virginia stood up, faced Malone with hands on her hips and demanded, "Where did Mary go?"

"South. She ran like a scared doe."

Virginia looked over at Bill and said, "I got to help poor Mary."

Her husband glanced over his shoulder towards the open door. He said, "Look at the lake. Seagulls coming ashore. Rough storm."

"She needs me," Virginia insisted. "Please Bill, hitch up the horses. I'm going."

"Where?"

"To her old cabin. That's the only place she can be," Virginia said, untying her apron. She put it on the sideboard, then walked to the bedroom and returned with a plain, muslin bonnet. Her rough hands trembled as she tied the ribbon under her chin.

Bill demanded, "Don't go. Look outside. It's getting bad.

Almost dark. Bet it hits before supper. Get awful nasty tonight."

Malone stood next to the open door, put his hand on the frame and leaned against it. He said, "I'm hightailing it home. The wife, you know."

"Thanks for the news," Bill said. "Two wives. Ain't right. That ain't right at all."

Malone straightened up and walked halfway out the door. He said, "Ain't no law against it. Do it out West plenty. Well anyway, thanks for the pie, Mrs. Ryan."

Bill watched the man leave. He scratched his bald head and said, "Looks like one hell of a storm. You can't go out there in that."

Virginia followed his eyes that studied the sky. "I know, but I feel sorry for Mary if she's alone."

29

*M*ary ran inside the cabin and bolted the heavy door. Her hands trembled. She sat down on the floor, leaned against a wall, and tried to slow down her heavy breathing. The dusty room made her cough.

It was still twilight. She looked about the cabin, empty of all her furniture. Across the room she saw an old quilt. On the day she had moved Strang had insisted, "Leave that quilt. It's too shabby for my new house."

Mary stood up, walked over, and picked up the quilt. She shook, then draped it over her shoulders. As she walked about, it snagged the floor splinters. Finally, she laid down and covered herself with it. The fading twilight outside the dirty windows eased the cabin into gloom. While she lay on the hard pine and smelled the dank floorboards, her eyes burned from crying. She couldn't sleep and heard the forest stir with wild animal noises and hoot owls. Eventually, the steady sounds lulled her to sleep. She dreamed of her new house at the harbor. In the dream Strang bent over the kitchen stove and stuffed wood inside while flames licked high in the air. Over the stove on the ceiling two nails held long strings. One string held an apple. The other a heart. All of a sudden each broke in two, showed they were rotten and fell into the flames. Strang laughed.

Mary awoke to strong winds that whistled through the crannies. She pondered the meaning of the dream until lightning illuminated the room phosphorescently, and thunder exploded. During the storm the flashes repeated. She cried out, "God! Save me! I miss my children. I don't want to die!"

Fear of the storm weakened her knees. With hands over her face she turned to the wall, but could not shut out the lightning. Thunder vibrated with terrible blasts, and the ground trembled as more lightning lit up the room. She turned over and looked as a flash of blue revealed the fireplace where she had popped corn for the children. Now all she breathed was dust and her heart ached with loneliness.

Lightning hit a nearby tree. The branches scraped and pushed against the cabin. When the falling timber became louder, she held her breath and stiffened with fear she'd be killed. As the sound amplified, her hands turned cold with fear. The next moment she heard a wolf howl in the distance. The animal stopped as a zig-zag bolt lit up the sky and the thunder boomed across Lake Michigan.

The storm grew worse and repeated its thunder like a thousand wagon wheels over the lake. Then the noise grew fainter and disappeared on the far away Wisconsin shore. When all became quiet, she slept. Within an hour the fury returned louder than before. Thunder rolled back and forth and boomed like a cannon.

Once again the sky lit up the bare cabin. In her fright it seemed that the old quilt covering her became a giant wheel, a kaleidoscope of scraps in triangles, squares and circles. Everytime the lightning glowed in the cabin, she recognized leftover pieces of cloth—green satin from her ball gown, Myraette's dresses, blue denim and linsey-wooly from James' work shirts. She closed her eyes, and clutched the quilt over her head. She remembered the fruit cellar, a good place to hide from the storm, but she was too scared to go below. The rain pelted the roof so fiercely she thought it might collapse at any moment.

The storm ended, and a northern breeze seeped through the cracks. It was a cold, restless wind that chilled her face. When it drifted away, Mary felt as if her eyes traveled with it. She imagined the new house and the children in bed. Tears flowed down her cheeks as she longed right now to tuck them in and kiss them goodnight. She visualized the unhitched buggy and Ezekiel in the moonlight. Her imagination traveled with the wind to the village where Bill and Virginia slept in their four-poster. Next, she thought about the grave where the stone angel guarded Leonora. Then, the pitiful little burial plot for her dead baby. Mary's mind traveled all over the island to the dunes, the inland lakes and the hill. She didn't want to think about Strang and Elvira.

There had been a time she wondered if she could live on Beaver and tolerate an unfaithful husband. She knew for sure that if she did, she'd be false to herself. Every day proved he only wanted her as a housekeeper. She made up her mind that to get his respect, she had to stand up against him. When the wind stopped blowing through the cabin cracks, she thought, *My love for him disappeared like that. I feel nothing for him.*

Once again she dozed off. She awoke the next morning to bright sunshine, cooler air, and birds singing. Laying on the floor she stared at the windows where dust motes coated the beams of light streaming to the floor. The specks danced before her eyes as she contemplated what to do. She got up.

The habit to be busy returned as she gathered evergreen branches to sleep on. After she used the outhouse, she found a worn broom and swept the cabin. While inside she saw a squirrel framed in the sun outside the door. When she collected firewood, he was her companion darting in and out among the maple branches.

She rubbed sticks together for a fire, hoping that Strang would see the smoke. When he came, she'd tell him her plans to leave the island. Later while collecting wood, the squirrel vanished, and instead of bird noises, the land was silent as if an intruder lurked. After she stacked wood next to the fireplace, she bolted the door with trembling hands, wondering if she'd been watched.

Mary threw the quilt over cedar boughs and laid down again. She wondered what Myraette and William thought of mama gone. Many thoughts surged back and forth as she searched for answers.

She felt soft wool material on the quilt and said out loud, "I bought that in Ohio." Her voice frightened her. It sounded so strange. Her fingers rubbed over gingham, tweed and silk scraps from dresses and shirts she'd sewed. At last Mary went back to sleep.

When she awoke, she went outside the cabin and heard hoofbeats. She laid down on the ground and pressed an ear to listen. She heard wagon wheels rolling on a nearby road. It had to be Mormons on their way to work the sawmill. No one came near her cabin. A fever began to spread from her head to her feet. She rested once again on the quilt, and heard a horse nicker. She became terribly afraid as she laid there hungry. She hadn't eaten since breakfast yesterday. If Strang didn't send someone to protect her, she was afraid of a wandering ruffian. She recalled that day at Whiskey Point when the renegade said, "Hey, girlee." She calmed down by telling herself, *Everyone knows I'm James Strang's wife. They dare not bother me.*

After she got up, she made her way to a spring in the forest where she found a large wood bowl. Myraette had used it to mold sand castles at the beach. The bowl brought a memory of her daughter and warm tears rolled down Mary's dusty cheeks. She rinsed out the bowl, then drank cool water from the spring. She carried more water in the bowl back to the cabin where she wet her dry lips and eyelids. *I must eat something,* she thought.

She pulled a large beech limb off a tree and returned to the cabin trap door. Mary forced the door open, dragged it aside and climbed down the ladder. It felt as if she descended into the hold of a strange, dark ship.

The cool cellar atmosphere chilled her body and she smelled the earthy dampness. Mary stepped from the bottom rung onto the dirt and in the semi-darkness found some apples. "Praise the Lord!" she cried out jubilently.

She climbed up the ladder, sat on the door step and ate two wrinkled apples. Her stomach felt better. One thought sobered her. To know. To finally realize. *Yes,* she thought, *to really know how I feel toward him.* He had cast others aside with criticism of their weakness and disloyality to the Church. She recalled Voree when some brethren had not paid their ten percent tithes, and women had been tried in Strang's court for blasphemy. *Now I will disobey him. What will he do to me? What are the other women saying about me?* She imagined Strang standing before the fireplace warming his hands in the cool of evening and saying, "Mary's obstinate. Mary is sulking. She will come home."

Mary bit into another apple and spat out a rotten part. She recalled her dream. She thought, *Rotten apple. Rotten heart. James kept the fire burning. I see now what the dream means. His heart is as rotten as an apple. He poked at the fire in my dream. Yes, he likes to have many irons in the fire, but he won't keep me.*

30

The morning after the coronation, Bill said he'd unwind dried nets from the reels and start packing. Before he left the cabin he told Virginia, "We'll hightail it out of here in a week."

"Not soon enough for me. Our friends are gone. Wish we sailed with them."

"Told you ten times. I'll be the last to leave. Captain always goes down with his ship. I'll hitched up the team, if you're going to visit Mary."

Before Virginia could leave, Mary walked up to the Ryan's front gate. When Virginia saw Mary she embraced her and said, "I was just about to leave. I heard you ran off to the woods last night."

"Yes, but I'm going home now."

"Come inside."

The women entered the cabin. Virginia noticed a determined

look on Mary's face. After she sat down Mary said, "I'm leaving soon as I can. I will not be part of a polygamous marriage. My marriage to James is over. No matter what he says, I'm not staying here."

"What if he won't let you go?"

"He will. I'm sure about that. Elvira's younger than me. I never expected my marriage to end like this. I've been forced into it. Polygamy drives me away. It robs me of my marriage."

Virginia set bread, cheese, cold beef and a glass of milk on the table. Mary put slices of meat and cheese between the bread and said, "Sure tastes good. I only ate old apples from the cellar."

Virginia said, "We're leaving too. Bill's packing his gear at the shanty."

"How soon?"

"Bill says a week. Sooner the better for me. Cooper shop shut down, but first they gave me barrels to pack china in. Won't leave nothing behind."

After Mary finished eating Virginia asked, "Want to lay down and rest?"

"No thanks. I got to find my kids. There is much to do."

Virginia noticed great excitement in Mary's eyes. Even the anticipated meeting with Strang did not discourage her. She moved about energetically, and helped clear the table of food and dishes. Next, she combed her hair and washed her face at the kitchen basin.

Virginia asked, "How can you stand the misery he heaped upon you?"

Mary said, "I made up my mind a long time ago. I saw polygamy destroy women. I won't let that happen to me. I can't love James like when we were first married. The evil of another woman in his life will not stop me from living. I won't end up like Lucy Brent.

"Lucy was only thirty years old. One afternoon she found out her husband took a seventeen year old girl as his wife. Poor Lucy aged and looked sixty. I didn't know her when she came to see me. I was weeding my flower garden back in Voree when she stumbled along the path next to my fence. I got up from my knees and went out the gate to talk to her. Her pretty hair, once brown, had turned white overnight. Her eyes were swollen from weeping. When she looked at me with all that agony, I hardly knew what to say or do. She carried a large pine cone in both hands like a wedding bouquet. At first, I put an arm around her shoulders and tried to comfort her. She finally told me what happened. When she dropped the pine cone, I took her hand in mine. Her hand was as limp as a mustard green. I held her hand and walked her home. She cried all the way. When I left, she thanked me. An hour later she blew out her brains with a pistol.

"Ever since then, I made up my mind that polygamy would not destroy me. I was shocked at first, but I've finished mourning over James and my marriage. I was more angry at myself than anyone that I let him and Elvira get away with that silly Charlie masquerade that long. I'll go home. Be a good mother to Myraette and William. It's my duty. When they grow up, I hope they understand why I left their father." She sighed, "I hope you visit me. You are my only friend on Beaver."

"You visit us too," Virginia said. "We'll ship out next week. Live with my sister, Martha Bigelow, in Pine River. She's a lonely widow. She always wanted us to live with her. When spring rolls around, Bill will build our cabin."

Mary said, "I'll settle in Voree, Wisconsin with my mother. She owns the biggest general store in town. Promise you will visit soon as you can."

"Sure we will," Virginia answered and patted Mary's hand. Mary knew she'd never see Virginia again. Like Beaver Island

and James, the Ryans would remain only a memory.

Virginia stepped forward and hugged Mary. Like an affectionate mother she kissed Mary lightly on each cheek. "Want me to go with you? Help pack? Go with you to the ship?"

"No thanks. I'd rather go alone. I don't know what kind of a mood he will be in. I'll face him by myself."

Mary lingered at the door. It was difficult to say farewell. Finally she backed a few steps away, and walked over the stone path to the gate. She stopped and waved a final time. As she walked down the sandy roadway, Mary felt watched. As soon as each Beaver family left, a Mormon moved into an empty cabin. To feel Mormon eyes stare from cabin windows didn't bother Mary. She had one goal. Get her children and sail away. Mary walked proudly with head held high. Her eyes looked straight ahead as she walked away to find Strang.

31

*M*ary passed Ezekiel chomping on grass at one side of the house. She walked quickly up the steps. When she reached the porch, the door opened. Strang stepped out dressed in dark pants and a white shirt, open at the neck where sparse red hairs stood up like those on a plucked chicken. He was hatless and his henna strands glowed even on the shady porch. His eyebrows arched in surprise and hazel eyes glared cat-like as he snarled, "So. You finally came to your senses."

If he had embraced her, said he forgave her, called her an endearing name and said he missed her, asked where she'd been and if she was hungry, then she might have weakened. When he didn't, she looked him directly in the eyes and said with great determination, "I'm taking my children."

"Where to?" he asked sarcastically. A sly grin spread over his face. He stood with hands at his sides and asked, "Back to your log cabin lover?"

His accusation repulsed Mary. She placed her right hand at her throat where a hard lump formed. She felt like vomiting. She swallowed hard and gasped, "How dare you! That's a lie!" He loved sarcasm to defeat enemies. Now she was an enemy. He accused her, not himself. He did what he wanted. Slept with other women, took a second wife. Mary felt if she begged on her knees to live here, he'd still spread gossip that she now had a lover. She knew all his tricks. She glared and shouted, "Liar! Liar!"

He eyed her with contempt and ordered, "Lower your voice in my house."

She replied with hands on hips, "Yes, it is your house, but I'm leaving with my children."

He glanced away at the harbor and said, "My children will not live with an unfit mother. Your actions were a disgrace at my coronation. You will be with them only if you live here."

"I will not live here. I'm leaving on *Zion* with them."

He folded his arms over his chest and said, "You can leave anytime you want. Alone. Myraette and William stay with me."

Mary wondered where the children were right now. Did Elvira have them? Her arms ached to hold them. She wanted to kiss them and explain why mama was gone all night. She didn't want anything from James. She just wanted her children.

Strang unfolded his arms, shoved his hands into his pockets and jiggled coins. Mary said, "You can't silence the heart, James. Not mine or the children's. If you keep them from me, the day will come. They'll learn the truth and turn against you. If you keep them here, I'll tell the whole world what's going on at Beaver. I will lecture against polygamy. You can't lie about me. I will tell the truth. Truth always wins. Truth shall prevail. My speeches will ruin you. There will be no paradise for you here or anywhere. Take your choice, James. I leave with Myraette and William. You stay with Elvira and your paradise. If I don't get my children, I'll talk against you the rest of my life. I'll see that you are ruined. Take your choice."

He snarled, "Don't threaten me."

"I have every right to speak up. I'll tell Elvira what I saw in your stateroom. You and that prostitute."

He sat down in a chair on the porch and stared at the floorboards. Mary knew she'd outsmarted him. He glanced up with a defeated look, and snarled in a hateful tone, "Leave! Go! Go home on the ship tonight. I don't want you here. I'll get the children."

Mary breathed a sigh of relief. She walked inside to the kitchen, pumped water into a basin and washed her face and arms. When she finished, she threw the water out the back door and hung up the towel. She packed a lunch of bread and cheese and put it in a picnic basket. On the stairs she looked below at the large stone fireplace, the sofa, chairs and the dining room furniture. She thought, *No house is big enough for two women. Elvira can have all this.*

In her bedroom Mary hurriedly shoved some clothes inside a black valise and a steamer chest. At the children's room she opened a foot locker and packed their clothes. The dolls and toy soldiers wouldn't fit, so she placed them on top.

She walked back to her room and found the same grey dress she'd worn to Beaver. She took off the dirty dress and pantalets and put on the grey dress that came to her ankles. She brushed her hair, then tied on a matching grey sunbonnet.

Mary walked downstairs and sat in a rocker on the veranda, just as the children ran up the main path to the house. Strang walked a short distance behind them. At first Mary thought she saw Elvira. As Strang approached, Mary recognized his fast stride like when he courted her. Back then in the store, she had kept her head down and pretended to be busy. He had sneaked up and put his warm hand over hers. She had pretend-ed to be startled. Now there'd be no more hand holding and kisses. He didn't love her. She knew the only solution was to divorce him when she reached mother back in Voree.

When Myraette saw Mary on the porch she shouted, "Mama!" and broke into a run. William followed. The two scampered up the stairs, climbed upon her lap and threw their arms around Mary's neck, smothering both cheeks with wet kisses.

Mary cried with happiness and through her tears recognized the woman walking behind Strang. It was Sister Phoebe. When Strang reached Mary, he lifted one child at a time out of her arms and said, "Go inside with Sister Phoebe. She will feed you."

"I wanna stay with Mama," Myraette begged.

"Me too," William cried out.

"Do what I say," Strang demanded. "Aunt Phoebe must feed you. Your mother's taking you on a boat ride."

"Where papa?" Myraette asked.

"Don't ask questions. Go!" he commanded.

Phoebe, now on the porch, walked over and took each child by the hand and said, "Come, my darlings. Aunt Phoebe will give you a nice supper."

As Phoebe led them away, Mary saw that the children wore their best Sabbath clothes. It annoyed Mary that Elvira had probably dressed them up. Strang said, "If they didn't love you so much, I wouldn't let them go. I don't want a nasty scene. I've watched how spite operates. I want to be charitable."

"Charitable!" Mary scoffed. "To whom? Not me."

She saw that he didn't like what she said by the way he folded his arms tightly over his chest and frowned. He said in a low tone between his teeth, "You would do well to practice charity." He unfolded his arms, and reached into his pants pocket and took out a small white envelope. He said, "This will be sufficient to get you home. I will establish a fund for the children in the bank."

She let the envelope lay on her lap. In a vexed tone he said, "Don't be careless. There's a goodly sum inside. Ship leaves in an hour. You can sleep aboard after it lands. At daybreak hire a carriage. You'll have a good start. Better pack your things."

"I packed."

"I'll see to the children," he replied and walked inside.

Mary sat and looked fixedly at the path, the trees and the distant harbor where *Zion* stayed tied up at the wharf. Phoebe came out the door and handed Mary her black leather purse. Mary had left it on the bed upstairs.

In an unconcerned manner Phoebe said, "Brother Strang says to give you this." She retreated inside, and the smell of food drifted out to the porch. The woman returned and asked, "How about a bowl of hot stew?"

Mary said, "No thank you." She sat in a rocking chair and looked at the lake. Her mother would be surprised to see her come home. Mary knew that loneliness would set in. Her husband's face would fade from her memory until he came to visit the children. She doubled up the envelope with money and stuck it into her purse. She sat there another ten minutes until Ebenezer arrived in a buckboard to take her to the ship. After a quick nod, he went inside and carried out one steamer trunk at a time, and at last her black valise.

When he finished loading the wagon, the children struggled to carry their toys. Mary picked up her purse, walked down the porch steps, then climbed into the wagon where she sat on one of the hard seats.

Mary expected James to come out and kiss the children good-bye. Phoebe helped the children into the buckboard and said, "Your papa will see you soon." As each child sat down, they snuggled next to Mary on the wide back seat. After Phoebe climbed inside, Ebenezer whipped the horses and they were on their way to the dock.

When they reached the ship, Phoebe took the children below to a stateroom. When she returned, she told Ebenezer where to store the trunks. She set the picnic basket next to Mary who remained topside. Phoebe said, "Here's the food. I know how kids dig in."

Mary leaned against the ship's railing and faced the sun, now a brilliant crimson that began to lower gently behind the evergreens. She looked at the wharf, where the only figures who moved about were *Zion*'s sailors who untied the ropes from the dock pilings. Mary felt her heart beat faster with excitement to finally leave the island.

Phoebe handed Mary a ladle. She said, "I brought the dipper from your kitchen stove." The woman tried to be solicitous, but at the same time Mary could tell she was greatly embarrassed to be placed in this awkward situation. She was a plain woman and Mary knew exactly what would happen tomorrow. Phoebe would blush when the other women cornered her for a first hand account of what had happened. The gossips would ask how Mary acted and what she had said upon leaving the island. Mary thought, *It will almost kill old lady Bowers that she wasn't on the scene*. Phoebe said, "I know how thirsty kids get. They can drink from the dipper. I got a jug of fresh spring water in your cabin."

Mary said, "Thank you for everything."

Phoebe reached for the gangplank rail and said, "I fed them good. Got all their toys down there. Nothing more I can do. Take care. Maybe we'll meet again someday. Good Lord willing."

She walked down the ramp quickly before Mary could reply. Phoebe appeared afraid that *Zion* might set sail with her aboard because the paddle wheel turned after the engine warmed up.

At last the chains scraped over the stern as the sailors pulled the big anchor on deck. The side wheel turned faster and the ship moved slowly away from the empty dock. After they passed a camp-fire at Luney's Point, the ship charged at the open water, and Beaver Island's evergreen aroma evaporated.

Mary watched as the sun blazed a final brilliant glow, then slowly the fiery ball turned into a soft shade of apricot. With every blink of Mary's eyes she watched the sun sink below the horizon. At last only a portion of sun remained like a candle's small flame above a pool of melted wax. As the sun weakened, the charcoal outline of Beaver Island dissolved into the inky harbor.

Later, when a full moon broke clear of the clouds, it shined on the lake. Mary stood topside and looked at the moon's ivory path shimmering over the dark water to the mainland.

Epilogue

*A*fter Mary left Beaver Island, Strang had four polygamous wives. The first, Elvira Field, wore male attire as Strang's "nephew," Charles J. Douglass. She was nineteen years old when she married him, and had four children by Strang.

Betsy McNutt, at age thirty-one, was teased as an old maid until Strang married her two and a half years after Elvira. She had four children by Strang, and one child died in infancy.

Four years later Strang married Sarah Adelia Wright, age nineteen. Sarah gave birth to Strang's twelfth and last child.

Three months after he married Sarah, Strang married her cousin, Phoebe Wright, who was eighteen years old. All polygamous wives were pregnant and gave birth after Strang's death. When he died, he left twelve children, Mary, his lawful wife, and four polygamous wives.

Despite Beaver's isolation from the mainland, the Mormons did not achieve the paradise Strang had promised. Strang's rules in his *Book of the Law of the Lord* deprived the people of freedom. Many resented his domination that affected their personal lives.

At Strang's First Church Conference on Beaver Island, he prohibited his followers to drink coffee, tea, liquor or to smoke tobacco. He ordered the women to wear a bloomer outfit, but many objected. Among them were the wives of Thomas Bedford, Alexander Wentworth and Dr. Hezekiah McCulloch. The official dress for Mormon ladies, called "Strang's bloomers," was full length calico pantalets covered by a matching, straight dress with a hemline at the knees. Strang insisted that the current dress fashion pinched the body and injured health. He claimed it would even create hereditary diseases. Although Strang said he designed the bloomer costume, Amelia Bloomer created this dress style and featured bloomers in her feminist magazine, *The Lily*, in 1849, as an attempt to reform women's clothes.

Thomas Bedford and his wife led a crusade against "Strang's bloomers." At the July conference Strang said that bloomers would be worn by "respectable women." He threatened that women who refused to wear bloomers did so over his dead body. His words were prophetic.

Women were harrassed for refusing to wear the bloomers, and also their husbands. Thomas Bedford was robbed of fishing nets, two boats and horses. Later he was overheard talking to a stranger in McCulloch's store that Strang had ordered a boat on Gull Isle "consecrated." Bedford was whipped thirty-nine lashes with a rawhide horsewhip after that conversation and he vowed revenge. Alex Wentworth and Dr. McCulloch joined him to plot Strang's murder.

Open warfare with the Gentiles continued to escalate. News about violence on Beaver Island reached the mainland from ships that docked at St. James harbor to buy wood. President Millard Fillmore authorized the Detroit U.S. marshall to send the steamer, *Michigan*, to Beaver. Aboard the iron-hulled warship the marshall carried a federal warrant to arrest Strang and other Mormons. They were transported back to Detroit to stand trial.

Mormons were accused of adultery, theft, arson, robbery, murder and counterfeiting. The murder charge resulted when a Mormon constable and a posse of forty men attempted to arrest the Bennett brothers at their house. The Gentile fishermen refused to obey Mormon laws. The brothers resisted arrest, and when the shooting stopped, Thomas Bennett lay dead, shot three times. Samuel Bennett's right hand was shattered from musket balls.

When Strang's trial ended, the Mormons estimated it cost the government $30,000 and Strang half that amount. The verdict was in Strang's favor because of his religious beliefs.

James Strang did not confine himself to Beaver. His youthful dreams of royalty and power yearned to be fullfilled. After being crowned king on Beaver, his next goal was to be elected a state representative in the Michigan Legislature. Although he served two terms in office, his election consisted of charges of fraud and other irregularities.

When Strang ran the first time, Mackinac authorities attempted to arrest him on a previous indictment, but he was released. Next, his political opponent who lost the election claimed Strang ineligible because he didn't live in Newaygo and Peaine wasn't part of the district. Strang debated in grand style for several hours and kept his seat in the legislature. While serving as Representative, he introduced three bills that weakened Mackinac. He campaigned and won to get Beaver divided into the townships of Peaine and Gailee.

Strang was elected the first time in 1851. When he was reelected in 1854, voting violations surfaced. "Charles Douglass," his first plural wife, voted, although women weren't allowed to vote. There were 177 unofficial names recorded on the voting record. A few were too young to vote. Others voted three or four times. Indians also voted.

Some Mormons continued to smoke and drink. McCulloch had a reputation as an alcoholic before he joined the Mormon Church. He continued to drink at bars inside lake boats when they tied up at Beaver. He was evicted from the church for this reason and for cheating customers at his general store. Strang had never trusted McCulloch and his fears were later justified when McCulloch masterminded Strang's assassination.

Although Mormons complained about McCulloch cheating them with store weights, they engaged in theft of Gentile goods that Strang called, "consecration." Mormons used the excuse of their "temperance cause" to invade fish shanties, ships and homes. They confiscated property and claimed they enforced the law, "No liquor sold to Indians."

Dr. McCulloch manipulated Strang's assassination, but the murder was executed by Thomas Bedford and Alex Wentworth. They shot Strang at the Beaver dock in front of a store on June 16, 1856. When the *Michigan* landed at Beaver, a ship's officer went to Strang's house and told him the Captain wanted to see him. When Strang reached the dock, two men jumped out from behind a pile of wood. Wentworth shot Strang in the head and Strang fell to the ground mortally wounded. Wentworth fired again with a revolver and the bullet hit Strang below the right eye. Strang rolled over and Bedford, holding a horse pistol, shot Strang in the back, then beat Strang on the head and face with the pistol. The assault was witnessed by sailors aboard the *Michigan*, and others in front of the Johnson and McCulloch store.

Twelve days later Strang, paralyzed from the bullet wounds, was carried aboard the propeller, *Louisville*, to the home of Strang's mother in Voree, Wisconsin. On July 1, he landed at Racine and was transported by train destined for Burlington, then Voree. He died July 9, 1856 in Voree, and was buried the next day.

After Strang sailed from Beaver, an armed mob arrived from St. Helena in a flotilla. They burned Strang's temple, sacked his printing office, destroyed his library and looted his home. At the time there were over 2500 Mormons living on Beaver. Church leaders and two hundred other Mormons left after he was shot. The mob went from cabin to cabin with guns and knives and forced the remaining Mormons to get out. One woman who had given birth three days before was forced to walk to the harbor. The Mormons departed with only the clothes on their backs, leaving behind horses, cattle and all their possessions.

In the fall of 1856, McCulloch, Wentworth and Bedford returned to Beaver with their families. The three men ran for various public offices, but were defeated.

Bedford stayed on the island until 1864. He joined the Union Army during the Civil War and died at age seventy-six.

Alex Wentworth also served in the Civil War. He was twenty-two years old when he shot Strang, and died during the war at age thirty. No one was ever arrested, convicted or sent to prison for the murder of James Jesse Strang.

When Strang lay on his deathbed, two of his polygamous wives, Betsy McNutt and Phoebe Wright, remained with him. Strang's first legal wife, Mary Abigail Perce, did not visit him before he died. Mary left Voree and moved to Elgin, Illinois in 1851. In later years she lived with her son and daughter in Terre Haute, Indiana.

Bibliography

Backus, Charles K. *The King of Beaver Island*. Westernlore Press, 1955, Original date 1882.

Bringhurst, Newell G. *Brigham Young and the Expanding American Frontier*. Little Brown and Company, 1986.

Fitzpatrick, Doyle. *The King Strang Story*. National Heritage, 1970.

Quaife, Milo M. *The Kingdom of St. James*. Yale University Press, 1935.

Riegel, Oscar W. *Crown of Glory, The Life of James J. Strang, Moses of the Mormons*. Yale University Press, 1935.

Strang, Charles J. *In Memoriam*. 1910.

Strang, Charles J. *A Michigan Monarchy*. *New York Times* Microfilm, 1852.

Strang, Clement J. *Why I Am Not A Strangite*. Papers. Detroit Public Library, n.d.

Strang, James J. *Diary of James J. Strang*. Michigan State University Press, 1961.

Strang, James J. *The Book of the Law of the Lord (1846-1850)*. The Wisconsin Historical Society microfilm. 1919.

Strang, James J. *Chronicle of Voree and Voree Herald* (1844-1849). Wisconsin State Historical Society microfilm, 1919.

Strang, James J. *The Northern Islander (1850-1856)*. Burton Historical Collection, Detroit Public Library.

Strang, James J. *Ancient and Modern Michilimackinac*. W.S. Woodfill, 1959. Reprinted from the original edition of 1854.

Taylor, Samuel W. *Nightfall at Nauvoo*. The Macmillan Company, 1971.

Van Noord, Roger. *The King of Beaver Island. The Life and Assassination of James Jesse Strang*. University of Illinois Press, 1988.

Weygand, P.W. *Murder on Beaver Island*. Rare Book Collection, Louisiana State University Baton Rouge, Louisiana, 1964.

Williams, Elizabeth. *A Child of the Sea* and *Life Among the Mormons*. Ann Arbor, Michigan. 1905.

Wright, John C. *The Crooked Tree*. C. Fayette Erwin, Harbor Springs, Michigan.